HARRIET

Persephone Book N° 97
Published by Persephone Books Ltd 2012

First published by Victor Gollancz in 1934
Afterword © Rachel Cooke 2011

Endpapers taken from 'Small Syringa', a woven silk
by EW Godwin for Warner & Ramm, 1875
© Victoria & Albert Museum

Prelim pages typeset in ITC Baskerville by
Keystroke, Wolverhampton

Printed and bound in Germany by
GGP Media GmbH, Poessneck on Munken Premium
(FSC approved)

9781903155875

Persephone Books Ltd
59 Lamb's Conduit Street
London WC1N 3NB
020 7242 9292

www.persephonebooks.co.uk

HARRIET

by

ELIZABETH JENKINS

✼✼✼✼✼✼✼

with an afterword by

RACHEL COOKE

PERSEPHONE BOOKS
LONDON

HARRIET

❧ I ❧

AT HALF-PAST FIVE on a January evening of the year
1875, Mrs. Ogilvy's drawing room was a pleasant
place; it was a small first-floor room and, though it
could not be said to be furnished with taste, there was
a warmth and brightness about it which made it very
comfortable on such a raw evening. The mantelpiece
under the ornate gilt glass was looped with rose-red
velvet; the curtains were a white chintz covered with
enormous roses and carnations in alternate rows connected with wide-flung sprays of green; the sofa was a
similar medley of red and white, but the armchair in
which Mrs. Ogilvy was sitting was a deep crimson,
and this, with the moss-green carpet, was pleasantly
mellowed by the bright-burning fire, and the lamp-
light which glowed on the many pictures framed in
plush and gilt, and on the piles of oranges, apples, and
grapes which covered the sideboard.

Mrs. Ogilvy, knitting with the precise click of
shining needles, had the room to herself except for
her little nephew, who was playing with marbles and
a solitaire board on the floor, half under the sleek
white fall of tablecloth. He was a retiring child, always slightly uneasy when addressed by a grown-up
person. He was not, in fact, Mrs. Ogilvy's own

nephew, but that of her second husband, a Unitarian
minister; Mr. Ogilvy was shy and unsociable, and little Tom took after the family. Mrs. Ogilvy's only trial
in connection with her husband was that it was so
difficult to make him really comfortable. He never
seemed to notice what there was for dinner or to find
any pleasure in his wife's pretty, comfortable household arrangements; however, she did not complain; she
was a lucky woman, she thought, as she sat knitting
before the fire, just glancing at the tea table with its
flowery china, its silver muffin dish, and a dark plum
cake, thickly iced. She was considering whether that
tea had stood too long, or whether it would do for
Harriet when she came downstairs; she had not had
tea with them, since she had been upstairs packing to
go on a visit to their relations.

Some people would have thought Mrs. Ogilvy,
despite her husband and her housekeeping, a very
unfortunate woman, and there were moments when
she gave way to the idea herself, though it could not
often prevail against the cheerfulness of her disposition. Harriet, her only child, was what the villagers in
Mrs. Ogilvy's old home would have called a natural.
Her intellect was not so clouded that intercourse with
ordinary people was out of the question; the deficiency showed itself rather in a horrid uncouthness,
the more noticeable in that she had a vigorous and
powerful zest for such aspects of existence as were in-
telligible to her; she was not easy to put out of the
way. In fact, her continued presence in any house-

hold was a strain, and consequently, since her mother's second marriage, an arrangement had been made by which she spent a month at a time with various relations; Mrs. Ogilvy had been comfortably "left" by the departed Mr. Woodhouse, and Harriet also had her own money: three thousand pounds at present, and a contingent reversion of two thousand more; so that some of their less well-to-do connections were glad to put up with the slight awkwardness of having her in the house for a short space, in consideration of the handsome boarding fee which was paid them for it.

Mrs. Ogilvy's feelings were not exalted, but they were strong in every kind, and she had not only the mother's special affection for an unfortunate child, but she often lost her temper with Harriet when she encountered in her an obstinacy and full-blooded determination the counterpart of her own. She had neither the enlightenment nor, for all her forcefulness, the self-control to preserve any detachment towards her daughter; but, not infrequent as the disturbances were, they were always lost sight of as one of Harriet's temporary absences drew near, and it was an eye of fond affection that Mrs. Ogilvy turned on her as she came downstairs to have a cup of tea before departing in a cab to Norwood.

"Now, girlie!" cried Mrs. Ogilvy, "I've let the tea stand, but Hannah shall bring you another pot if it's got too black." Harriet came with little bouncing steps towards the tea table and looked into the teapot.

"This is do, Mama," she said; she sometimes confused small words, though she could always make her
meaning clear. At the age of thirty-two she had a
sallow countenance, with strongly marked lines running from the nostrils to the corners of the lips; her
chin receded, and her eyes were the glutinous black
of treacle. Apart from her expression, and the slightly
slurred enunciation of her words, however, her appearance was one of rather particular neatness and
cost. Her scanty brown hair was crimped in a fringe
and elaborately bunched at the back of her head in a
series of small wiry plaits. She was wearing garnet earrings and a shield-like brooch of pinchbeck pinned to
the front of her dress, which was a handsome blue
silk; it had just come home, and Mrs. Ogilvy looked
at it critically and approvingly.

"Miss Marble makes up very well," she said; "that
silk wants justice doing to it, and it has it, in my
opinion."

Harriet looked down complacently as she sat drinking her tea and eating a piece of cake; but suddenly
her expression changed to one of peevish anxiety. "My
boots!" she said, and stared about her.

"There, bless me, I was forgetting," said Mrs.
Ogilvy, rising in rustling amplitude and fetching a
parcel from under the sideboard. "Here they are, now.
Tom fetched them on his way home from the dentist,
didn't you, Tom?" Tom, still half under the tablecloth, pursuing his solitaire, raised his head and assented shyly. Harriet snatched the parcel and tore off

the wrappings. Inside were two elaborately cut but-
ton boots with narrow toes which had been neatly
though heavily soled in shining leather. As she turned
them over, her face relaxed into a smile, showing almost the whole depth of her teeth.

"A really nice job he's made of it, that I will say,"
said Mrs. Ogilvy; "I'll put them on the hearth, dearie,
to warm while you finish your tea." She took the
boots and herself turned them over, examining them
with satisfaction. One of the points of warmest sympathy between her and Harriet was the latter's acute
enjoyment in anything concerned with food or dress;
on these topics her intelligence was perfectly normal,
and Mrs. Ogilvy's pleasure in promoting her enjoyment and in sympathizing with it was the more intense for being restricted in other respects. She now
returned to her armchair and watched Harriet finish-
ing her tea; to her eye, misted by affection and use,
the traits in Harriet's face which shocked a stranger
appeared hardly more than a slight blemish, rather
endearing than otherwise. She was called to the door
by the maid's bringing down Harriet's box. "Fetch a
cab for Miss Hatty, Hannah," she said, and went upstairs to make sure nothing had been forgotten. Harriet meanwhile was eating and drinking in great content; Tom, crawling cautiously out of his semi-con-
cealment, glanced up at her and inadvertently caught
her attention; she was about to take a currant bun
onto her plate, and something, perhaps, in its glossy
roundness struck her drolly. She held up the bun to

him and gave a loud laugh. What goes on around and above the heads of young children is seldom comprehended by them except in a series of striking vignettes; in after life the most vivid impression of his cousin which Tom Ogilvy retained was the sight of her holding up a bun and laughing with great heartiness but apparently with no meaning.

"Now, Papa," Mrs. Ogilvy was saying as her husband came out of his study into the hall, "you'll tell the cabby where to go, won't you? You know I don't like them to see Hatty without someone at the back of her." Mr. Ogilvy said yes, in an unenthusiastic manner; he opened the front door and saw the cab coming up the street; it drew up at the door while Mrs. Ogilvy was saying all the usual farewells to Harriet and recapitulating the instructions Harriet was to give as to her own comfort once she arrived at the destination, concluding with a perfunctory message of goodwill to their cousin Mrs. Hoppner. The cab lamps shed a misty radiance across the humid dark, and Harriet, in a pelisse and a smart straw hat, bundled in while the luggage was hoisted onto the roof. Mr. Ogilvy directed the man to drive to Norwood, and they drove off, Mrs. Ogilvy watching the last of their disappearance from the lighted hall door.

❦ II ❧

ALICE HOPPNER was sulkily arranging dresses of her own behind the curtained space which was already occupied by her mother's, and jerking open dressing-table drawers to find a hiding place for various little matters that she did not care to have under anyone's eye but her own. Her mother, faded and harassed, came into the room behind her with a nightgown and a brush and comb which she had brought from Alice's own bedroom.

"I was fetching them myself in a minute," said Alice with suppressed irritation.

"Well, I've got to get on with the room," said Mrs. Hoppner defensively; "I can't get the bed made and the dressing table done with your things lying about."

"It's detestable," Alice burst out. "Having her in the house at all is bad enough, but being turned out of my own room is beyond anything. Just when—just when I *want* somewhere to dress myself properly."

"You can dress yourself properly in here; what's to hinder you?" Though usually she shrank from arguments with Alice, Mrs. Hoppner was too tired with endless housework to resist the opportunity of leaning against the wall for a moment.

"The glass is in the wrong place," complained

7

Alice; "besides, I can't, with another person in my way the whole time."

Mrs. Hoppner might have said that she could hardly be much in Alice's way, unless Alice had chosen to dress herself at the kitchen table or the sink; but she was too much occupied with the imminent incursion of visitors to trouble about self-justification; she merely advanced the argument most likely to pacify the girl.

"You know as well as I do," she said, "it's the money we can't do without, if you're to have that dress you want. I'm sure it's no pleasure to me to have Harriet in the house—extra to do for, and no help either; but Jane Ogilvy pays well to get her off her hands, and I'm sure I don't wonder. It's a good thing for her she's got the money to do it, and eight pounds for the month is what I can't do without, not if you're to have all your flummeries." She straightened herself and moved off to the linen cupboard.

That dress! Whenever Alice had devised a toilette, the whole of her existence seemed narrowed down to its achievement. It was now January, and though she had wanted a stiff silk dress to wear in the house—a claret colour or blue—she had decided to forgo it and to concentrate all her resources on one which she would wear indoors during the early spring and outside with the first warm weather; it was to be of crêpe, in that faint but clear lilac known as *soupir étouffé*; the skirt, as was all the way just now, looped in front to suggest an apron, and caught up at the back in a bunch of drapery that stood out behind the waist, giving the wearer the *tournure* of a swan. With this, when she wore it out of doors, she would have a small white straw hat, tilted up at the back and pulled well down over the eyes, encircled by a wreath of wild roses. It was cruel that she should have to do without a silk dress, a watered silk that would rustle in that way that seemed to inspire every movement with grace, but the sacrifice must be made if she was to have this delicate, heavenly creation for the coming year. Her mother could not afford to give her any regular allowance for dress, and all her clothes were obtained by her own examining and apportioning of the family exchequer. Mrs. Hoppner did not demur; she accepted it that Alice was to have the best of everything their meagre income allowed, and Alice herself was too hard-headed to run into foolish extravagance or debt. Mrs. Hoppner acquiesced in her passion for self-adornment, but she did not altogether approve the forms it sometimes took. She supposed she could hardly object to the girl's covering her face with cold cream at night, nasty, messy habit though it seemed; and Alice's dark hair was touched with something that smelt strongly of heliotrope: well, there was no harm in that, perhaps; bandoline she had always thought dirty and unhealthy, but, all the same, there did seem something a little fast about this mysteriously fragrant compound with which Alice coaxed the smooth waves over her temples and the small clusters of curls that rested, delicately intact, behind her ears. A skin like creamy milk she knew her daughter had by nature; but that coral bloom in her cheeks, could that be natural too? Mrs. Hoppner refused to contemplate the idea of Alice's painting, a practice indulged in only by actresses and street-walkers, so she merely shut her mind to the question when it now presented itself again as she began laying clean sheets on the bed.

Alice meanwhile was emptying the corner of a drawer, and arranging in it, behind glove box and handkerchief sachet, a paper of Spanish wool, which, when passed over the cheek, left that transparent flush, above which her excited eyes shone like peridots. Beside the paper was a small pot of red paste for the lips. She hid these appliances, not from any fear of the objections she knew her mother would make, but rather prompted by a savage dislike of interference.

She had much to think over just now, so that to be deprived of a separate bedroom was a real hardship. The reason she had had to vacate her own was the unfortunate coincidence of Harriet's arrival with that of Alice's married sister and her husband. Elizabeth Hoppner had married an impecunious young artist of twenty-two, four years younger than herself; they had been living with Patrick's brother Lewis in a small villa at Streatham; but, the lease having now expired, circumstances combined to make them feel that living in the country would be in every way better— more economical and more suited to the pursuing of Patrick's profession. A small brick house, scarcely larger than a workman's cottage, outside the Kentish village of Cudham, had been fixed upon; and while the two children, born of the first two years of the marriage, had been packed off down there, in the charge of a general servant, to settle in, their parents had come to spend a few days at Elizabeth's home.

Patrick's brother Lewis, who was employed as clerk to an auctioneer, was coming over, it being Saturday, to spend the afternoon and evening with them; and it was Lewis Oman who was occupying Alice's thoughts and making her particularly difficult to live with just at present. The Omans were, without being socially of a different order from Mrs. Hoppner's family, exciting in that they were both worldly and unusual, though the former quality preponderated in Lewis and in Patrick the latter. Mrs. Hoppner was inclined to be slightly awed by her son-in-law, but, as he made scarcely a penny and kept Elizabeth in such a poor way, she felt more able to stand up to him than she would otherwise have done; and if Lewis thought he was going to marry Alice, she supposed that could hardly be done on what he earned, either, unless she herself made some sacrifices. Still, Alice seemed set on him, and he was the sort of man likely to make his way; the only wonder was that he had not bettered himself already. Besides, if she had Alice off her hands, she could dispose of the house and find some comfortable rooms where she would be waited on; in any case, it was no use determining against what the younger people wanted.

Mrs. Hoppner washed up the tea things in the scullery while the others sat in the firelit parlour; Elizabeth usually helped her mother when she was at home, but she had arrived looking so pale and exhausted that Mrs. Hoppner had made her keep still. She now sat, wan and with dark rings round her eyes, and her hair, which she wore loose behind her ears, hanging lustreless. None the less, she was a beautiful woman, with large features and brooding blue eyes; she sat in perfect silence and repose; the animation of the party was supplied by Lewis and Alice. The latter, in a pea-green merino gown, twisted and turned with all the grace of her long delicate limbs as she sat by Lewis's side on the sofa, sometimes with her arm on the sofa behind his neck, sometimes leaning her elbow on his knee; when she gave him a light for his cigar her hand curled over his; her charming shrill laughter was constant, and at every second word she turned her little face towards him. She was not beautiful like her sister, but the perfect roundness of the apricot cheek, the long neck, and full reddened lips made her ten times as seductive; that her countenance betrayed no evidence of mind whatever did not detract from her charm; she was an exquisite little brute, and Lewis Oman liked her the better for it.

"I am looking forward to the pleasure of meeting Miss Woodhouse," he was saying with a grin; his thick pale lips looked the paler for his black moustache, but he was handsome in a somewhat melodramatic manner.

"Oh," screamed Alice, "I can't bear to be reminded of her!"

"I believe Alice is jealous," Lewis observed to the other two. "I know Miss Harriet is a stunner; I'm going to be very attentive to her."

Alice clasped both hands on his shoulder. "Seriously," she cried, "you must be careful, Lewis. If she thinks you are making fun of her, she'll complain, and her mama will fetch her home; and then we shall lose eight pounds. You want to see me in my new dress, don't you?"

"Of course I do," he said earnestly, patting her knee. "But you'll see," he continued; "she's going to fall a victim to my fascinations. You keep a straight face, and we'll have some fun." They went on joking together while Elizabeth sat still and looked, not at her husband, but at the air above his head, in that luxurious security when to know that a movement of the eyelids will bring the beloved object into view is almost more delicious than the view itself. Lounging in a low chair, Patrick Oman was busy with the pieces of a child's toy; he wore the one decent suit he possessed, a dark brown broadcloth, which had that special freshness and becomingness that belongs to clothes only worn on holiday occasions. He did not join in the conversation; to listen to Lewis was entertainment enough; his brother, with his capability, his good looks, and his peculiar force of character, commanded Patrick's whole devotion. He worshipped Lewis with a silent, unquestioning acceptance, entirely oblivious of the fact that, of the two, he himself was by far the more gifted and distinguished man.

"I should have taken a pair of horses over from Streatham," Lewis was saying; "we could have put them up here at the Half-Moon and gone for a spin tomorrow. It would have done Lizzie good, and Alice wouldn't have objected to come, I daresay."

"You wouldn't have had room for me," said Alice pertly. "You'd have had Harriet on the front seat."

"So I should," said Lewis. "What a galling thing to think of, now! And I can't do it simply because the old man won't give me a rise. I've been with the old skinflint two years, and practically run his business for him, and he still won't give me more than twenty-five shillings a week."

"Swine," said Patrick in a low, vindictive voice.

His wife turned her gaze full upon him; her face lighted up as she said, "Don't vex yourself with Alfred's jack-in-the-box."

"I'm not vexing myself," he answered carelessly, continuing his scrutiny and manipulation of the little apparatus. His head lay a little to one side, his legs stretched out to their long length, while he held the spring and its gaily painted box close to his eye. His face, though so young, was gaunt; the big eyes, habitually narrowed with the effort of visual concentration, were rayed with dark lashes like spider's legs. His wife, dwelling on his face, did not tell herself he was the most attractive man she had ever seen; she was merely not conscious of ever seeing another man at all. She fed her gaze, in this quiet and care-free interval, on those features which were known to her better than her own, and always of new interest; he had two little moles under the left eye, which would have been kissed away by now if laid there by any means but the indelible hand of nature. His thin mouth looked to her, as it rested slightly open, everything that was sensitive and beguiling; she had never noticed the significance of its appearance when it was shut.

❧ III ☙

THE SUPPER TABLE, at which Mrs. Hoppner presided, with some slight remains of grace in her worn appearance, had the addition of Harriet, who came downstairs, very affable and smiling in her blue silk, and prepared to be condescending and friendly to her poor relations. She greeted each of them except Mrs. Hoppner, who had already received her, by repeating their names:

"Well, Elizabeth; well, Alice."

"This is Mr. Patrick Oman," said Elizabeth.

"Mr. Patrick Oman," said Harriet.

"Mr. Lewis Oman," said Elizabeth.

"Mr. Lewis Oman," Harriet repeated, and seemed at first surprised at Lewis's leaning towards her with his teeth exposed in a smile under his black moustache; she quickly accepted his attention, however, and presently was seated beside him, eating heartily the corned beef and custard pie, and drinking the stout which had been provided in honour of so much company. Alice's darting eye rested on her in scornful amusement as Lewis gallantly pressed her to take a second bottle of stout; Harriet was plainly delighted by the notice of this handsome stranger, and every time she met his flashing smile her own lips parted in a wide grin; a sensation of pleasure was rapidly forming in her mind, which was a crystallization of all the unapprehended dreams and vague, sensuous moments which had their place in the background of her consciousness as in that of another's, and which was now diffusing its warm rays through her, bringing no clearer an understanding of itself, but making itself moment by moment more strongly felt. She took no further notice of Patrick and Elizabeth, beyond a glance at the former which plainly expressed the feeling that he was very insignificant beside his brother: a common sort of man with no beautiful black whiskers.

Patrick meanwhile was giving his attention to Mrs. Hoppner in his happiest vein of liveliness and good nature.

"The children are very well indeed," he was saying in answer to one of her questions; "they get more amusing every day."

"More naughty," said his wife somewhat regretfully.

"Not when they're with me," said Patrick, "but of course I don't see as much of them as Lizzie does. That's one advantage of being a man; I'd rather support any number of brats than look after one."

"He is very fond of them really," said Elizabeth in anxious defense. "They think there is no one like Papa."

"I hope you will be able to make a little more

money with your painting now, Patrick," said Mrs.
Hoppner, "once you are settled in the country."

Patrick paused a moment, looking at the gas
bracket with unseeing eyes, his mind hovering over
the impossibility of explaining to his mother-in-law
anything of his actual position, either of how difficult
it was to make a decent living by his work, or how
impossible that he should give it up and take to anything else. His temper was set fair for the evening,
however, so he went off at a tangent and said, "What
a lucky devil that Rossetti is!"

"Who may he be?" asked Mrs. Hoppner.

"A painter. He's got an old cove to push him—
Ruskin. If Ruskin says to the public, 'Buy these pictures,' they buy them, and Rossetti has nothing to
do but live with his girl and turn out as many can-
vases as he can between breakfast and supper."

"Well," said Mrs. Hoppner, with the air of one
who scorned to understand mysteries beneath the
notice of a sensible person, "it seems a pity that this
Mr. Ruskin can't do the same for you; but people
who need the money aren't usually the ones to be
taken notice of, by what I see of the world."

Elizabeth did not like what appeared to verge on a
criticism of Patrick, and always faintly resented the
fact that it was his poverty, dear angel, which made
her mother feel that she could adopt that tone with
him.

"I am sure Patrick will make enough for us all once

we get into the country," she said. "It is living in town
that makes it so difficult to paint, naturally."

"No, it doesn't," said Patrick. "You can paint in
London as well as anywhere else. Rossetti has a house
over the river, but it stinks with the mud."

"Well, I shouldn't think that can be very nice,"
said Mrs. Hoppner doubtfully. She leaned across the
table and said, "Harriet, won't you try a piece of
marzipan? You like it, I know. I got it on purpose."

"Thank you," Lewis answered for her, "we're getting on very comfortably down this end." Harriet's
eyes became round with satisfaction, and Lewis was
about to take the dish when Alice snatched it impatiently and, starting up, cried, "We'll take it into the
parlour. Everyone's finished supper, haven't they?"

The parlour fire was a coagulated mass of embers,
but on being poked it blazed up bravely; they all
trooped in, Elizabeth having persuaded her mother to
leave the supper table uncleared and sit with them a
little. Lewis conducted Harriet to a chair and sat
down beside her, taking the plate of marzipan and
handing it to her as he did so.

"Pray try a piece, Miss Harriet," he said. "It looks
very good! Sweets are meant for the ladies, but if you
offer me one, I shall have one too."

Harriet gave her nasal laugh. "You can have one,"
she said.

It darted through Alice's mind that she herself
would have made Lewis entreat for one and finally

receive it as a favour. She watched the pair. Harriet was already practising small gestures, preenings and turns of the head, which she had never used before in her thirty-two years of life, but which had been called out by half an hour of Lewis's company. There was an inhuman vigour in all her movements; they were so full of life, and yet they had not the lithe sureness of an animal; it was as if nature were breathing her inspiration into some curious replica of a living being, neither animal nor human. Alice, standing for a moment on the opposite side of the hearth, caught Lewis's wink. She became convulsed with laughter like a mischievous school-child, and, to conceal her mirth, she ran round the back of the sofa and squeezed herself in beside her half-recumbent brother-in-law.

"Come on, Patrick," she cried, in her shrill, silvery treble, "have half of this with me!" She broke a bar of marzipan in half and daintily poked the glistening fragment into Patrick's mouth; she glanced round as she did so, but the gesture had been lost on Lewis. Was the game turning out to be quite so amusing, after all? She became suddenly quiet while the others went on talking, watching Harriet like a cat at a mouse's hole; and now, for the first time—it was no wonder she had not noticed it before, for who would look twice at such a creature if they could help themselves? —she saw what a very handsome dress Harriet was wearing. The house was badly lighted, and at first she had had the impression that this was a black poplin; but now, as the firelight streamed over a wide breadth of skirt, Alice saw that it was a silk, a deep jay's wing blue, and so stiff that it stood out by itself. She knew how much that sort of material cost. O God, how wickedly, monstrously unfair, that this creature should have such a dress, while Alice herself, whose poise and limbs gave her a natural right to everything that was lovely in colour and sheen and fold, had nothing but—here she disdainfully reviewed her own wardrobe; even the lilac crêpe, when she should have it, would not be half so handsome as this, and Harriet no doubt had many more. Here the thought struck her that Harriet, who had so much and was so stupid, might perhaps give her something out of her own wardrobe; not this dress exactly—though, after all, why not? What pleasure could Harriet get from it compared with the satisfaction it would be to Alice! —but if not that one, another: or a piece of jewelry or a scarf. On the whole she was glad now that Harriet was paying them this visit; when Harriet was out of the way she would go into her bedroom and look through all her belongings to see exactly what she had. Oh, what a dreadful, shocking idea! But if anyone were to come in and see her, she would say that she had left something of her own behind there.

They did not sit up very late. Mrs. Hoppner toiled upstairs with the jug of hot water into Harriet's bedroom, while Elizabeth went to clear the dishes from the supper table, and Alice, left alone with the two men, was immediately conscious of the freedom that comes from an absence of feminine surveillance. She twined her arm in Lewis's and, looking up into his face, she said:

"I see you've quite thrown *me* over. You'll ask Harriet to make me a bridesmaid, won't you?"

Lewis caressed her shoulders without speaking; then he kissed her. "Hadn't you better help Lizzie with the dishes before your mother comes down?" he said. This idea did not commend itself to Alice, who pouted and began to rub her cheek up and down against his sleeve. Patrick, divining that his brother wanted a moment's conversation with him before returning home, turned round at once and said sharply:

"For shame, Alice! You idle little bag of bones! Go and give Lizzie a hand with the clearing up."

Alice straightened herself abruptly, and with a heightened colour walked out of the room. Lewis immediately strolled up to his brother and leaned against the mantelpiece. He opened without delay.

"I wonder how much that —— has of her own," he said.

"Lizzie mentioned five thousand pounds," said Patrick, "but these things are always exaggerated."

"Christ!" said Lewis.

"It's a pity Alice can't get some of it out of her," continued Patrick, "but Alice has no notion of making herself agreeable when she doesn't feel like it."

"No," said Lewis absently. "It would be interesting to know exactly," he went on presently. "If it were anything like five thousand pounds it would be quite a fortune."

"Yes," said Patrick. "I should think she must be about the only woman with so much money who'll never be married for it. She's awful, isn't she?"

To his surprise, Lewis gave an actual shudder. "God —awful," he said.

"It's a pity she's got to be here just now," Patrick went on, but Lewis interrupted him decidedly.

"I don't know about that," he said.

Patrick supposed Lewis thought that no connection with money, however ephemeral and remote, was to be shunned, and he himself was quite of the same opinion. It made one writhe and gnash one's teeth to see how money was distributed in this world; with half of what that outlandish —— had to spend on herself Lewis could be a gentleman, driving his own dogcart; it was a vision of his brother, invested in all the attributes of independence and power, sleekly attired, bowling along behind a snowy chestnut, which rose faintly on Patrick's mental vision, and in that visionary flash the whirling spokes and hoofs, the impression of covert coating and the tilt of a sporting bowler, made for him an image joyous and sacred as that of a hero charioted by a team of leopards yoked with lions. What he himself would do with money was a question quite secondary to this aspiring conception of his brother's greatness.

"Well," he said, "I daresay Lizzie can find out from Mrs. Hoppner how much there is; if only there were any way of getting at it! Why don't you give Alice a hint? But she's so damned flighty, I don't suppose she'd take it."

"No," said Lewis, "I've not much hope of that. Well," he continued, stretching and bestirring himself, "I may as well be off before the old girl comes down. Say good-night for me. I'll be round first thing tomorrow." Patrick accompanied him out onto the front doorsteps and stood a moment leaning with his hand on Lewis's shoulder; he was a head taller than Lewis, who was, indeed, scarcely of middle height, but he always gave the impression, even when they stood side by side, of looking up to his brother. He watched him now as Lewis strutted off down the street, while the lower rooms were darkened and, above, candlelight rayed across the walls of the bedrooms. Harriet found her bed quite comfortable and dug herself down into it with a grunt of satisfaction. Mrs. Hoppner and Elizabeth finished the washing up in the scullery, while Alice, in her frilled flannel nightgown, lay back against the pillows of the double bed, her hands clasped behind her head, her heart beating wildly, and her brilliant eyes staring at the ceiling.

☙ IV ☙

PATRICK and Elizabeth did not remain with Mrs. Hoppner more than a day or two, and to the latter, at least, their stay was all too short. She was beginning to know that sensation of perpetual, dull weariness, sometimes accentuated to actual pain, which was, in fact, her mother's ordinary condition. Alice would never know it, for Alice was not one of those women who devote themselves to a household; what Alice could not get done for her she would leave undone, and no man would like her any the worse for it; though children in her care would not, perhaps, thrive, unless they should happen to be as hardy as she was herself. But to Elizabeth a short space in which she did not rise at half-past six and sit sewing until long after dark was haven of tranquillity and repose. It reinspired her and made her look forward with pleasure to seeing the children again. On the morning of their departure she was collecting her belongings and Patrick's, all of which had to be stowed into a battered old portmanteau and a shawl bundle; she was finding the usual difficulty in this operation when her husband came into the bedroom.

"Will you bring me your slippers, love?" she said, rising from her stooping posture over the bed.

"They're here," said Patrick, indicating a pair of worn-out carpet slippers, embroidered in pansies, which Elizabeth had once worked for him. "How shabby they are!" she exclaimed, beating the soles together. "I must work them over when we are at home again."

"Listen," he said abruptly, "did you ask your mother how much money Harriet Woodhouse has belonging to her?"

"No," said Elizabeth, surprised. "I don't believe I did."

"But I told you to find out."

"I remember—but it went out of my head. Why do you want to know?" Patrick's face darkened.

"Of course," he said, "if it's too much trouble to do what I ask, I'll know better another time. But I should have thought that when you've had nothing to do here except gossip with your mother, you might have found time to ask a simple question."

Elizabeth looked bewildered and unhappy. "I'll find out if you really want to know, Patrick," she said, "but it seems so strange to ask." She could have no idea that this implied a criticism of Lewis, but as such it exacerbated Patrick's already uneasy temper.

"Don't trouble yourself, then," he said vindictively. "I should be sorry to put you out." And he turned to leave the room. With a low exclamation that was almost a wail, Elizabeth pushed past him and ran downstairs into the kitchen. "Mother!" she exclaimed, confronting Mrs. Hoppner at the sink.

"What is it, dear?" The sight of the questioning face, however, instantly aroused Elizabeth's instinct to conceal anything censurable in her husband. "I forgot to ask you," she said. "Does—does Harriet stay here long?"

"About another three weeks, I daresay."

"I suppose—no, it would hardly do—I suppose it is no good suggesting her coming to us in the country for a bit? We could do with the money."

"I don't think so, dear. You've your hands so full already, I doubt the extra money would be worth it. And then, I don't believe she'd go so far from London."

"I see." Elizabeth paused. "She's very rich, isn't she?"

"Well," said Mrs. Hoppner, "to our way she is."

"How much has she? I suppose no one except she and her mother has any idea."

"Oh, dear, yes," said Mrs. Hoppner, with the readiness of her kind to display information. "Harriet has three thousand pounds of her own, and when one of her aunts dies she will have two thousand more. That's what they call a reversionary interest."

"It sounds a great deal," said Elizabeth wistfully; then she turned slowly about. "I must finish our packing," she said.

"I've got a beefsteak pie for you to put in," said Mrs. Hoppner, drying her hands on a piece of rag and following Elizabeth out of the kitchen.

"How good you are, Mother. That'll save me a lot."

But Elizabeth, who knew that she had no head for figures, was anxious to impart her information to Patrick as soon as possible, before her mind confused it; she evaded her mother, therefore, and discovered him in the minute strip of garden in front of the house. She went up to him as he stood smoking his pipe by the railings, and said casually, albeit lowering her voice so that there should be no chance overhearer from an upstairs window:

"Three thousand pounds now, and two thousand more when an aunt dies—what is called a reversionary interest."

Patrick received the information in silence; it sank into his brain with the sureness of acid burning through wax to bite its impression on the copper plate beneath. He removed the pipe from his mouth, and, without his saying anything or altering his gaze across the sunny street, his presence somehow communicated to his wife an expression of benevolence. She leaned slightly against him, following the direction of his eyes with hers, over to the opposite row of yellow brick houses, all with identical railings and front doors. A passer-by, seeing them standing tranquilly in the sunshine, would have thought them a singularly dignified couple, with that speaking gravity on their fine faces.

When they arrived at their new abode that afternoon, dusk was already stealing over the Kentish woods. The little raw brick villa, containing four rooms downstairs and three above, was two miles

from the railway station and almost as far from the
village, and only to be approached through a lane
winding between hedgerows, or else, more directly,
provided one knew the way, across a waste of fields,
through gaps and gates. Behind the house, a coppice
stretched along the side of other fields, forming now,
for all its leaflessness, a background dense and dim,
over which a faint star or two sparkled intermit-
tently.

Their arrival was prepared for: a small fire and
lamps glowed in the front of the house, and at the
front door Clara Smith appeared with little Julia in
her arms, while Alfred was hopping in and out over
the threshold. Elizabeth alighted from the hired trap
and took the children in her arms with a rush of maternal feeling. Her arrival, however, was only part of
the general excitement. Alfred was but three, and in
his mother's absence he had got on as well as he usually did; indeed, rather better, for, as Clara had had
everything on her hands, he enjoyed, in between her
impatient sallies on him, unrestricted leisure and en-
largement. His father, however, he recognized at once
as a mysterious and attractive element which had returned to his life. As they sat at high tea, a meal of
which Mrs. Hoppner's cold pie formed the basis,
Elizabeth held the baby on her lap, while Alfred stood
at his father's knee, his finger in his mouth, staring
wide-eyed at that absorbing face. Patrick quite
acquiesced in his position as a parent, whatever strange
and unseemly outbursts his temper might sometimes

betray him into; it was true, as he had said, that he
did not care to look after children, but when he had
to do so, he went through with the thing and had
more than once washed and dressed Alfred and put
him to bed. Now, in the intervals of his own meal, he
cut and handed to Alfred pieces of pie crust or cake,
very small, as suited Alfred's capacity, which were
eaten with due thankfulness. Elizabeth presently went
upstairs with her baby, while Clara Smith began to
clear the table and carry the things into the kitchen.
Clara was a girl of about fifteen, distantly related to
the Hoppners, and an arrangement had been in force
for some time by which she was general servant to
Elizabeth; she received no wages, but on the other
hand she was understood to be more or less one of the
family. Besides food and lodging, Elizabeth undertook to provide her with clothes, and Patrick had
promised that she should have some pocket money
from time to time when he could see his way to it.
The arrangement had been made between the Omans
and Clara's parents, who were glad to get rid of one
of many children, and to secure her what, on the surface, appeared a good enough place, the drawback of
no payment being atoned for by her receiving a home
among relations. If Clara had been a girl of the cali-
bre of her cousin Alice, or indeed of a practical turn
of mind at all, she might have directed her attention
to doing better for herself than her parents had done
for her; but in actual fact she was a bulging-eyed
creature whose happiness it was to feast upon any

form of emotion; exaggerated surprise over the most trivial happenings, being shocked to death when Alfred perpetrated one of his many minor misdemeanours, gaping with admiration over the fine clothes or accomplishments of anybody else, all made a life, which to many people would have been one of drudgery and excruciating boredom, perfectly acceptable to her. Her chief indulgence was a slowly accumulating collection of penny-press novels and stories of crime, the latter illustrated with grotesque drawings of the protagonists; she had few opportunities for reading, and could, besides, only spell out the print with difficulty, so that one of these productions lasted her a considerable time, and, scanty as were her opportunities of replenishing her store, she was seldom without something to finish. She kept the dirty-looking paper-covered books in the tin box under the bed which she shared with Alfred in the small back bedroom. It was a fourposter, although it had no curtains, and there was plenty of room for them both in it. The baby had a cot in the large front bedroom occupied by Patrick and Elizabeth.

This bedroom was the best, indeed the only properly furnished room in the house. It had a carpet, a bed with chintz hangings, some oil paintings in elaborate gilt frames, a large dressing table, a wardrobe, and a washstand. The back bedroom had nothing in it except the curtainless fourposter and a chair, and a curtain hung before a row of pegs; and, indeed, it was so small that there would scarcely have been room for anything else. Clara had to wash herself downstairs in the scullery; as to a looking glass, she did not use one. Occasionally she stole into the front bedroom to look at herself in Elizabeth's mirror, but then the foreign splendours of the apartment so startled and unnerved her that as often as not she saw only the carpet reflected in the mirror, since the latter had a trick of slanting forward, and she would come away without appearing to realize that she had not achieved what she set out to do. The downstairs rooms also contained the minimum of furniture, the one to the right of the front door being the family sitting room, while the one opposite was empty except for Patrick's easel and paints, Alfred's toys, and some tools and odd stores which were indispensable in a house so isolated from neighbours and shops.

As Elizabeth prepared for bed that night she felt a strange mixture of gladness and apprehension; she could see that the loneliness appealed to Patrick; already he was prowling about the premises as if he were happy and at home, although he said nothing; and she herself, as she drew back the scanty curtain and looked out at the expanse of faint starlight, was inexplicably touched and soothed. But to be two miles away from the village shops! Dependent for every mouthful they ate on visiting tradesmen! Would not the shops neglect them in bad weather, such parsimonious customers as they would be? And suppose the children were suddenly taken ill? Or the house burnt over their heads? But it did no good to think of such things; a long steady struggle was in front of her to keep everyone happy, and, that being so, the sooner she got to sleep and revived her energy the better. She told herself she was devoted to the well-being of the family, and she was indeed prepared mechanically to undergo any hardships which the children's welfare might make necessary, but the inspiration of her life was the wish to secure Patrick's happiness. Her love was so heavy on her heart; the burden of a nation has been borne more lightly than the weight of this one man. She drew back from the window and finished undressing in the darkness; she had not troubled to light a candle; she was accustomed to the simplest ways.

The next morning, when they had breakfasted and were all astir, Elizabeth began to examine her domain; there was—what she had not previously noticed—a small vegetable garden at the back of the house, where Patrick was already doing some work with a hoe. How clever he was, she thought; there was nothing he couldn't turn his hand to and accomplish with that easy, firm dexterity. She stood a moment, enjoying the warm burst of January sunlight which gilded the landscape, and saw, away to the left, a building half hidden by a turn of the lane.

"Why, there's a house!" she exclaimed.

"Three," said Patrick. "They're developing the sites. In some years' time this will be part of the village. A town, it may be then. If I'd a sixpence I'd buy the next bit to ours and speculate." He leaned on the hoe.

"It would be convenient to be part of the village," said Elizabeth. "The shops are so far away, darling!"

Patrick straightened himself. "You won't want much with the shops," he told her. "There's a barrel of flour in the kitchen and a side of bacon, and we've got cabbages here. You won't be buying anything oftener than once a week, and they send the boys round then."

"I'm not extravagant," said Elizabeth, smiling, "but if we are suddenly out of some little thing—tea or butter——"

"We do without it, that's all," said Patrick, beginning to hoe again. "And Lizzie!" he called as she was going back to the house. "About those neighbours——"

"Yes, dear?"

"I suppose you'll want to know them?"

She smiled rather ruefully. "They mightn't want to know me! I'm so shabby and down at heel, and we'll hardly have a parlour."

He gave his rare, slow smile. "You'll be the most beautiful woman in the parish, I don't mind betting. But we don't want people always out and in."

"No," said Elizabeth with dignity. He was crouching over the path and put his arm round her knees, leaning his head against her.

"It's a pity we can't eat snails, like the French," he

said. "The undersides of these cabbages are covered with them."

"I daresay we could cook them!" she said, smiling. "Would you like a little plateful for supper, just to try?" She caressed his hair and left him stooping over the cabbages; as she went up the path to the house, she thought, "I am so happy! So happy! What had we better have for midday dinner? A batter pudding, perhaps, and the remains of Mother's pie for supper. It isn't suitable for Alfred."

Clara's round, staring face met her at the side door.

"Fancy, madam!" she exclaimed, "if the baker's boy hasn't been already! But I said you was talking to the master. So he's coming on his way back, after he's been to the new houses up the lane."

Elizabeth would have had no objection to Clara's calling her and Patrick by their Christian names; but Clara seemed to derive positive enjoyment from treating them in an obsequious manner. The girl worried Elizabeth rather, as a busy woman is apt to be fretted by an assistant whose main interest is in posturing and anticking rather than in performing the actual work in hand. However, she was capable enough and flew to do what she was asked. Elizabeth could not have formulated any reasonable objection to her, had she been asked for one, and on this of all mornings Clara's deficiencies were blurred in a roseate light. She entered the scullery with a slow, queenly step, saying, "Never mind. Watch out for him while I dress the children; I am going to walk to within sight of the shops. Hurry up with the breakfast things, and have the kitchen table ready for me to make a batter pudding when I come in. You might ask Mr. Patrick to cut us a cabbage." She went upstairs to collect the children's outdoor clothes and her own and heard the baker's boy come whistling down the lane as she did so.

V

AT MRS. HOPPNER's things were going quite smoothly. Mrs. Hoppner missed the visitors, but their absence meant less work; it depended upon her own degree of tiredness as to whether she were more conscious of the loss of Elizabeth's society or the relief of having less cooking and washing up to do. Harriet was indifferent to the change; Elizabeth had been slightly stiff and awkward with her, but she had not seen very much of the Omans. She always took her breakfast in bed, coming down late and sitting in the sunny parlour when it was all neatly dusted and made ready for her reception. She was, however, active and vigorous and fond of walking, and nearly always passed some of the day in walking in the half-urbanized country behind Norwood, or in making expeditions, sometimes into the West End, to shop. She also liked going to theatres, and to these Lewis sometimes accompanied her; he stipulated that Alice should come too, and he always paid for the party; Alice thought somewhat resentfully that Harriet might have contributed to the expenses of the evening (naturally she herself was not able to do so); but Lewis would not have accepted anything even if it had occurred to Harriet to offer it; he saw well that she was not only careful with her own money, but that she admired open-handed generosity in other people; and he spared nothing in the way of oyster suppers after the play and boxes of sweets on his visits to the house, to increase his glory in Harriet's eyes. Alice was all this while vaguely puzzled and at a loss, and a faint frown began to develop itself over her clear eyes. The open-mouthed admiration which Harriet showed, and a certain uncouth possessiveness which she was beginning to exhibit towards Lewis, had long ceased to be amusing; surely anyone must feel that; and sometimes, as when they were obliged to delay their departure from the theatre while Harriet carefully smoothed on her gloves and adjusted her hat and tippet and collected her reticule and umbrella, Lewis's gallantry and attention prolonging rather than hastening the process, Alice, who liked to start away like a gazelle at the fall of the curtain and could not endure being overtaken and crushed and impeded by the surging crowd, could hardly contain herself. Then, sometimes Lewis would scarcely speak to her as he escorted them home, but with Harriet on his arm would entertain the latter with anecdotes of a curious but simple nature, and try to draw her out, asking her, for example, whether she cared for the stars. Yes, Harriet said, she was partial to stars; she sometimes wondered that you couldn't see them in the daytime. Lewis gave her to understand that he could if necessary explain to her the reason for this, but it was difficult and uninteresting, and he had rather spend the time talking about her and what she liked and disliked. He had heard her say one day to Mrs. Hoppner that she did not care for anything sweet served with the meat; did that mean that she never took apple sauce with pork? He himself felt that it was the making of the dish, but he wanted to know what she thought; and he insinuated, perhaps more by his voice and his pressure on her arm than by anything he actually said, that he should be very anxious to have her opinion on anything to do with housekeeping, because he knew what a fine house she would have when she set up for herself, and how lucky anyone would be whom she allowed to live in it. When they arrived at Mrs. Hoppner's door that night, Harriet and Lewis arm in arm, Alice stepped aside onto the grass as the door opened, revealing Mrs. Hoppner's lamp, because she had to conceal a great sob of vexation that was rising in her throat. Harriet, having bid Lewis goodnight, said, "Come along, Alice!" in the tone of a matron addressing a child, and passed into the hall, eager to recount all the doings of the evening. Alice stepped onto the path to follow her, rigid with fury, tears sparkling on her lashes; but Lewis put his arms round her and in the shadow of the house gave her a passionate kiss. It was over before she realized what had happened, and he had walked away and swung the gate to after him; but she went upstairs in a state of mingled disappointment and excitement.

The next morning, after a night's sleep and some careful reflection, she arose feeling quite confident

and happy; that second in Lewis's arms meant more
than long evenings of exasperation and days of suspense; and she now began to think, as Harriet's visit
was drawing to its close, that she might as well bestir
herself and see whether there was any plunder to be
gained from her. She was particularly pleasant with
Harriet that morning, and another person might have
been touched to see in how childlike a manner Harriet
responded to a show of interest and good-will; affection it was beyond Alice even to simulate. They were
in the parlour while Mrs. Hoppner and the daily
woman were busied in other parts of the house, and
Harriet's handsome workbox was on the table. It was
of polished wood with a painted china medallion let
into the lid, and the inside was elaborately ruched and
padded with turquoise velvet. Alice admired the box
and praised the picture on the lid, and Harriet began
to show her all the little treasures it contained: the
carved mother-of-pearl boxes; the needlecase with
the little hole, which, when applied to the eye, disclosed a whole prospect of the front at Llandudno; a
Bible two inches square; a pincushion made in an exact replica of a large strawberry; a tiny silver-gilt
vinaigrette; all these much cherished objects she laid
confidingly in Alice's hand, one after the other; she
was willing and anxious for her to see and handle them
all. Alice was really rather interested in them for a
moment, and the lining of the box was exquisite, that
silky light blue velvet; what would not one give for a
dozen yards of it! Aloud she reminded Harriet that

the latter had said she wanted some help in putting a new set of lace into her blue silk dress, and by this means she got her upstairs into her bedroom. Here it was easy to lead her on into displaying the contents of her wardrobe. Harriet liked her possessions to be admired, and she was beginning to feel that Alice was quite a pleasant sort of girl and that she was now for the first time getting to know her. Besides, there was in her own breast such a sensation of blind happiness and content that she felt kind and good towards everyone; and Alice, as a sister-in-law of Mr. Lewis, was an object of special interest to her now. She was standing by the wardrobe fingering the row of her dresses, and she thought that she would like to give one of them to Alice; any that Alice liked. She would turn round and say, "Alice, you may choose one of my dresses. You may have whichever you like, however expensive it is." Of course, her very best dresses were not here at all, but at home, but any of these would be a very handsome present to anyone so poor as the Hoppners. The impulse sent a glow through her, and she turned round, the words on her lips. Alice was standing by the dressing table, so that she was reflected in the glass; she was trying on a brooch of Harriet's, the large garnet cluster which had been left on the china tray on the dressing table. Her face, as she earnestly regarded herself, was so startling, for all its youthful roundness, in its expression of vanity and greed that Harriet stood petrified. She saw a violent, impudent attack on her own property, and she advanced with a sudden start of rage. "That's mine!" she said, and gnashed her teeth. Alice dropped the brooch. "I was only looking at it," she said, terrified. Harriet made no reply but put the brooch into her jewel box, which she shut with a snap, and, having closed the wardrobe door, she went out of the room, muttering under her breath.

Alice remained a moment, pale and shaking. Keen disappointment, a sense of having been cheated of something to which she had a right, made together a positive hatred; she sought for epithets with which to express her rage and loathing, but could think of none that were not quite childish. She hurried out of the room and saw her mother on the stairs. If Harriet had complained of her—not that she *minded* what her mother said, but she really could not endure another commotion just now. She drooped her eyelids and sailed demurely downstairs. Mrs. Hoppner did not say anything and was merely coming upstairs to get a clean tablecloth out of the linen cupboard. She was at present quite out of sympathy with Alice because she saw that Lewis was less marked in his attentions to her, and she thought it a good thing. While she supposed their marriage to be inevitably coming on, she was prepared to submit to it with a good grace, but if anything were to put it aside, why, so much the better. Alice need not want for admirers, and men with a decent income, even if they were less smart and clever than Lewis; she had no doubt Alice would make a fine to-do when she discovered Lewis

really didn't mean to have her; but, then, she was not
exactly pleasant at the best of times, and it was all in
the day's work. Reflections of this sort, however inspired with fortitude, do not make for friendliness and
conversation, and Mrs. Hoppner rarely said anything
to Alice nowadays. She did not suppose Alice cared;
Alice did not; she retired into herself now, and it was
difficult to say what she did with herself all the time,
but she became, in a day or two, thinner; her lovely
throat that supported the round head, with its delicate curve of jaw and chin, became more sharply
defined in all the outlines, and all round her eyes the
skin had a faintly bruised look; though she had had
plenty of annoyances, she had never before experienced any real anxiety or trouble, and a feeling of
strangeness in all her unhappiness gave her an air of
surprise and pain which was moving to anyone who
noticed it; but this mysterious shade was frequently
dispelled by her outbreaks of savage irritation, when
she became merely a vulgar little shrew. For the re-
stored confidence which Lewis's kiss had given her
was dwindling away now, and as Alice became more
uncertain and unbalanced, Harriet grew ever more
preening and serene. She had quickly got over her
burst of indignation over the brooch, and treated
Alice with increasing good nature. Alice flung away
from these demonstrations as openly as she dared, but
the consciousness that there was no one now who was
completely devoted to her interests and on whom she
could rely made her very cautious and self-contained,

and she even avoided the sitting room when company was present, preferring to crouch upstairs over a candle with some sewing, or reading a novel bought in Holywell Row, lent to her by a fast girl with whom she was acquainted, and kept under the mattress of her bed; she had not gone back to her own room, because Mrs. Hoppner had not liked to put Harriet to the trouble of moving, so she had gone into the room vacated by Patrick and Elizabeth.

On the last evening of Harriet's stay Alice had been feeling slightly more cheerful; surely things would be better once the creature was out of the house. How revolting she was, to be sure! Alice rose from the pillow against which she had been lying and began to straighten her skirts. One candle on the dressing table showed a reflection, not of the shabby room, but a deep interior of rich light and sombre shadow, in the middle of which she herself appeared, flushed and untidy, here deep coloured, there blotted out in shade, so lovely that she advanced towards the vision with delightful consciousness of how impossible it was that any human man could relinquish her; she was positive that Lewis was in love with that girl in the glass, and she felt how silly and morbid she had been, giving way to exaggerated fancies, making out that everything was much more significant than it really was. It was no wonder if Lewis had got a bit tired of her, going on like that! But he was here this evening, downstairs even now; she would tidy herself and then run down and charm him as she knew perfectly well how to do. It did not occur to her that she had found this easy when she had only a fancy for him, and that the bad time she had had just lately might mean, among other things, that she was not altogether her own mistress, and could not command her gaiety and radiance when she wanted to shine with them. She was now eager to be presentable and downstairs. Nine o'clock! She had refused any supper on the plea of feeling bilious, but Lewis had not been in the house then, and if she chose to come down now, her mother was too experienced in Alice's vagaries to comment on her quick recovery. She shook out her skirts and ran downstairs; in the hall she paused; a light in the scullery showed Mrs. Hoppner washing up, and the parlour door was open too. By the fire Lewis stood, with his back to her, bending over Harriet, who sat on a low chair with her netting, looking incredibly simpering and silly, Alice felt sure, though she could not see her face.

"Then you will tell your mother as soon as you go home tomorrow?" he was saying in a low voice. Alice stood behind the door, transfixed. What secret could Lewis possibly have with Harriet that the rest of them didn't know? Harriet's answer was inaudible, and to the listener the whole scene became indescribably intense and remote; she saw both people as if for the first time. Then Lewis took Harriet's hand and kissed it, and she, dropping her work, seized his hand in both hers and pressed it against her cheek. Lewis raised his head and glanced towards the open door;

he wore the strangest expression, but Alice did not stay to examine it. She fled upstairs in an agony of rage and horror and locked herself into her room; but no one was troubling his head about her.

Mrs. Hoppner was called in from the scullery to give her reserved congratulations, and, though Harriet looked round and said, "Where's Alice?" she was speedily diverted by a remark from Lewis. The latter did not stay very long, and his attendance at the auctioneer's office would prevent his seeing Harriet on the morrow; but he promised to come over to Mrs. Ogilvy's on the following Sunday, and Harriet, shortly after his departure, took herself up to bed.

Mrs. Hoppner remained in a slightly puzzled but passive condition. She supposed her cousin Ogilvy would not be best pleased with the match. Well, she was a masterful woman: she and Lewis could fight it out together. Harriet would not give up her young man without a struggle, that was clear. It did occur to her that Mrs. Ogilvy might hold her responsible for Harriet's ever having come in contact with Lewis, but who in the world could have helped that? Lewis had been about the place as Alice's lover: that ought to have been safe enough, specially considering the difference between the two. Anyhow, if Mrs. Ogilvy did take on, the worst she could do would be to deprive them of the pecuniary benefit of any further visit from Harriet, and *that* they would not be having in any case if the marriage came off. No, the pressing problem before Mrs. Hoppner was how to bear with Alice; she hoped, however, that the commotion would not last. Alice must look about and take up with somebody else, someone with a competence this time, who would be able to look after her without any more sacrifices from her mother.

Alice's behaviour after Harriet's departure was better than Mrs. Hoppner had anticipated; she made no outward complaint whatever, and her mother refrained from mentioning Lewis in her hearing. She did not, at first, even cry, so far as could be known. On the following Monday, however, a fine day with the promise of spring in the air, she was coming back from the post office when, just a few paces from her own door, she encountered Miss Croker, the local dressmaker. Miss Croker conducted her business in a neighboring road, in a yellow brick house with a brass plate on the door, and she and Alice were on rather friendly terms; many an anxious consultation had taken place behind the heavy lace curtains of Miss Croker's front parlour, where the cheval glass and the sewing machine and the sofa littered with scraps and threads gave a professional air somewhat at variance with the rest of the room. Miss Croker took an interest in her work for Alice, because the latter, although exacting and particular to the last degree, always knew exactly what she wanted, was clear in her directions, and such a credit to Miss Croker in her appearance once the dress had come home. Her clever ideas, too, when slightly altered, served Miss Croker over and over again in her dealings with unimagina-

tive customers, and gave her a reputation for style
and knowingness which she was entitled to use, in
consideration of the very low rate at which she
worked for Alice, and her obligingness in not pressing
for her moderate accounts. She now stepped across
the road to her, and said, "Miss Alice, that heliotrope
crêpe of yours that we fixed on—I wonder if you'd
like it begun on now? I'm doing a lot of work for
Mrs. Samuelson, of The Pines, next month, and by
then likely we'll have the warm weather and you'll
wish you had your dress!" She paused, amazed, for
Alice did not answer. She merely stared at Miss
Croker with a white face, and, muttering something
unintelligible, rushed through her own gate and into
the house; that evening Miss Croker received a brief
note saying that Alice could make no arrangements
at present. "It's peculiar," thought Miss Croker,
"very! If money's the trouble, she might have said so,
and it could have stood over a bit." She was disappointed, for she had looked forward with a workman's pride to making the mauve crêpe dress; it was
to have been something altogether distinguished and
out of the way.

From this time onward Alice did seem to give way
to tears. Her eyes were often red, and sometimes, sitting in the parlour, she would not exert herself to hide
the fact that she was crying. This did not worry Mrs.
Hoppner; people who merely sat about and cried were
no trouble.

❧ VI ☙

MRS. OGILVY was appalled. Harriet had arrived home saying, "Mama, I am going to be married to a very handsome young gentleman, a brother of Elizabeth Hoppner, who is now Oman," and Mrs. Ogilvy had thought it a fantasy engendered by this man's good-natured attentions, whoever he was. She thought gratefully of him for having been kind to poor Hatty and letting her have a little fun like other girls, and perhaps he hadn't understood that it might have been as well not to be too good-natured, as she would be sure to build on it more than she ought and take some time in forgetting him again. But gradually, as the evening of Harriet's home-coming wore on, and Harriet talked of nothing else but Lewis and his generosity and his beautiful black moustaches, and of his gallantry at the play, and finally of his proposed visit on the following Sunday, Mrs. Ogilvy began to be seriously disturbed; she was not immediately alarmed, because the whole affair was quite preposterous; but she began to see now that she had taken a very great risk in allowing Harriet to go about so much by herself, and that the wonder was this sort of thing had not happened before. But Harriet's condition, making her marriage utterly impossible to be conceived of by any decent person, had blinded Mrs. Ogilvy to the fact that the world contains many people who are far from decent. Then, too, Mrs. Ogilvy herself had always been so comfortable in her circumstances that she had, for so sensible a woman, been surprisingly oblivious of the bait which Harriet's fortune would offer to the needy. But, now that her eyes had been opened to the position, she saw the whole thing as clear as day. When it was a question of an actual attempt upon property Mrs. Ogilvy did not take money and comfort for granted at all; she knew to a sixpence the value of every article she possessed, and every detail of Harriet's present and presumptive fortune, and the more she looked about her and reckoned up the family estate, the more impudent and atrocious did this barefaced robbery which Lewis proposed to commit appear to her. "For robbery it is," said Mrs. Ogilvy, "and no one can throw dust in *my* eyes about it!" At first blush her feelings about Lewis had been, in an intensified form, those with which she would have regarded him had he been discovered in making off with her silver tea service or Harriet's jewelry, which had been left to her by will from her aunt Bowaters; but that night, when she was in Harriet's bedroom waiting to put out the candle, as she always did, Harriet, seeming to have forgotten the rather strained and unsympathetic manner with which her mother had put by her other remarks about Lewis, said in an innocent and awestruck tone, "Mr. Lewis drives a dogcart when he is on his holiday!" Mrs. Ogilvy said nothing, but as she kissed Harriet and put out the light she told herself that Lewis was a black-hearted scoundrel, and she was not thinking about the property when she did so.

On Sunday she prepared to receive Lewis herself, alone, in the drawing room. Harriet wanted to be there very much, but Mrs. Ogilvy managed, partly by entreaty, partly by commands, and partly, though her heart was wrung as she did this, by the insinuation that when gentlemen came on an errand like this it was not suitable for the lady concerned to be present at the interview with her parents, to send Harriet upstairs as half-past two approached. She settled herself, in a majestic gown of black bombazine which had been part of her mourning for Mr. Woodhouse. One might almost say that she felt herself widowed afresh in this crisis; but she would not allow any of the present situation to fall upon Mr. Ogilvy's shoulders, and that for two reasons: she had, when she married him, been half conscious that, owing to his dread of his studious and retiring habits being disturbed, it was only her own determination which finally had brought the marriage about, and therefore she always felt it her duty to screen him from any trouble and worldly interruption, more especially when it concerned her own family apart from him; and secondly, she felt she had a good many things to say to this young man which she would be sorry to entrust to somebody else. She was revolving them in her mind with some satisfaction when Lewis was announced.

If there had ever been in Mrs. Ogilvy's breast some faint, delusive hope that this man might turn out to be someone who was fond of Hatty—who would see what a poor, sweet girl she was, in spite of her little queernesses; to whom she might, although she felt marriage for her to be very wrong, confide the care of her, with Harriet's own money to keep them comfortable—that hope, if it could be said ever to have lived, died as Lewis crossed the threshold. Mrs. Ogilvy knew quite well that no one except herself really cared about Hatty, and that everybody, in his heart of hearts, had rather that she were not there. She did not blame them; she was too sensible for that; but if she could have found one person who showed a spark of anything beyond the civilized toleration and forced kindness with which her daughter was universally treated, she would have come forward to that man with all her sympathies, her support, be he who he might. But she never expected to find anything of the sort, although that ghost of an irrational hope must have been there, to account for the double bitterness with which she surveyed Lewis Oman as he came jauntily into the room.

Lewis had a part to play which required so much effrontery that to attempt deceit as well, and make himself out a disinterested lover, would have been beyond the capacity of anyone human except King Richard III. Lewis was no bottled spider, nor had he been born in the eyrie which dallies with the wind and scorns the sun; his scope was altogether more limited than that redoubtable monarch's; but what he was, he was with his whole being; his intensity of purpose gave him an ascendancy over people much cleverer than himself, like his brother Patrick, and as he now sat down opposite to Mrs. Ogilvy, a pert, undersized, vulgarly good-looking person of the lower middle class, he impressed even her stalwart bosom with a sense of foreboding. He for his part was relieved to see that she was the sort of woman on whom falsities would be thrown away, and that all he had to do, all he could do, was to declare his intention of marrying Harriet, and to carry out that intention as soon as possible.

"I believe, Mrs. Ogilvy," he said, laying his bowler hat and stick on the floor beside him and crossing his legs, "that your daughter has told you of our engagement."

"My daughter," said Mrs. Ogilvy, "has told me that you have paid her considerable attention and has certainly spoken of an engagement with you, but you must be aware that her marriage is out of the question. Quite out of the question."

"I don't see that at all," said Lewis slowly. "In fact," he added, "I am naturally anxious that we should be married as soon as possible."

"You needn't try to throw dust in my eyes," said Mrs. Ogilvy peremptorily. "I need not discuss with you the question of my daughter's being unfit to be married at all; but, even if she were not, how, may I ask, have you the impudence to propose for her? Have you any connections? Any prospects? I wonder if you are quite aware, Mr. Oman, of what sort of people we are?"

"Perfectly," said Lewis, with a grin. "With regard to my prospects, I earn twenty-five shillings a week at present, and I may have thirty by midsummer. Your daughter has five thousand pounds, ain't it? Don't you want somebody to look after it for her when you're gone yourself? You won't last forever, if I may say so."

This last he delivered in a tone of rational expostulation, which made it difficult for Mrs. Ogilvy to charge him with insolence and have him turned out of the house. She said, in great anger:

"You have yourself given very good reasons why the marriage is impossible in a worldly point of view, Mr. Oman; it's indecent from another point of view —and what's more, I may tell you, though my daughter is a natural, she's my own flesh and blood, and dear to me, and I won't see her the prey of a shabby, cold-blooded sneak of a fortune hunter."

Lewis said with gravity, "You talk as if the good luck would be all on my side. I may state that there are several people who'd be glad enough to marry me —in fact, I'm causing disappointments, a thing I don't like to do: and there'll be a good deal of surprise at *my* marrying your daughter, quite as much as at *her* marrying me."

Mrs. Ogilvy attempted to awe him by calling up all her dislike and contempt into her face, but Lewis sat unmoved under her gaze.

"Might I enquire why?" she said, with laborious interest, but before his impervious attitude, tinged with a sneer, her tones fell flat. Lewis did not hurry in his reply; he recrossed his legs and rested one hand on his knee.

"I am considered handsome by the ladies," he said.

It was too much for Mrs. Ogilvy; with a blast of disdain, unmeditated as lightning, bold as thunder, she exclaimed:

"Handsome! Yes, you are the sort that housemaids call handsome!"

For the first time Lewis showed himself vulnerable; he flushed, and for a moment his face wore such an expression that no one could have called him good-looking. He quickly recovered himself, however, and said:

"Your daughter seems to be of the same opinion."

"My daughter," said Mrs. Ogilvy, "we need not discuss."

"And why not?" asked Lewis coolly.

Mrs. Ogilvy appeared to strive for patience; she rose to her feet and said with an air of finality:

"Once and for all, Mr. Oman, it is quite out of the question, as you ought not to need telling, that my daughter's friends should allow you to have any opportunity of repeating your proposals to her. *Any* marriage for her is quite impossible, and one with you could not be thought of for a single instant!"

Lewis had not got up when Mrs. Ogilvy had risen; he remained, his thumbs in the armholes of his coat, tilting back on his chair, so that he was looking up into her face.

"And may I ask," he said, "how you propose to put a stop to it?" He saw that she was for a moment nonplussed and went on, "Your daughter is considerably over age; she is her own mistress; her money's her own. I want to marry her—she wants to marry me. May I ask you again what you think you have to do with it?"

His brutality of address was partly inspired by the realization that in no circumstances could he hope anything from Mrs. Ogilvy's assistance, and therefore that it might even be to his advantage to employ roughness; and partly—how much he perhaps did not know—by her remark about his appearance.

"Mr. Oman," she said, with some dignity, "I will ask you to leave the house immediately."

"Right," said Lewis, getting up, "but you ain't heard the last of me, I can tell you. It's my belief that you're pretty comfortable on Harriet's money and that you've your reasons for wanting her to stay single." He stood a moment, listening. Someone was fumbling with the door handle.

"Harriet!" exclaimed Mrs. Ogilvy as the door opened, "go away—I told you——"

Lewis's eyes glittered with excitement: this was a

piece of luck and no mistake; he'd expected to have to hang about, watching the house, for a chance to speak to her in the road. He went up to the door and, taking Harriet by the hand, led her into the room. The creature gave an odd chuckling cry of pleasure and held his arm with the other hand.

"My dear," said Lewis, in a tone so different from any which he had used to Mrs. Ogilvy that the latter almost started, "I've come all this way to see you, but your mother orders me out of the house. But never mind. You'll see me soon: I shall keep calling to see you, and if anyone tries to stop me, I'll bring a policeman. And we'll arrange about our wedding as soon as we can—whatever anyone may say, won't we?"

"Yes, our wedding," said Harriet, in tones of delight, not moving her eyes from his face.

"And you'll be true to me, won't you?" he asked. She gazed at him speechlessly, her face distorted. "You're my own, aren't you?" he said.

"Sir!" burst out Mrs. Ogilvy, aroused from her stupefaction, "how dare you! Get out of my house this instant!" Lewis gave her a look of cool defiance.

"I'm going," he said. "I've only got a present to give my sweetheart." So saying, he took a small paper package from his pocket, unloosed Harriet's hand from his arm, and placed it within it. Then he was gone. Mrs. Ogilvy hurried, rustling, after him to the head of the stairs; but his departure was so speedy that the front door slammed almost before she had reached the staircase. She returned to the drawing

room, trembling all over with indignation and dismay, to find Harriet unwinding tissue paper and
drawing out a pinchbeck gold thimble studded round
the rim with ruby glass. She held it up in ecstasy.

"Look, Mama!" she exclaimed. "How kind! How
sweetly pretty! Isn't it beautiful?" Her pleasure in
the bauble seemed for the moment to have taken
away the sense of her lover's hurried departure, but at
her mother's face she altered her tone and said re-
proachfully, "Why were you so unkind, Mama? Why
didn't you ask Mr. Lewis to stop to dinner? He came
all this way, and then you sent him out of the house!"
The corners of her mouth drooped as if she were going to cry.

"Hatty, my darling," said Mrs. Ogilvy, "I'm not
unkind; don't think it, my sweet girl. But you must
believe that Mama knows best; you must never see
that man again." Harriet turned on her a face of
blank incredulity. "Never!" repeated Mrs. Ogilvy.
"He's cruel and bad; he wants to take away your
money, and then he won't care what becomes of
you." At the mention of her money Harriet looked
grave; but then her glance fell on her hand, where
she wore the latest proof of Lewis's munificence and
regard, and her face brightened again.

"That's nonsense, Mama," she said; "he gives me
ever so many things! Besides, Mr. Lewis said you
would do this; he said people's mamas don't want
them to marry. You want me be old maid. But I
won't!" she cried suddenly, facing up to Mrs. Ogilvy

with that odd lift of her upper lip over the teeth. Mrs. Ogilvy's concern for her likelihood of being miserable outweighed at first all other feelings, and, though she from the first persevered in the attitude that the whole thing was impossible, refusing to pacify Harriet by deceptive promises and consolations, she tried at the same time to soothe and comfort her with an unusual display of tenderness and affection. But Harriet showed no response; ordinarily very fond of her mother, and a good, amenable creature, she was now possessed by one desire; to get and keep something which instinct told her she ought to have. To all Mrs. Ogilvy's persuasions she turned a deaf ear, and when she spoke it was only to repeat her determination to be married as soon as possible. It began to dawn on Mrs. Ogilvy, with slow and chilling horror, long resisted but finally overpowering, that there was, ultimately, nothing that she could do. Harriet was not only independent in the eyes of the law, but she had the strength of purpose to carry out her own designs. The dependence on her mother which had seemed so marked a feature of her existence was not owing to incapacity so much as to the fact that, having the mentality of a young child, she had also a child's pleasure in being made much of, liking to receive protection and indulgence as much as her mother liked to give it; but if she chose to look for these things elsewhere, she was quite capable of transferring her dependence to someone else. Mrs. Ogilvy realized that her mere authority, which had sometimes carried the day from strength of habit, was going to be useless now; all she could do was to confess Harriet her equal and plead with her, frantically and humbly, that she would consent to take her advice. In an access of feeling that she had never known before, she besought her, with tears in her eyes, to stay with her and do nothing without her consent. But Harriet seemed to have lost all feeling of comprehension of any matter except one; with dogged persistence she repeated that she was going to marry, that no one should stop her, that she would leave the house and go and marry straight away.

Mrs. Ogilvy, conscious at last of her disordered cap strings, her streaming eyes, and her unusual position before the chair in which Harriet sat, got up from her knees and recomposed herself. Harriet said once more: "I shall be married, whatever you say!" her head hanging forward with a look of immovable obstinacy.

Mrs. Ogilvy, glancing at her as she settled her cap in the mirror, suddenly had a fierce revulsion of feeling, a great burst of exasperation. "You're a bad, ungrateful girl!" she exclaimed. "I've no patience with you! And after all I've done for you!"

She retired upstairs without saying anything further, and shut herself up in her own room in a state of brooding indignation and ill usage. She felt that she had exercised, during Harriet's adult years, a remarkable degree of patient, long-suffering affection; that she had been truly self-sacrificing. It had never struck her so before, because she had never, until now, claimed the reward of her conduct by demanding Harriet's obedience in anything very important; but now that she did so and was refused, she was made forcibly aware of how faithfully and lovingly she had discharged her difficult maternal duties; and she expected, unreasonably, a recognition of this from the very person whose mental deficiency had made their discharge so difficult. In addition to this, the irritation of a sensible person who sees another wilfully embarking on a foolish step, and the irateness of a masterful woman who is, for the first time, defied in her own house, made Mrs. Ogilvy's state of mind so pitiably sore and angry that, in a most unusual weakness, she went to lay her troubles before her husband and ask his support and advice. "For there are some things," said Mrs. Ogilvy, wiping her eyes, "that are too much for me, bear up as I may."

Mr. Ogilvy hated disturbance and was usually only too happy to be relieved of worry; but he wished now that the matter had been left to him from the start. When the circumstances had been explained to him as clearly as Mrs. Ogilvy's diatribes and exclamations would allow, he supposed that very little could be done with Lewis now; his back had been put up, and if he could not be kept off by force there would be no hope of getting rid of him at all. Whether, if he had been taken in time, he might have been amenable to some arrangement, and agreed to clear out for a small consideration, needed now not to be considered;

and, in any case, though Mr. Ogilvy would not have
recoiled from bestowing a small sum on him to relinquish a project he ought never to have had the impudence to attempt, Mrs. Ogilvy's stomach would have
found the idea intolerable. In any case, it was now
no use thinking about it, as Lewis's influence with
Harriet had been seen to be so powerful, and he himself was perfectly well aware of it. The question of
Harriet herself, and the possibility of any appeal to
her, next presented itself to Mr. Ogilvy, but one
glance at her in her mutinous stubbornness convinced
him that any idea of reasoning with her would be
impracticable; he was intensely shy and self-conscious
in his dealings with her always, and secretly relieved
at the obvious uselessness of talking to her on the present occasion. As, therefore, dealing with either of the
two parties was out of the question, it became necessary to see whether outside help might not be available, for if a woman of thirty-two and independent
means chose to marry in the face of her family, there
was, on the face of it, nothing the family could do.
Mr. Ogilvy would not be party to romantic schemes
of incarceration or kidnapping; but the idea then
occurred to him that it might be possible to have
Harriet declared of unsound mind, and placed under
the protection of the Court of Chancery. He hesitated a little before mentioning it to his wife, but,
when he did so, she accepted it much more calmly
than he had expected; indeed, when he had explained
it to her, and made it clear that if an affidavit could

be procured and Harriet placed under the protection
of the Court, she would be unable to marry without
the consent of the Court—a state of affairs which
would permit Mrs. Ogilvy in person to lay before the
judges her objections to the suitor—she seized upon it
as a means of deliverance. "She would stay at home
with us just the same," said Mrs. Ogilvy; "it's not as
if we'd be putting her in one of those shocking asy-
lums; for have her out of my sight I couldn't nor I
wouldn't, for in everything else she is as sane as you
or me, and she need never know a thing about it."
She was all in a glow of hope, and wrote at once for
the doctor who attended them to come and supply
the necessary evidence of Harriet's condition.

"At the same time," said Mr. Ogilvy, "I think you
should see whether something can't be done about the
property, to tie it up completely to Harriet in the
event of her marrying. I don't say it can; in fact, I
should be inclined to think, as the money doesn't
come from you, that you can't do anything. Still, you
may as well find out. Of course, if the Court will take
charge of the matter there will be no need for anything further."

Mrs. Ogilvy felt excessively grateful and com-
forted by all this; and, as she left her husband once
more in possession of his study, she felt that there
was nothing like a man's way of going about things.
Though in some ways Mr. Ogilvy was as helpless as
a child, still, when it really came to something serious, his calm and clever mind guided and steadied her

amid her tempests of agitation. She posted, at the
same time as her note to the doctor, one to the family
man of business, saying that if convenient she would
call on him the day after tomorrow. He should take
charge of the doctor's affidavit and see it lodged with
the proper authorities and also advise her as to
whether anything could be done in the meantime to
make poor Hatty's money less of a danger to her. Her
indignation against Harriet was purely transitory,
and now she was only anxious to show her as much
affection, and reconcile her to her home as much as
possible. Harriet, on her part, bore no malice against
her mother; she would have retreated into her sullen
attitude had the forbidding of the marriage come up
again, but Mrs. Ogilvy was completely silent on the
point. She exerted herself instead to interest Harriet
in other concerns—a new mantle and some dresses for
the spring, and, among other distractions, a visit to
the Crystal Palace. Harriet always responded to
kindness like a child, and her whole life had been surrounded by her mother's kindness. Nothing but a
deep, primeval instinct, beyond her control as the
tides are beyond the control of man, could have in-
duced her to set herself up against her mother. Now
that the cause of disagreement was shelved she went
on exactly as she had always done: deriving intense
enjoyment from small pleasures, outings, purchases,
the playing of a musical box; and as her mother made
no motion to check her in her frequent mention of
Lewis and their approaching marriage, she was alto-

gether happy. Mrs. Ogilvy was preparing all her resources to meet the storm that would burst on them presently when Harriet should know that Lewis was going out of her life altogether, and she did not want to break up the serenity of the present. "Though it goes to my heart," she told her husband, "to see how her mind runs on that worthless scamp." She had no hope at all of Lewis's image fading in Harriet's mind; she knew her obstinate tenacity too well; they would just have to spoil her a good deal extra, that was all; perhaps take her away for a long holiday, as the summer was coming, and make it up to her in every way they could. She no longer reproached Harriet for being ungrateful to her; she blamed herself for having been so careless as to let her come in contact with Lewis Oman. She made no communication whatever to Mrs. Hoppner beyond sending her the cheque for Harriet's board and lodging; her scorn and repulsion were too deep.

Dr. Williams was an old friend of Mrs. Ogilvy, and had attended Harriet for many years, though her physical health was so good that she had never had any illnesses beyond the usual epidemics. Mrs. Ogilvy received him in private the next day, and, telling him all the circumstances, explained her husband's suggestion, and finished by practically demanding an affidavit of him there and then. Dr. Williams had shown in his good-natured red face the greatest sympathy while hearing the story, but he began to look a little gloomy when he heard Mrs. Ogilvy's proposal.

"I am sure, doctor," she said, "you won't have any hesitation in stating your opinion as clearly as possible."

"No, ma'am," he said, "but I shall have to consider rather carefully what my opinion is, you know. This is not quite a straightforward sort of matter, you see."

"I don't see at all," said Mrs. Ogilvy. "There can be no doubt that the fellow is after her money, and that if he knew he had to get the permission of the Court to marry her, he'd be off directly."

"Yes, yes, yes," said the doctor soothingly; "but the point is, I should have to give it as my professional opinion that Harriet is not fit to have the control of her own fortune."

"Of course she isn't fit!" exclaimed Mrs. Ogilvy. "Doesn't the way she's behaving show that she isn't?"

"My dear madam," said Dr. Williams, "I agree with you that the marriage would be a catastrophe, and that it must be stopped if in any way possible. But if every young lady who wanted to make an unsuitable marriage could be put under judicial restraint, the judges would be busy."

"But surely—surely——" expostulated Mrs. Ogilvy.

"It is not quite so simple," went on the doctor. "You see, you yourself have never felt, up till now, that she required any sort of restraint, have you? She has always lived at home like an ordinary daughter of the house and stayed away without you. And yet

I don't know that we can say her condition is any worse now than it has ever been."

"But everybody has always known——"

"What have they known? That she was not quite normal in point of intelligence, certainly. But if the Court take the matter up, they'll want to be satisfied that she really isn't fit to be trusted with herself."

"But she isn't!" cried Mrs. Ogilvy. "Just look at all this!"

"You must see," said the doctor, "that what she's doing now is done by hundreds of young women who are to all intents and purposes as sane as we are: alarming her friends by wanting to throw herself away on a worthless young man. There isn't anything in that to convict her of lunacy, not in the medical sense of the word. And, you see, you'd appear, at first sight, to be in rather a dubious position; they'd say, 'This lady never seems to have thought it necessary to trouble about her daughter's deficiency until it was a question of her money going out of the family!' I'm sounding horridly unfair, I know, but we have to think of what will be said. I'm only trying to point out that the business won't be as easy as you think!" Mrs. Ogilvy almost wrung her hands in distress.

"Anyone who could see Lewis Oman would realize the necessity of putting her under restraint immediately," she said.

"Now that, my dear lady, is just what I take leave to doubt. That he's quite penniless certainly puts his motives in a very disreputable light; but people *will* marry these men. I take it there is nothing physically impossible in a girl's falling in love with him."

"Perhaps," said Mrs. Ogilvy reluctantly. "But," she added, with increased energy, "when you know what's right to be done as plainly as we know in this case, I think you ought to stretch a point in your evidence."

The doctor felt all the difficulty of explaining the fallacy of this argument to a woman, but he said solemnly:

"Mrs. Ogilvy, it would be as much as my professional reputation was worth to do such a thing." His tone spoke finality; Mrs. Ogilvy was bitterly disappointed; she had built so much on this hope; it had seemed a heaven-sent deliverance to be had merely for the asking. She would not question Dr. Williams's judgment as things stood, though privately she felt that if women were allowed to arrange these things a great deal of trouble and nonsense would be prevented, and that she herself could, in Dr. Williams's place, have settled the point without the slightest trouble. Aloud she said wistfully:

"It seems then, doctor, that you can't help us?"

"I don't say that, ma'am, I don't say that. I will urge everything I can in my report, you may be sure; all I say is, you mustn't build on it too much. There *is* a chance they'll see fit to hold an inquisition, and then perhaps a word or two in explanation of the circumstances might be put in. I know this will come hard to you if we can't manage it, but you see what

it would be if you were to tamper with medical evidence in cases like this, and get the Court to restrict a
person's liberty where there was no medical reason for
it: the safety of the individual person would be gone.
For one case where it would be in the patient's interests, there'd be a hundred where it would be a gross
imposition. Still, don't despair. I'll do what I fairly
can; I'll send my report straight to your legal man,
shall I? You can instruct him in the meantime; and
I should get away with Miss Harriet as soon as possible. The longer you keep him out of her sight, the
easier it'll be in the end; I don't suppose, if you use
a little justifiable deception, that there'll be much
difficulty in getting her to go on a holiday with you.
As for the marriage ever coming to anything, I don't
think there is grave danger; there's her affection for
you, for one thing: that's bound to count for a great
deal."

"She's so *set* on him," murmured Mrs. Ogilvy
wretchedly.

"Well, you know," said the doctor, preparing to
depart, "those obstinate fits are part of the trouble;
when a poor creature has nothing to go on but her
own desires, it's only to be expected. You and I would
be just as unreasonable over everything we wanted if
we hadn't the sense to see reasons why we should control our wishes."

"Doctor," said Mrs. Ogilvy in a last desperate
attempt, "suppose I called in another medical man
who might be inclined to take a stronger view of the

case than yourself; you wouldn't be offended, I know
—but you wouldn't feel obliged to go to him and
contradict him and make him alter his views, would
you?"

"I shouldn't say a word," said Dr. Williams cheer-
fully. "It would be nothing to do with me unless he
consulted me himself; but I must tell you that I think
you'd do better to stick to me; partly because, as
your own medical man who's had the charge of your
family for several years, my opinion, given even mod-
erately on your side of the question, would have more
weight than most, and also because, as I have known
Harriet for so long, I am likely to take a more definite
view of her weakness than someone who examines her
for the first time. So keep up a good heart, ma'am,
though I know you've a great deal to put up with."

"I am sure I'm much obliged to you for your kindness," said Mrs. Ogilvy, a little relieved by the doctor's encouraging manner.

From that time forth she began to feel a little
calmer. She could not hope that Harriet had in any
way forgotten Lewis; she received from him, two or
three times every week, a letter or a picture postcard,
usually of the type sold at Christmas or for St. Valen-
tine's Day, frilled with paper lace and ornamented
with sparkles and roses. Her rapture and satisfaction
with these knew no bounds, and really she preferred
them to his letters; though no pains had been spared
to teach her, she had never been able to reach more
proficiency in reading and writing than enabled her

to make out a clearly written line or two, and to express herself on paper with the spelling and composition of a backward child. Lewis had not realized this at first, until, having on one occasion written her word of his going down to Patrick and Elizabeth for the week-end, he referred to it on their next meeting and found that she had not assimilated the contents of his letter beyond the endearments and the time he hoped next to see her. So now he bought the gaudiest cards he could find in his locality and wrote on them in a large hand such messages as "Always thinking of my dear one, from her faithful Lewis," or, "Absence makes the heart grow fonder, of yours till Doomsday." Mrs. Ogilvy would have liked to suppress these missives before they got to Harriet, but, for one thing, Harriet was remarkably quick at detecting, when the post was delivered, anything that might be for her, and sometimes, when Lewis had not written, would not be satisfied until she had turned over all the envelopes to make sure there had been no mistake; and then, too, she was so good-humoured and happy while this correspondence was continuing, perfectly satisfied with her position as a young lady with a romance, of which the symbols were these elegant postcards, so brightly coloured and with such sweet, kind messages written on the backs, that Mrs. Ogilvy felt to interfere in any way would be stirring up a hornet's nest; and as long as the affair continued to be one merely of postcards and occasional boxes of bonbons—of a very cheap and highly flavoured variety, as Mrs. Ogilvy did not fail to observe—there did not seem cause for immediate alarm. Harriet kept all the postcards, wrapped very neatly in silver paper and tissue paper, inside her workbox, and she retired to her bedroom to eat the sweets he sent, as if they were too precious to be shared with anybody else. Not that anyone else in the house would have cared to venture on the sinister-looking pieces of raspberry hardbake, the glassy green peppermints, or the strongly perfumed confections of rose and violet sugar; but though Harriet herself had always been accustomed to what was pure and good in food, she saw nothing amiss in Lewis's sweets, but sucked them, her eyes half shut in keenest satisfaction. As long as she had these reminders of him, she did not fret in his absence or make efforts of her own to see him; she was as intimate and fond with her mother as ever, and Mrs. Ogilvy began to hope that perhaps the mere idea of a romance would be enough to keep her happy; they *would* go away, certainly directly there was a prospect of warmer weather, but really, with the nipping winds they suffered at present, there was no idea of moving to the coast just yet; to bundle off and find themselves obliged by the weather to stay indoors in lodgings, in a place where they knew nobody, was just the way to unsettle Harriet again; it was far better to stay where they were while she was so comfortable; and every day brought nearer the decision of the Court on Dr. Williams's evidence which was now before them. The natural hopefulness of Mrs.

Ogilvy's disposition was wearing out the effect of the doctor's warning and making her look towards a favourable answer as almost certain. Altogether it was better to be thankful for the present quiet and risk nothing that might upset it. Mrs. Ogilvy did not realize, as she helped Harriet to choose the trimming for a new bodice, or gazed and exclaimed with her as they watched the antics of bears at the Zoo, or urged her willing acceptance of some special dainty at the tea table, that Harriet's childlike cheerfulness and good-nature were the result of a deep sustaining confidence that quite soon something very wonderful was going to happen to her; that the forcefulness of Lewis's character, which Mrs. Ogilvy herself had been struck with, had inspired Harriet with absolute faith in his power to dispose of her future.

Lewis in the meantime was not attempting a personal interview; since the occasion of his precipitate departure from the house, he had seen Harriet twice: once, by appointment in a letter in which he had asked her to meet him on a Saturday evening outside the garden gate and, under cover of darkness, had walked with her for ten minutes up and down the road, the whole quite unknown to Mrs. Ogilvy; and the second time when he had unexpectedly met her and her mother coming up the road as he was approaching the house from the opposite direction to spy out the land. He had boldly walked up to them, there being no policeman in sight to whom Mrs. Ogilvy could appeal, and had insisted upon Harriet's accepting his arm as he walked with them to their gate. He had said nothing to the purpose, but merely made some remarks on the fineness of the day and the ample repayment that it was for his trouble in coming so far, to see Harriet even for these few moments. At the gate he lifted his hat to them and eyed Mrs. Ogilvy with malicious triumph as she swelled past him in silent indignation. He was not blind to the fact, as Harriet lingered on the doorstep, with her idiotic smile and her waves and gestures of farewell, that her mother's attitude to him, so plainly expressed, would do nothing to increase her influence with Harriet or to strengthen the bond between them.

He was at present biding his time, secure that he could afford to do so; he had actually very little time to secure interviews even if he had been a lover; for his office kept him employed the whole week, except for the latter half of Saturday afternoon and Sunday; and he had a good deal of business to arrange in the limited hours at his disposal. He had discovered through Mrs. Hoppner, not without some inaccuracies, all of which had to be rectified at the expense of a good deal of time, who exactly were the relatives from whom Harriet derived her fortune. There were her father and her aunt, of course, and he spent two Saturday afternoons in examining their wills in Somerset House. Then there was the matter of this reversionary interest—not to be disregarded, since it comprised two thousand pounds, two fifths of the whole. It was necessary here to pursue a separate line of investigation and examine the will of whoever had left this property to the aunt who now enjoyed it. It turned out that the lady did not inherit it from her father, but from an uncle, fortunately of the same name, so that, though Lewis's researches were lengthy, they were fairly straightforward, and the interest that inspired them deprived them of all tediousness, rendering them, on the contrary, more absorbing than any form of printed matter which had heretofore come under his notice.

When he had examined the financial position to his complete satisfaction, he next turned his attention to finding a suitable house. He had been in a very humble "single gentleman's" lodging since the expiration of the lease of the house he had shared with Patrick and Elizabeth; but he felt it absolutely necessary now to provide himself with a house; he must tell Harriet that he had one ready for her reception, and though in ordinary circumstances he would not have objected to telling a lie, or to telling any number, still, the fact remained that he must have somewhere to take her. He meant that everything which could be done beforehand should be, to ensure the smooth achievement of his design. He would not be too particular in his choice, as in all probability they would not stay there long; still, while he was about it, he might as well take a house rather than lodgings. For one thing, he longed to be tasting the joys of an owner of property and the sensation of being master in his own house; and for another, it would be a good thing to have quarters to offer Patrick and Elizabeth. Lewis felt that he would want company.

To find a house which he could take on a quarter's lease, in a part that suited him, took him another fortnight or so; he fixed finally upon a decent little villa in Laburnam Road, Norwood; it was very similar to the one he had occupied before with the married Omans, but as he strolled through the unfurnished rooms, lighted by dusty windows, all empty save for litter left in the middle of the floors, the general greyness and gloom, the chill, and the hollow sound of his feet on the uncarpeted boards filled him with exultation. To own the whole house, without a landlady on the ground floor ready to call up if the gas were left burning, seemed to him a prospect of stimulating delight. He explained to the landlord that for the moment he could not, owing to his circumstances, make a positive decision, but he would let him know in a week's time. He then went, on the following Monday evening, to a large warehouse of furniture and upholstery and arranged with them that, unless they received a cancellation of the order, they were, next week, to furnish the front bedroom and both downstairs rooms of the house in Laburnam Road. This done, he was now faced with the last step in his plans.

He had not troubled to see Harriet, because he never doubted his complete ascendancy over her, and that he had nothing to do but, when the time came,

complete the purely practical details of his scheme.
He was as courageous in his impudence as could be
imagined, and thoroughly believed himself to be master of the situation; but, even so, he did not want another scene with Mrs. Ogilvy; even their *rencontre*
outside the garden gate had not precisely fluttered or
alarmed him but left him anxious not to risk a repe-
tition of it. It was something in her contempt of his
person and attractions which subtly wounded him
and gave him an unfamiliar sense of weakness; her
rage and bluster would not have caused him to turn
a hair. Despite the callous self-seeking of his disposition, he was not, even excluding his physical passions, a cold man. He depended on Patrick's loyalty
and affection in a way that no man of frigid temperament would have done; he really liked to stand well
with people, to be admired, that is to say; he was not,
of course, sensitive to criticism of his morals; but
though there was, most unmistakably, something
about him of the ruthless cruelty of an adder, he was
yet capable of feeling hurt by slighting usage, like a
small boy who is misunderstood.

He determined, therefore, to take his time over
the last step and not, if he could help it, damage his
sensitive feelings in the process. Now that the prospect was near, he felt less and less inclination for
haste. When he had had that evening walk with Harriet under the gas lamps, her manner of hanging on
his arm, her attention to his every syllable, had revealed a strength of passion which he had not till

then suspected; and by turns it repelled him and exercised a perverse atraction. He did not shudder now, as he had done on the evening of their first meeting, at the idea of marrying her, but he was in no hurry to do it. He would be perfectly equal to the situation, but as he now sat on the bed in his gentleman's apartment, during the process of taking off his boots, he glanced round the dingy room, where his watch and chain lay on the chest of drawers, his bowler hat hung behind the door, and the dressing table was covered with such objects as his pomade, his razors, his brush and comb, and his purple cotton handkerchief, and felt, as he did so, so free and snug, like an animal in its lair, enjoying the present moment and in no hurry for the next; though actually he was quite aware that what caused this feeling of care-free happiness was the near prospect of five thousand pounds.

The extraordinary pleasantness of the last days of a holiday does not make a determined man want to be on holiday forever; he enjoys each second with peculiar gusto just because he is prepared to leave at an appointed time. Lewis savoured a pleasure in this little space of solitude and independence such as he had never known before, for as a rule he enjoyed society of his own choosing. But now, in these evenings, he planned little excursions for himself. Sometimes it was a visit to a music hall, at other times something to which he was prompted by his curiosity and love of practical affairs. He and Patrick had often said they would like to go down to the docks, though it

was a thing they had never happened to do. But now
he set off one evening as soon as his work was over
and spent raw, damp hours with all the rapt oblivi-
ousness to discomfort of a schoolboy, watching the
wonderfuly mysterious and suggestive panorama of
the Pool of London: the great ships, their masts loom-
ing up to be lost in the fog, the myriad lights, some
twinkling stationary on bulk and masthead, some
glimmering up and down the sides as men embarked
and disembarked by the swaying rope ladders: the
whole spectacle, for all its solidity and weight, tremulous from the keen night breeze and the rocking of
black water, invisible except where a patch of light
showed the oily scum and the clotted refuse covering its surface. Hoarse cries sounding from the water,
unintelligible words ceaselessly filling the ear, the perpetual hurrying to and fro of figures in the gloom,
made an atmosphere so enthralling that hours passed
unnoticed; and as Lewis stood amid this stir he knew
that a power was coming to him too, that he was
about to enter the sphere of those who moved the
world by their activity; that whole tracts of his own
being were waking to life which had lain stagnant
in the routine of poverty and restricted labour. Another evening he walked late down the Strand, where
the windows of jewellers and goldsmiths were still
flashing; their radiance, which before he had hardly
noticed, and the glimpses of the fashionable world
hurrying from theatres into carriages and hansom
cabs, which before had passed him by as things of no

meaning, now filled him with confused sensations of luxury and pleasure; at that moment he would hardly have changed places with one of those glorious beings; the anticipation of the humbler pleasures he had always wanted was so sweet.

This was perhaps the only time in his life when he tasted the wild happiness of a spiritual adventure. However, he did not regret it when the moment came to put an end to all this and to achieve the final step of his design. It was simple—merely to walk up to Mrs. Ogilvy's house and ask Harriet to leave it in his company so that they might get married. He had now arranged everything; the house was cleaned up, and two rooms in it were furnished—a double bedroom and the front room downstairs. The kitchen contained the necessary utensils, but otherwise the house was bare; the furniture establishment was one which gave large credit, and Lewis, when his prospects had been explained, was felt to be a good customer; there would have been no difficulty in providing three times the amount of cheap maple wood, bamboo, and plush; but Lewis saw no point in unnecessary expenditure at this juncture. It was by no means certain that he would wish to remain in Laburnam Road, and if he did, once he had his hands on the money he would go to better warehouses, where one needed ready money, but where really stylish things could be bought; if Patrick could spare Lizzie, she should come with him on a grand shopping expedition, for Lewis knew how to value a lady's taste. He did not picture to himself the pleasure of giving Elizabeth things of which her own home must stand in need, but he liked to think of the pleasure she would have in his good fortune. He did not spend much time on anticipation now, however, for the practical details requiring his attention were many. He had interviewed the necessary authorities with regard to the marriage itself and had persuaded Mrs. Hoppner to have Harriet in her house for the three weeks which she must be resident in the neighbourhood in order to have the marriage solemnized in the district. Mrs. Hoppner, when she realized how forward matters were between the young couple, had agreed, albeit doubtfully, to having the wedding from her house. If Harriet were once married to Lewis, Lewis would be a party more to be reckoned with than Mrs. Ogilvy. Lewis was her friend already, while Mrs. Ogilvy would be at enmity with her to her dying day. There was nothing further to be expected from Mrs. Ogilvy in the way of financial benefit, while Lewis had made considerable promises to her, which she believed he would fulfil; and in this belief she was doing him no more than justice. The indifference with which they viewed the rights and feelings of the rest of the world made all the more remarkable the strong clan spirit of Lewis and Patrick and gave the few people who were of their party and allied to their interests a feeling of confidence and security in their friendship stronger than is often excited by persons who are humane and just to everyone. Of course, had

Harriet been under age, or if there had been anything
in the way of the marriage except the strong disapproval of Mrs. Ogilvy, Mrs. Hoppner would never
have been party to it; she was not one to run the risk
of getting herself into serious trouble; it was merely
that where there was a prospect of gain to her own
family she was prepared to endure anything in the
way of unpleasantness and inconvenience; it would
have been difficult to say whether she was really dead-
ened to it, or whether, in spite of having allowed herself for so long to be dragged at the heels of her more
independent relations, she still retained a sense of her
progress being very rough and uncomfortable.

At present, however, she was glad to throw in her
lot with Lewis; he was so sprightly and considerate,
always behaving with courtesy and attention; it was
quite a relief to have him about the house; it inspired
Mrs. Hoppner to take a firm line for once and to tell
Alice straight out that she must go down to Patrick
and Elizabeth for a month until everything was over.
"For have them all in the house is what I can't," she
said, "and no sense in it either. It's much better for
everybody Alice should be away just now." Elizabeth
was quite of her mother's opinion; she and Patrick
were strongly in sympathy with Lewis and looked
forward eagerly to his match with Harriet and the
consequent fortune, which they had come to look
upon as Lewis's natural right, and any interference of
his claims to it as an outrage, arousing that sort of
affectionate indignation which is felt in the relations

of some man who has spent his life in the devoted service of his country and then finds, as the hour of retirement draws near, that his pension is in danger. But while Patrick regarded Alice merely as a possible impediment to Lewis's plans who must be kept away from the sphere of action, Elizabeth had some sisterly sympathy. The intimacy between the two had never been very close, Elizabeth having always been the friend and ally of her mother and resentful on her mother's account of Alice's rapacious selfishness; but while she made her full share of such remarks as "How can you go on so?" she was always ready to say, "I'll mend your stockings," or, "That becomes you very well." She would do her best now to be good to Alice, though she feared that there was nothing down here which could take her out of herself. She would not care for the children, and they had no society. Perhaps Alice would bring plenty of sewing; she usually had some renovation or little matter on hand; she would be certain to bring some novels. Elizabeth only hoped that having a not very amiable aunt in their already close quarters would not upset the children. She did not fear that Alice's peevishness would upset Patrick: Patrick had his own ways of dealing with female annoyance.

Alice herself, to everyone's relief, made no opposition to the scheme; she packed her trunk, refusing passionately all her mother's offers of assistance, and went down to Cudham, hardly opening her lips to anybody.

Lewis pondered for some time whether he should send Harriet a letter announcing his visit on this important occasion; he decided finally against it, the risk of finding her out when he called not weighing against the possibility of her family's getting wind of him and secluding her in some way, or concealing his arrival from her. He dressed in his best on Saturday afternoon, and towards tea time, when he was almost sure of Harriet's being at home, he boldly presented himself at the door and asked for her. He met with a piece of good luck he had not dared to reckon on; Mrs. Ogilvy was in her bedroom under the hands of the hairdresser; the drawing room was lighted but empty, and Harriet came hurrying downstairs to him alone.

Strong delight and absolute, serene trust gave her face at that moment a look in which intelligence needed to play no part and was not ugly in its absence; as she crossed the room to him, holding out her arms, her face flushed, her eyes irradiated, her hair looser than she usually wore it, she looked for that one instant like any girl coming to her lover, and Lewis, relieved and elated at finding her alone, gathered her in his arms and thought with quite a glow of gratitude, "She really isn't a bad old stick after all!"

"Listen, my dear," he said. "Do you know what I've come for?" She raised her face mutely, her eyes shining. "I can't tell you," he said, "unless you are going to be very clever and sensible and do everything I tell you."

"I shall do everything you say," she said. Both her hands clutched his arm, and though ordinarily he was repelled by the way she would fasten upon him, now he derived comfort and assurance from her powerful grasp.

"Then, dearest, I have come to take you away so that we can get married." He paused; he was afraid of some wild demonstration of joy which would prevent his giving her his instructions as rapidly as he wished; but she gave no sign of the kind. Instead, she merely smiled and slightly nodded her head. She had lived in the fullest expectation of this moment; it gave her no surprise or shock now that it had come. He went on hurriedly but distinctly:

"Should you like to come to Mrs. Hoppner's? We must wait a little while before we can marry, because of having our banns asked. But your mama will not be kind if you stay at home——"

"No," she interrupted, "I won't stay at home."

"And Mrs. Hoppner is very glad we are going to marry. She will like to have you, and I can come and see you every day. Will you like that?"

"Shall I come now?" she asked.

"That's what would please me," he said, conscious as he did so that after that he need not fear the influence of anyone who tried to keep her in the house. She drew away from his arm and said, "I'll go and put up my things"; without another word she left

the room, leaving Lewis on the hearthrug in a state of
fierce exultation and a defiance that was born of
apprehension at being alone in Mrs. Ogilvy's house.
That quiver of the nerves and thrilling of the blood
which he had felt when he was looking at the enormous ships trembling on the tide he now felt with an
acuteness that was almost painful, as he stood with his
back to the fire in this bright and comfortable room;
he realized that he was laughing, and clapped his hand
over his mouth just as Mrs. Ogilvy entered the room.

Mrs. Ogilvy's appearance, for all her handsome
skirts and her freshly ringleted hair, was that of a
woman who is making her last stand. The information simultaneously received—that Lewis was in the
drawing room and that Harriet was upstairs packing
a bag—had brought with it the realization that the
last moment had come. It had brought hardly surprise to Harriet, but to Mrs. Ogilvy it was a sickening
shock, like the ring of an axe at an oak tree's roots.
For weeks she had hoped that the idea of Lewis was
becoming fainter and fainter in Harriet's mind; day
after day had strengthened her in her expectation of
a favourable reply from the Court of Chancery
which would guard finally against this and any other
danger of the kind. All the little plans and arrangements she had made for the immediate future—every
church activity, every tea party—added to her sense
of ruin as they were torn down and annihilated in the
gulf before her. Why was it that she could do nothing? How could it be that, with every argument of

decency, propriety, humanity, and common sense on her side, there was nothing to help her against this single-handed, upstart blackguard? With a great effort to control the agitation of rage and despair that was making her eyes misted and the voice thick in her throat, she said:

"Mr. Oman! Is it possible that you have the effrontery to push yourself into my very drawing room?"

"Just so, ma'am," said Lewis, with a grin that was a menace. "I've come to remove your daughter to Mrs. Hoppner's, where no restrictions will be placed on her freedom until we can get married. She is at an age to decide for herself in this matter, and she has chosen to accompany me to the protection I have found for her until I can make her my wife."

Mrs. Ogilvy's florid face had become ashen.

"Mr. Oman," she said, "I may tell you that you are incurring a risk of legal penalties you've no idea of. Negotiations are at the present moment going forward with the Court of Chancery to have Harriet put under the protection of the Court as of unsound mind; I expect their warrant at any moment from my legal man, Mr. Winterbourne. He will be able to tell you better than I can what the results will be to you if you dare to attempt a marriage, or any form of interference with my daughter, without the express permission of the Court—which," she added on a stronger note, "you no more dare apply for than any other criminal."

They stood facing each other with the width of the room between them. When she had finished, Lewis, who had never moved his eyes from her face, slowly altered his features into a look of almost fearful triumph. How it was that a person consciously guilty of a misdemeanour, and habitually in slight apprehension of the forces of law and order, should have been at this moment able to disregard the element of real danger which Mrs. Ogilvy's remarks had disclosed, and to seize instead upon that which was to his own advantage, can only be explained by the theory of intuition and inspiration working in moments of strong excitement.

"Indeed," he said, in a voice hardly above a whisper, and precisely at that moment of all others, to suit his purpose, Harriet, her outdoor clothes hastily and untidily put on, a package under her arm, entered behind her mother and ran up to him. He put both hands on her shoulders and said:

"Harriet! Do you know what your mother has done to stop your getting married?" He paused, and added in a ringing shout, "She is trying to have you signed in as a lunatic!"

No one, since she was born, had consciously allowed Harriet to hear any discussion of lunacy or the control of lunatics; no one had ever suggested to her that she was anything but her mother's favourite, to be specially petted and cared for; and if anyone had attempted to make her understand any other subject of which she might be supposed equally ignorant, it would have required endless explanation to make sure that she had grasped the outlines of it; but of this subject, of such vital importance to herself, the mere mention was all that was needed. Her comprehension took light like tinder from a fatal spark; she seized hold of Lewis with one hand and, advancing towards her mother, trembled and gnashed her teeth in a hideous paroxysm. She tried to speak, but nothing came except an inarticulate gibber. Lewis put his arm round her waist, and instantly she turned and clung to him with all her strength, so that he almost shook in her grasp.

"We've had enough of this," he said roughly. "I'm removing your daughter from your persecutions. If you dare to follow us, you'll know where to find us. Come, Harriet."

He picked up the bundle she had dropped and led her to the door. Mrs. Ogilvy was as helpless as if she had been in the pangs of death.

VII

ELIZABETH tried to carry out her intention of being good to Alice when the latter arrived at the Woodlands, but Alice repulsed her steadily, and she had no leisure to spend in conquering such a settled reserve. It was hoped that presently Patrick's work would put them in easier circumstances; he was at work now on a series of four small pictures illustrating the seasons, a kind of thing in considerable popular demand, and which he was doing for a dealer in Canterbury; but until these were finished, how they were to live was, not a mystery—nothing so vague and glamorous—but a hard, unending struggle of arithmetic. Alice's board would be provided by the thirty shillings Mrs. Hoppner had sent down with her to cover the period of a month, and a few shilings would remain over, as Mrs. Hoppner had meant they should; these would buy some cakes of paint, and also tobacco for Patrick and some Stilton cheese, of which he was fond—luxuries which otherwise he must have done without. For the rest, existence was translated for Elizabeth into shillings and pence. She made a firm resolve that Patrick must have meat at least twice a week, and so she bought him a chop on Wednesdays and Saturdays from the basket of the visiting butcher; and the re-

mains, a bone and a fragment, were carefully stewed
to make a teacupful of something approaching broth
for Alfred. She, Alice, and Clara ate no meat except
bacon, and eggs from the three hens on which Patrick
had spent a terrifying number of shillings, but which
even Elizabeth's fearfulness had now to admit a sound
investment. The variety of their food depended on
the number of things that could be made from flour,
eggs, and butter: omelettes, batter puddings, pastry,
girdle cakes, and bread: the latter spread with golden
syrup or condensed milk, which, with rice and tea,
were the only other articles bought from the grocer.
The garden provided them with potatoes and cabbages, and Elizabeth hoped that next year they might
have currant and gooseberry bushes and perhaps some
raspberry canes.

Each morning, while Clara lighted the fire and laid
the breakfast in the kitchen, Elizabeth washed and
dressed the children and herself, and after breakfast
the baby was tied into an armchair while she and
Clara did the housework and cooking, with Alfred
under their feet as little as good luck allowed. He had
a few toys, however, and would sometimes remain
for hours dragging a little cart up and down the garden path; or he would sit on the floor near Patrick,
building with a few wooden blocks to which he had
made additions of his own—an old shoe, half a real
brick, some cardboard boxes and bits of firewood. He
loved to sit near his father's chair, although Patrick
would turn him roughly out of the way, and struck

him outrageously if he touched anything he ought not; on the other hand, he once painted the sides of a block alternately red and blue, and once he gave Alfred a little piece of rag all over coloured smears. Alfred, although he cried at the time, accepted the ill treatment with perfect philosophy, and regarded the rarer acts of goodness as blessings from heaven.

In the afternoon Clara took both the children out, carrying Julia, so they did not go far; but in their absence Elizabeth washed, mended, sewed, and did the hundred and one different things that claimed her attention. Patrick, after he had taken a walk in the morning, painted nearly all day. He was industrious and conscientious, and was making a determined effort to do his duty as the provider of a family; but whatever their needs, he set his face against taking money before he had delivered the work. Elizabeth had once suggested his doing this; the Canterbury dealer was a good client and would certainly have advanced him a little money; but Patrick merely refused to consider it, giving no reason, but with such a look on his face that Elizabeth felt sure that their stores might run out to the bottom of bin, crock, and canister, and they would still have to wait round the easel for their next meal. However, even so, she could not feel unhappy; they had no actual want, although their commons were so short that they all of them developed a strong appetite, and poor Alfred tried to eat everything he could lay hands on. It was only the fear of want that made the future occasionally black;

and the spectre was dissipated by the fact that Patrick
actually had work, and the prospect of more. Besides
his connection in Canterbury, he made his morning
walk a means of exploring their immediate neighbourhood and working up a small circle of clients.
The mania for overdecoration which raged at the time
made people pay willingly for an elaborate frame of
velvet or gilt, and not grudge a shilling or two for
something to put inside it. Patrick was quite clever at
hitting the popular taste with something small,
luscious, and bright, and where he found anyone who
appeared interested in his work, he produced bigger
pictures in which he had really interested himself;
usually a sketch in oils of the neighbouring scenery.

The evenings were bound to be times of idleness for
him, unless he occupied himself with some household
job, for their faulty lighting, consisting of firelight,
one low-powered lamp, and farthing candles, made
even the working up of sketches impossible; and it
was in the evenings that Elizabeth at least really
found happiness in their new home. Clara went up to
bed soon after eight o'clock, and she and Patrick had
the living room to themselves. The dim light concealed all the deficiencies of furnishing; the fire was
like the hand of Midas; and, free at last of all the occupations and anxieties of the day, she could feel the
influence of the countryside; be conscious of the absolute stillness, and notice the stars behind their uncur-
tained window. Almost every night she said. "It's
quiet, isn't it?" and Patrick would say, "Not a

sound," or else speak of something quite different and make her equally content.

But now that Alice was with them, things could not be quite the same. Alice kept herself very much to herself, but in such close quarters the mere presence of somebody else spoilt these few hours of silent happiness. Still, Alice as an inmate was, in the whole, much better than many might have been. Her state of mind made her keep aloof from the family conversation, and it was possible to talk quite freely before a person so utterly indifferent that she might have been unhearing; and then, too, she had deft personal ways and was as delicately retiring as a cat. She occupied the small slip of bedroom which overlooked the fields and woods, and here she kept every one of her possessions; nothing left in the sitting room betokened her presence, except when she was actually there with her work-box. She made her bed in the morning, and if she ever ate anything when the rest were not having a meal, she prepared it herself and washed the dishes afterwards; otherwise she took no part in the household duties; sometimes she would go for a walk by herself, roaming about because she was too restless to sit still, not because the country had any charm or interest for her; she spent long hours sewing in the window corner; she was making herself a grey delaine dress, for which she had bought the stuff very cheaply and with such a lack of interest as she had never shown even in childhood on a question of dress; she could bear to do it because it gave her

something to do, and because it had been started upon
after her life had altered and did not remind her of
hopes and expectations that she could not endure to
think of now. She did have something of an acquaintance with Clara: Clara was quite wild with astonishment at Miss Alice's elegance and her beautiful things,
at the way her hair was curled, and at her cleverness
with her needle; then, too, there seemed to be about
her something of the world which Elizabeth did not
suggest: Alice's scornful impatience with the make-
shifts of the house, her contempt for whatever Clara
had been accustomed to think fine or pleasant, made
Clara feel that she must be a young lady of very great
experience, and she prostrated herself before her in
admiration and amazement. Alice had no use for such
a girl, naturally; she did not want Clara to do anything for her; but it did soothe her a little to know
that there was one person in the house who would
have done anything she liked to ask, and thought it a
favour. In one respect she did make use of her: she
discovered that Clara had a hoard of novels in her tin
box; and as the two or three with which she had provided herself were soon exhausted, she was glad to
have Clara's to go on with, though she turned up her
nose at the tattered, dog-eared pages; she took care
not to lend Clara any of hers, in case she should reduce them to the same condition; besides, Alice's were
rather different from the merely crude, sensational
stories Clara had; they were wonderful novels, but
they would not do Clara any good.

She did not have much conversation with Patrick. He was pleasant to her when they met at table, and she somewhat abated her weary impatience when she spoke to him. She had an odd mixture of feeling with regard to him as Lewis's brother: he was more interesting to her than anyone else in the house, and yet she bore him malice; she knew that his influence with Lewis would be all against her. She was very, very unhappy, as only the selfish and mindless can be; in her trouble she was like someone confined to a treadmill; nothing about her could give her any relief from herself. The weather was getting warmer now, and the trees and hedges were covered with thick, delicate bright green; but this was no consolation; she felt less acutely when the days were grey and dark and one could do nothing but crouch indoors with one's hands pressed to one's temples, reading by the light of the hearth. These bright, balmy days, with sunshine pouring from a high sky, seemed to reveal her desolation as they revealed the landscape. Alice had never read any poetry, and her ideas of beauty were all confined to pretty clothes and handsome furniture and good-looking men and women; she knew, rather than felt, that flowers were lovely; had she been going to the opera in a low silk dress and diamonds, she would have appreciated a bouquet in a silver filigree holder. But when in one of her solitary walks she came across a thicket of whitethorn, standing in ethereal brilliance against the dark wood-side, it gave her a pang of such sharpness that she almost felt her unhappiness had never really come upon her till this moment. She retraced her steps in horror, and from that time she half unconsciously shunned anything beautiful in scent or sight or sound that the countryside offered; she was town-bred, and had never associated any idea of pleasure with the land, but no one in the midst of these budding fields could be quite oblivious; the rest of the household were rejoicing in the spring, and Alice was conscious of it as being, in some way, a perpetual aggravation of her misery. Her keenest wretchedness was reached when the time of the full moon grew near. She would wake within the narrow space of four bare walls, the patches of radiance reflected on the wall as if through prison bars, and the great golden face gazing in upon her, forbidding her to sleep; forbidding her, in that strange silence and light, to cry; drowning her in gulfs of loneliness and despair, so that she longed for daylight, until the morning made her long for the night again.

In the small bed under the living-room window a few scillas and anemones were wavering in the breeze, which were a great source of joy to Elizabeth, particularly as she had thought the bed empty except for weeds, among which she had not distinguished the little green shoots. She was stooping down to look at them one morning, with Alfred beside her, when she caught sight of Alice standing a little way off in the lane; she picked the largest scilla, that of deepest blue, and put it into Alfred's hand, which immediately closed round it with the intense grasp of a small child;

Elizabeth opened his hand again and tried to make it hold the fragile stem more loosely. "There," she said, "now you take the pretty flower to Aunt Alice." Alfred hurried unsteadily down the lane and, stopping in front of Alice, held up the scilla; she put out her hand to take it mechanically, and Alfred trotted off at once; he was never disposed to talk to Alice.

"Was Aunt Alice pleased?" asked Elizabeth as he came in at the back door.

"Ess," said Alfred; he felt very busy that morning, and, having performed his errand, was anxious to get on to more important things. Alice meanwhile had crushed the flower between her fingers until it was all, petal and stalk, an indistinguishable clot, dark and livid like a bruise. She was thinking that at some time she would be returning to her mother's house; in a week, most likely; she really did not care whether she went or stayed.

VIII

MRS. HOPPNER received Lewis almost like another son-in-law when he brought Harriet to the house; indeed, she was on more familiar terms with him than she was with Patrick. For one thing, he was connecting himself with money, so that she could approve of him; for another, he had so much gallantry and agreeableness and was so much the ordinary gentleman, with nothing about him to make one feel at a loss, that she was able really to take a pleasure in his society. The matter of Harriet was not quite so pleasant, though that too had something to be said for it; directly they were married, Lewis would pay for these three weeks what Mrs. Ogilvy had been accustomed to pay for Harriet's board, and give Mrs. Hoppner ten pounds besides. At first she had thought of using that for new curtains and a carpet in the sitting room and some other things for the rooms upstairs; the whole place was shabby enough, goodness knows, she thought. But then the idea occurred to her that if only she could get Alice settled somewhere, she would prefer to get rid of the house and realize her dream of going into furnished rooms, with a landlady who would look after her. It was impossible to make definite plans at present, but in the meantime ten pounds was a nice little sum to have lying by one, and she would not break into it. Harriet herself was not very much trouble; in fact, Mrs. Hoppner told herself that she had never seen her so near to ordinary. The intense excitement and interest of the present had stimulated her feeble intellect, and made her seem much more able to take part in what went on around her; she would, for instance, sit in intelligent silence while Lewis or a visitor talked to Mrs. Hoppner, instead of, as she had often done, breaking in upon the conversation with some remark quite at random; and when she was spoken to she showed an eagerness and pleasure which, but for that slight but unmistakable flaw of utterance, would hardly have allowed a stranger to notice anything wrong with her. She was on this occasion particularly friendly towards Mrs. Hoppner. Whereas before, partly guided by her mother's attitude, she had regarded Mrs. Hoppner as a lodging-house keeper while she herself was an important lady, she now looked upon her quite as a friend, and especially agreeable as someone who was favourable and helpful towards her marriage, whereas her mama had been wicked and cruel. The idea that her mother had wanted to do that dreadful thing to her did not cause her the horror and dismay which a more sensitive and intelligent person would have felt, labouring under the same mistake; she merely felt exceedingly indignant, but quite safe now that she was under Lewis's protection. All her mind was taken up with the preparations for the wedding. She had sent a scrap of paper with a request that her clothes might all be packed and sent to Mrs. Hoppner's, by the hand of the daily servant. Mrs. Ogilvy had, when she received this, received the same day the information from her solicitor that the Court of Chancery could not see sufficient evidence of mental deficiency, as set down in the deposition, to warrant the interference of the Court, Miss Woodhouse being at the present time over thirty years of age; and that they felt to hold an inquisition would be needlessly trying to Miss Woodhouse's feelings. After that it seemed quite natural to Mrs. Ogilvy to pack up all Harriet's things, clothes for both summer and winter, ornament and possessions of every kind; it took her a good part of the day, and in the evening she had them, packed in two large cabin trunks, sent away in a cab to Mrs. Hoppner's.

Harriet was greatly pleased to have her own things about her again; she had always derived great satisfaction from her possessions; but, all the same, she wanted to buy a lot of new clothes; she knew it was the right thing before a wedding. Lewis, who spent every evening in their society, heard about this from Mrs. Hoppner and said it must be discouraged as firmly as possible. She had quantities of things already, and where was the use of buying any more? Nothing would make her look any better, and he had other uses for the money than allowing his wife to spend it on herself. Mrs. Hoppner agreed with him, but she could not but tell him she thought it unwise to thwart

Harriet altogether. Having a more intimate knowledge of her than Lewis, she knew what her stubbornness could be; and who could tell but that she would
take it into her head to think herself ill used and go
straight back to her mother? Lewis did not think that
at all likely; still, he did not want to take any risk;
fifty pounds or so laid out now, to make the whole
secure, could not be grudged; and it would be in his
power to prevent her spending another sixpence on
dress as long as she lived, if he wished it. So he said,
very well, merely asking Mrs. Hoppner to remember
that he wasn't *made* of money; neither of them saw
anything odd or unreasonable in his speaking of the
fortune in such a way.

Mrs. Hoppner suggested to Harriet that she had better concentrate all her energies on a handsome bridal
outfit and offered to go with her to buy it; when
Harriet agreed, she had expected to have to do all the
choosing and ordering for her, and she was amazed at
the practical and sure manner of Harriet's proceedings. Harriet knew the name of the big and very expensive shop in Regent Street at which everything
was to be bought—her own and her mother's best
dresses had always come from there—and when they
arrived, she went straight to the silk department,
which she remembered. Mrs. Hoppner realized that
she was going to choose a white wedding costume and
tried tentatively to suggest something else; she felt
that Lewis would consider such an impractical gown

an extravagance, and told herself uneasily that in the circumstances it was not "suitable." But Harriet brushed aside her suggestions with good-humoured indifference; she thought Mrs. Hoppner must be very silly not to know that people were always married in white. With the aid of an attentive and good-natured shopman she chose a thick white corded silk, with a trimming of white silk fringe; a pair of white satin boots, white silk stockings, and a complete set of very fine underlinen. Her glee as she settled upon these purchases was indescribable; when she finally led the way out of the shop, with an air of elated proprietorship, Mrs. Hoppner could only follow in awed submission, thinking, as she passed among shining bales and glowing folds, how well Alice would have looked in these beautiful things. She was for the moment quite put down by Harriet's complacency in surroundings where she herself would never have ventured, so that she had not the presence of mind to suggest to her how much Alice would love to have that deep crimson satin or the sea-green glacé silk; but she determined in her own mind that she would persuade Lewis after the wedding—that period from which all their joys were to begin—to give Alice something of the kind. Now that Alice was not present to be a burden with her obstinacy and sullenness, Mrs. Hoppner's maternal feelings were especially strong, and, though she had not wanted her to marry Lewis, she could now feel that Alice had been somewhat injured because she was not allowed to. Lewis might well take the opportunity of doing something handsome.

The wedding was arranged to take place in ten days' time, and there was to be a wedding breakfast at Mrs. Hoppner's house, after which the couple would go at once to their new house. The number of guests was small, being merely Mrs. Hoppner herself, the clergyman, and Patrick; Alice was naturally not asked to come up, and Elizabeth did not care to leave the children at present; Mrs. Ogilvy was not mentioned even by Harriet; they might, since the marriage was viewed by all the parties except one merely as a business arrangement, have dispensed with the function altogether. But Lewis rather liked the idea of a good meal immediately afterwards: oysters, roast fowl, a cake, and plenty of champagne; it was a pleasant first use of his money, and he and Patrick would enjoy something good; they had very seldom been able to indulge themselves in eating and drinking, and, though they were both temperate men, they were by no means indifferent to food. When they were boys, sleeping in the same bed, they would often beguile the time before going to sleep with planning banquets, consisting sometimes of dishes they had never tasted but knew only by hearsay.

Patrick was going to spend a fortnight or so in London; he could not stay in Laburnam Road, since Lewis had furnished only one bedroom. Lewis regretted this now, and determined to furnish at least one other room right away. Meanwhile Patrick would stay with Mrs. Hoppner, but during the day he would be free to be with Lewis.

One of the greatest delights of Lewis's present situation was that he had given in his resignation to the auctioneer. In his extreme prudence he had not done so until the actual eve of the wedding; he had something within him which assured him that his plans could not fail now, but nevertheless his native caution prevented his running a risk and finding himself without fortune or employment all at once. But, once the ceremony was over, the breakfast eaten, and his hat hung up on the stag's antlers in Laburnam Road, he could defy fate. He was complete master of his own time, a pleasure Patrick, for example, could hardly enter into, as Patrick's work was done at his own hours instead of under a rigid routine; he had a house of his own, more money than he had ever dreamed of possessing, and the society of his brother, which made all these things just twice as pleasant. Patrick was of enormous support and help to him in the business of enjoying himself, which was not quite as simple as it seemed. With Patrick to drive with him down to Epsom or Newmarket, to sit with him after dinner smoking good cigars, to be idle and talkative and merry and luxurious, he was able to bear up against the fact of his wife's existence, to be good-natured and even tolerably affectionate. He was not fastidious; the only woman who had ever really attracted him was Alice, but he knew how to get a certain amount of pleasure out of any woman who was disposed to be attached to him and not altogether a monster. Patrick could not have done this, even for money; he did not care about women as a whole, and he often thought he had been fortunate in meeting with Elizabeth, since there was certainly no other woman in the world with whom he could have brought himself to live; even she could give him nothing to equal the pleasure he had in being with his brother. That Lewis was different from him in this matter did not cause him any surprise; he accepted him altogether without comment.

Harriet in the meantime was very happy, although, as time went on and she was left a good deal to herself, the burnishing of her intelligence, which had been noticeable over the elopement, began to dim. It was not good for her to be without constant sympathetic society; her mother's attention and treating of her as a companion had drawn out her powers and not allowed them to atrophy; and though Mrs. Hoppner's society had been nothing like so skilful and stimulating in itself, yet the excitement and interest of things in general had more than made up for the difference. But now, though she was very happy, she began, with the responsibility of the house on her hands, to be puzzled and confused; Lewis had engaged a daily servant who did the housework and cooking, so that Harriet had not much to do except see that meals were ordered and commissions not forgotten, but these were just the things she was least capable of doing; if Lewis had required her to make him a dozen shirts or to do the sweeping and dusting with her own hands, she would have found less difficulty in such tasks than in giving a coherent message to Patrick or in substituting an appetizing meal when what had been originally ordered was not procurable. Then, too, when Lewis was out with Patrick for the day, she began to find time very heavy on her hands; there was, of course, infinite delight in wandering about in her very own house, although only three rooms in it were properly furnished; and her satisfaction in her husband was so great that her general state could hardly be otherwise than one of contentment; but, nevertheless, there were hours when she was really puzzled to know what to do with herself, with no one to tell her. She kept all her own belongings in great neatness and order, but she seemed incapable from the first of keeping the house shipshape; at home, she had been brought up to look after her clothes and take a great interest in them, whereas everything to do with the household had been managed by Mrs. Ogilvy and the servants between them. If there had been anyone at hand to put her in the way of things, she could have picked them up quite readily, but, as it was, there was no one but the servant, and Harriet's sense of dignity would not allow her to take directions from her, even if the woman had been inclined, by pointing out deficiencies, to make more work for herself.

Lewis, although he had had an inaugural burst of

spending, had no intention of being extravagant; he
had as yet no definite plan of laying out the money,
but in the meantime he was as prudent and as anxious
to have no waste as if he had earned every penny with
the sweat of his brow. When Patrick went down to
the country again, he had no further incentive to
recklessness, and having, besides, more time on his
hands, he began to be more closely aware of Harriet's shortcomings. He pointed out to her that she
should not leave the back door unbolted when the
house was empty, and that half-eaten dishes should
not be thrown away but turned to some use; that the
kettle should not be put down on the carpet, and that
the curtains should be neatly drawn after dark. Harriet perfectly agreed to all this in the abstract, and
wondered how anybody could be so foolish as to doubt
it for a moment; yet it somehow happened that she
made these mistakes over and over again. Lewis became at times violently irritated by her; his temper
was not improved when, among other accounts, he
had to pay the bill for her wedding clothes. He could
not say to her what he thought; if he had put it into
words she would hardly have understood him; but
forty-eight pounds for dressing up such a creature, in
clothes that would never be worn again! He had paid
Mrs. Hoppner the money he had promised, and she
had said as yet nothing about a present for Alice; she
had not quite been able to bring her tongue to it, and
she felt that perhaps Lewis's good-nature might
prompt him to it. Lewis had at present no intention

of spending money on Alice; but he remembered a hundred times a day what she had looked like in her cheap and pretty dresses, that fitted so closely round her slender waist and fell in stately folds or elegant and coquettish ruchings round her feet; and how her neck and hands came out of narrow little frills of goffered lace; she thought a lot about her dresses, too, but she was quite right; that was another matter altogether. Lewis did not grudge reasonable expenditure; but he determined that Harriet should not spend another penny on clothes; she had enough to last a lifetime.

When Patrick went down to the country again he was necessarily thrown more upon her society, and in those early weeks he did feel something for her that was almost fondness; she was so very fond of him, her face lighting up whenever he spoke to her in a way that could not but be flattering, at first; the sense, too, that she had conferred a considerable advantage on him without ever seeming to be aware that she had done so made him feel rather tenderly towards her. Physically speaking, also, she was not disagreeable; she was always richly dressed—too richly!—and her clothes were always neat and fresh; she spent a good deal of time and trouble on her appearance, always appearing just as she should. Neither was she a difficult companion, for she would be contented during his long absences if he would kiss her and say something kind when he left her and when he came back. He was, after all, a man to appreciate a smooth domestic background, and as long as he had it they really got on very well; but the trouble arose when Harriet's deficiencies as a housekeeper became apparent. Lewis not only liked comfort, he was a vigilant guardian of property, and he became indignant at the carelessness which Harriet showed about the house. At first he pointed out to her what she did wrong and was mollified by her hearty agreement with him; but as the mistakes were repeated and repeated, he grew violently irritated and spoke to her sharply. Harriet was in a confused state of mind because she did not actually realize that she herself had done these foolish things; when Lewis complained about a tap that had been left running and flooded into the sitting room, she knew it was a sad mishap, but she thought it was unreasonable she should be blamed for it, since she was able to see how tiresome it was just as well as he. Everybody knew that water should not be allowed to soak into a handsome rug. She became gradually rather sobered, and though on the whole she was willing to put up with anything from him, the unfamiliar sense of being found fault with began to upset her.

Mrs. Ogilvy had been so completely ignored by them all that she had had ample time to overcome her indignation and resentment; her affection reasserted itself in her loneliness; she longed to see Harriet, and her animosity towards Lewis had slightly abated. The hopefulness of her temperament made her incline to think, once the marriage was over and her violence could be of no use, that perhaps, after all, things might not be very bad.

She thought he must be tolerably good to Harriet now he was altogether in charge of her; Harriet herself was devoted to him, as they had only too much reason to know; and though the distress Mrs. Ogilvy had undergone was something she would never quite recover from, still, she thought that if she could see Hatty fairly happy, and well, she would be satisfied. She did not even know the exact address of the married couple, but she found it out from Mrs. Hoppner, and then she wrote a short, affectionate note to Harriet, not mentioning their past disturbance, but merely asking if she should come and see her in her new home. Harriet had not quite forgotten that dreadful discovery, but she felt so safe with Lewis that it did not now weigh very much with her; and, though Lewis was beyond expression the chief object of her affection, she felt that she would like to see her mama again, if Lewis did not object. Lewis was quite agreeable; he did not want Mrs. Ogilvy much about the place, but he, as well as Harriet, had no fear of her now, and he preferred to have things pleasant where he could. So he told Harriet to ask her mama to come on the following Tuesday afternoon.

Mrs. Ogilvy came, fully determining to make the best of what she saw and not to be unduly critical; she brought with her a box of sweet biscuits that she knew Harriet was fond of, and a scarlet geranium in a pot. Lewis opened the door to her and passed off the difficult first moment very well; he greeted her quite cordially, and was genuinely pleased with the geranium, which he put in the parlour window. Mrs. Ogilvy's anxious, fearful eye longed and was yet unwilling to search Harriet's face: but it was no use; in spite of the embraces and the bright conversation, she could not help noticing that Harriet had about her an air of quiet sadness, utterly unlike the sullenness which in old days used to mark her being out of temper. She did not look unwell, but Mrs. Ogilvy could not help saying with eager earnestness, "And how do you find yourself, my love?" Harriet said, "Pretty well, Mama; middling." Mrs. Ogilvy stopped, feeling that Lewis would resent closer questioning; but Lewis, as if divining her thoughts and determined to be amiable, said to Harriet, "Take your mama upstairs, my love, and show her the rest of the house."

When they were upstairs and had seen the bedroom, Mrs. Ogilvy was more than surprised to find that the other rooms were unfurnished. She could not help commenting on this to Lewis when she came downstairs again, and at the same time asking him whether he and Harriet would not be more comfortable with a resident maid. Lewis said that both these improvements would be made shortly, and his demeanour did not encourage any further conversation on the matter. When the house had been seen, Mrs. Ogilvy was really at a loss for anything more to say; any confidential or fond talk with Harriet was impossible; the first she was afraid to venture on, anxious above all things not to cause any trouble, and the second she felt in some subtle way that Harriet did not want. It came to pass, therefore, that this long-thought-of and much-desired visit lasted rather less than twenty minutes; Lewis accompanied her to the door with a suspicion of his disagreeable grin on his countenance, although his leave-taking was pleasant and simple. Mrs. Ogilvy had kissed Harriet good-bye in the parlour, and as she went down the road she looked to see if she could catch a glimpse of her through the window curtains, but there was nothing to be seen.

When she got home, her husband asked her how she had found matters.

"Don't ask me," she said. "Least said is soonest mended," and pursed up her lips.

"But," said Mr. Ogilvy, "she was quite well, at any rate?" His wife gave an involuntary sigh that made him want to show some sympathy, but he could do nothing but stand over her with his fingers locking and unlocking.

"I wouldn't say she was ill," she said. "I've seen her look better, certainly. But there! Don't ask me. There's nothing for it now but to make the best of it." So saying, she got up from her chair and went slowly upstairs to take off her bonnet. Mr. Ogilvy stirred the fire and then hovered about uncertainly while Hannah brought in some tea. There was nothing he could do to assist in the preparations for his wife's comfort, but at least he forbore to retire to his study.

It was two days later that she received a letter from Lewis enclosing a note from Harriet. Lewis said:

DEAR MRS. OGILVY:

Liking to have everything pleasant, there was no objection to your visiting us the other day; but you must be aware of how you have forfeited Harriet's confidence by your monstrous conduct and any right to see her. Consequently should esteem it a favour if you would abstain from coming to the house; otherwise I shall have to take steps which cannot fail to be mutually disagreeable; or rather to me, since I know you have no objection to things which no decent person would demean themselves to do. I think I have now said all that is necessary on the subject; Harriet is writing to tell you what she thinks, since we have but one thought in the matter.

Yours truly,
LEWIS OMAN.

"What *she* thinks!" exclaimed Mrs. Ogilvy, as she unfolded Harriet's note, and read:

DEAR MAMA:

Dear Lewis says you not come to the house I think it best. He says we do not want anybody but us and you was very cruel. I am your affectionate daughter
HARRIET.

The spelling alone was enough to tell Mrs. Ogilvy that this did not come from Harriet unaided; and the letters at once broke down the restraints she had imposed on herself, even in her thoughts, letting in a flood of impressions which before she had refused consciously to notice. She could not now think of Harriet with any equanimity; that she seemed fairly contented she did not deny, but with how little reason! "The base wretch!" she cried. "Three thousand pounds with her, and not even a decently furnished house!" Mr. Ogilvy thoroughly agreed with her, but he said gravely:

"You must take a hold on yourself, Bessie. You said yourself it was no use to worry. The young people may do all right yet. He's a most objectionable young man, no doubt, but many people's daughters do even worse, my dear. You have done all you can; you must have faith now."

Mrs. Ogilvy allowed herself to be talked into a calmer frame of mind, but she could not be at ease.

❦ IX ❦

LIFE went on in Cudham with little variation except that Alice had gone back to her mother. The variety of their existence, such as it was, was occasioned by Patrick's sometimes having quite a comfortable little income, when they would have beef or a leg of mutton in the house, and apples and bananas, and butter as well as treacle on the bread, and at other times having practically nothing, when all these pleasant things would disappear from the table. The people who enjoyed these bursts of prosperity most were Alfred and Clara; they were naturally a relief to Elizabeth, but more of a spiritual than a sensuous satisfaction. Eating, however, was so far almost the greatest pleasure in Alfred's life, and Clara was hardly behind him in her enjoyment of grocer's pound cake or the toffee-like taste of treacle over butter. The hardness of so much of their life, enlivened as it was by these pleasures, had the strange effect of binding Clara still more closely to her cousins; whereas most people would have left such a situation at all costs, the rigours she endured seemed to act upon her like hardships undergone by soldiers on a campaign, or by shipwrecked mariners, creating a bond between the fellow sufferers that nothing can unknit. In spite of the original understanding, Patrick never gave her any money, and it never occurred to her to ask for it; so that not only would she have found it very difficult to go far by herself if she had wanted to escape, she would hardly have known how to take the first step, for her sense of direction was so feeble that it was only the necessity they were under of not going farther on their afternoon walks than the baby could be carried which brought them home safely at all.

Elizabeth was by now quite inured to their way of living. She did not mind the hardships and inconveniences for herself very much, having none of Alice's imperious impatience of discomfort; and she was, too, endowed with something of her mother's faculty for overlooking what she did not care to see. What did affect her, and that acutely, was anything of an emotional disturbance in the house; it fretted her when Clara had a bilious turn and the consequent depression; when Patrick was moody she never showed anything, but she felt in such a state of tension that it seemed as if her brain must give way at the slightest added annoyance.

Towards the end of the summer, when everything was going well with them, Lewis sent to ask Patrick whether Lizzie might not come up to him for a few days: he thought of buying the extra furniture he had talked about for so long. Patrick saw that Elizabeth was jaded and thought some days in town would do her good; besides, he was glad if she could be of any use to Lewis. So though not very anxious to make a closer acquaintance with her sister-in-law, she went up to town and spent some interesting days with Lewis in the big shops; he deferred to her taste in everything, and only disagreed with her about the necessity for such strict economy; he wanted a properly furnished home at last, he said; he did not explain why he should have waited till several months after his wedding to achieve one, nor did Elizabeth enquire. Together they chose a suite of pretty blue-covered furniture for another bedroom, quite like a young lady's boudoir; and they replaced most of the shoddy bamboo furniture in the living room with things in better style. Lewis further insisted upon a white fur hearthrug and some elaborate lace drapery for the mantelpiece.

Harriet did not accompany them on these expeditions, but she was delighted with the things when they came home. When the mantelpiece was dressed in its new ornament she fingered the folds with interest and admiration. Lewis saw her doing this and stepped forward angrily.

"Keep your hands off it," he said. For the first time it seemed to strike Harriet that she ought not to be talked to like this; she looked at him with something of that expression he had seen on her face during the quarrel with her mother. She muttered something under her breath and turned away. From that time onwards she showed open anger when she was reproved, and stopped even trying to remember what Lewis wished to be done with regard to the new things. He could not prevent things being spilled on the white rug, and when he told her to keep out of the blue bedroom, she rushed into it in an outbreak of rage and overturned the chairs, pulling the bedspread from the bed and throwing it about the floor. Elizabeth had gone back to Cudham, her return having been hastened by Alfred's coming out in a rash, so that Lewis had no one to sympathize with him, unless he wrote to his brother, which he accordingly did.

MY DEAR PATRICK:

Many, many thanks for your kind messages by Lizzie. No one knows, dear Patrick, what I have had to put up with from Harriet; her temper is something frightful. I have talked to her for hours together and tried to reason with her, but it is all no use. From the time she gets up in the morning until the time she goes to bed, she does nothing but try to aggravate me and make me as miserable as she possibly can. I have been quite disheartened and cried for hours to think I should have laid out money to have things nice, and no one to take any interest in the place. I am indeed truly unhappy; but oh, dear Patrick, I can never thank you and dear Lizzie enough for all your kindness to me, but rest assured I shall not forget it.

Your ever affectionate brother,

LEWIS OMAN.

Such a letter could not but prove to Patrick the absolute need of someone to act as housekeeper in

Laburnam Road. Lewis partly believed that it represented his own state of mind, but above all he was anxious that whatever course he might adopt, though it were misunderstood by other people, should at least have Patrick's sanction.

One afternoon, in the dispiriting brassy glare of a December sunset, Alice was upstairs sorting ornamented buttons on her counterpane; she had entered into a sort of partnership with Miss Croker the dressmaker, who had always admired her taste and skill in dress, and whose clientele had increased so much that she was glad to take in such a valuable assistant; Alice worked for her because she thought that when she had by this means saved a little money she might do something—she did not quite know what—begin a business of her own, perhaps, or else go to America; she worked well and had already proved worth her weight in gold, as Miss Croker said; but she no longer took any interest in her own personal appearance. As she stood now against the afternoon light of the window, her head bent, her hands languidly sorting the buttons, her hair no longer curled but combed into an irregular wavy mass behind her ears, and wearing the plain grey frock she had made during her stay at Cudham, she was hardly recognizable as the radiant, elegant, spirited creature of a few months back. Her mother came into the room, but Alice did not raise her head; it required an imperative appeal to her attention nowadays to rouse her from the abysmal indifference she showed to everything outside her working hours at Miss Croker's. The next moment, however, she looked up, with a wondering, startled gaze. "Lewis is in the parlour," Mrs. Hoppner said. She repeated it, but, before she had time to add anything else, Alice was out of the room and halfway down the stairs; there she paused, trying to tell herself that he had merely called on some business arrangement with her mother, but it would not do. She hurried on in spite of herself, and, when she reached the parlour, Lewis met her at the door, holding out his arms.

If there were anything gracious or good in Alice's nature, it showed itself now. She did not say, "You made me cruelly unhappy, and you don't deserve that I should ever speak to you again." Nor, for that matter, did she once consider whether she ought to speak to him in such a frame of mind as she now was. She flew into his embrace; the look of age went from her face, and tears rained down her cheeks; Lewis could not see them because her face was over his shoulder, but he felt them on his neck, and clasped her so tightly that neither of them could say a word. At last he whispered in the nearest approach to an everyday tone that he could manage:

"Harriet is going to have a child; I want you to come and look after the house." Alice twisted so that she could look at him, and gazed with heaving sobs and lips parted in the mast ecstatic smile. "If your mother can spare you," went on Lewis with the old familiar laugh.

"Yes, yes, of course she can."

"Listen," he said, drawing her to a chair. "When can you manage to come?"

"Now, now."

"Right away? Then I'll wait for you while you pack your bag."

Alice had managed to let go one of his hands, and she put her free one up to her hair; as she did so, she suddenly realized what a fright she must look; weeks of neglect, and now all in tears! "Oh!" she gasped, "I must get tidy—I'm a perfect sight—don't look at me!"

Until that moment Lewis himself had not noticed that there was anything different about her appearance; he had only been conscious of her rushing into his arms in the way he had half expected but which none the less gave him a shock of thankfulness and joy. Now, however, he saw that she did indeed look a poor little washed-out creature; but whereas Alice felt ashamed of her looks and wished ardently to be rectifying them, to Lewis they made no difference at all at the moment. Still, he said kindly:

"How long do you want to put yourself to rights, eh? Shall I come back for you later?"

"Yes," cried Alice; then she sat quite silent, with his arm round her, looking at the carpet. It seemed as if they said nothing about the situation, past or present, by mutual consent. The idea of consulting Mrs. Hoppner about Alice's accepting the proposal, or even of ascertaining her views of it, did not occur to either of them for a moment. Alice, in fact, thought

of nothing; it was enough that from utter barrenness
and futility she had been translated to unspeakable
bliss; she seemed already to have left the last months
behind as a horrid dream, and to be looking about her
now with eyes newly awakened to familiar objects.
Lewis got up presently, and, as he went out to the
back of the house to talk to Mrs. Hoppner, Alice flew
upstairs and dashed into her bedroom. She began to
brush her hair and curl it round her fingers, and
laughed at her own clumsiness, reminding herself that
there was no violent hurry; then she found she could
not paint her face because she was crying so. She sat
in front of the dressing table, leaning her forehead
on her hands, trying to become sensible again. She
did not visualize what all this meant, though, had she
stopped to ask herself, she would have discovered that
she knew perfectly; she was overwhelmed with the
sensation of unutterable joy, not entirely caused by
the fact that Lewis, that man and no other, whose
place no one in the universe could fill for her, was
come back; it was as much a feeling, as divine as air
to a suffocating creature, or water to someone dying
of thirst, that her life had now come right again; a
satisfaction, whose sweetness was past expression, that
all the things she ought to have she would have; that
life had become full and glorious and she would never
endure that degrading misery any more. It was not
only that she did not reason and argue to herself; she
was entirely content to leave the future to Lewis. All
she had to do was to stop crying and make herself

look presentable; she raised her head slowly, pushing away the tears with the back of her hand, when suddenly she sprang up and nearly overturned the chair. Fool, fool, that she had been! The lilac dress which she had stopped Miss Croker from putting in hand! What an occasion this would have been! To have had it now would have been worth making any number of sacrifices. The mirage-like vision she had of herself going down to Lewis in this cool, whispering, *soupir étouffé*, which made such a lovely contrast with a clear rose pink in the face and dark silky hair, made her feel for a moment that the happiness was all withered; then common sense reasserted itself, and reminded her, though forcing its way with difficulty against feminine convictions, that to a man one pretty dress is very much like another, and that if a woman looks charming it is ten to one that he won't know why. Besides, the thought came to her, as, standing bare-armed in her petticoat, she laid out her long-neglected dresses on the bed, that the time would come when she would have not only the lilac dress, but as many others as she wanted. In the meantime there was a good deal to be done to the few she had, in the way of odd stitches and fresh frills of muslin or lace; she was very busy for an hour or more, and glad of the excuse to remain upstairs and avoid any discussion with her mother. She felt intuitively that her mother would rather she stayed at home, and she did not want any trifle, however light, to interfere with this rapture.

When she came downstairs at last she was as swan-like, as brilliant-eyed, as glowing of cheek as she had ever been; the dark curls had all come back, and her mouth, half open as she looked up at Lewis, was as red as the deepest strawberry. She said nothing to him, but asked the daily woman to bring down the tin trunk from her bedroom. Mrs. Hoppner had been giving Lewis a cup of tea and seemed on perfectly good terms with him. Alice, however, said nothing to her either, except that when they were all at the door and her box was being put on to the cab, she turned half round and said carelessly: "Tell Miss Croker I shan't be coming any more. The buttons she wanted me to cover are in my room. I've done some of them." With that she got into the cab, and it was left for Lewis to say a polite and gracious good-bye to Mrs. Hoppner. He put his head out of the window as they were driving away and said:

"I'll see she comes to no harm." Mrs. Hoppner waved a rather uncertain farewell.

"Whatever did you say that for?" Alice scolded him, clasping her little gloved hands on his arm. Lewis roared with laughter and pinched her knee.

"Well, I must look after you now," he said; then they both laughed. The thought in his mind was, as he felt all the renewed delight of Alice's presence and saw again all the quickness of her movements, the vivacious changes from frowns to smiles on her face, and felt, as she sat beside him with her arm tucked in his, the sensation of a being in absolute sympathy

with himself, that he had been wonderfully patient
with Harriet and borne with her as very few men
would have done.

As they drew near to their journey's end Alice began for the first time to be a little apprehensive. She
did not quite know how she would meet Harriet, and
then, too, it was dreadfully hard that at this moment
she and Lewis should have to begin behaving as if
they were nothing at all to each other. She was quite
chilly now after the fever she had been in, and shiv-
ered a little as she got out of the cab. Lewis, however,
seemed quite at ease; he directed the luggage to be
taken in, paid off the cab, and then, taking Alice by
the elbow, led her into the parlour. A bright fire lit
up the walls, though the lamp was not lighted. Alice
looked round and saw to her relief that the room was
empty. As Lewis was turning up the lamp wick, an
elderly woman came into the room.

"Nurse," he said, "this is Miss Hoppner, Mrs.
Oman's friend, who has come to look after us while
Mrs. Oman is upstairs."

At that moment the light went up and revealed
Alice in all her damning charm. The nurse said nothing, but stared and made a sort of curtsey before she
passed through to the kitchen. Lewis waited till she
had come out and gone upstairs again. Then he drew
an easy chair up to the hearth and made Alice undo
her cape.

"Doesn't she come down?" she asked rather nervously.

"Oh, yes," he said, "but she goes upstairs early. But now, wouldn't you like to see your room?"

The reluctance Alice felt to encounter Harriet had become a positive dread. She looked up at Lewis speechlessly.

"Come, darling," he said kindly, and helped her to her feet with a protectiveness he had never shown before; he seemed all encouragement and tenderness; she went up the stairs with his arm round her waist, and saw with some reassurance that the doors upstairs were shut. In another moment Lewis had opened one, and there before her was the prettiest bedroom, all upholstered in blue.

"There," said Lewis, "Lizzie chose these things. I thought, you know, we should be wanting to have you with us when this happened, so I had everything got ready in time."

"It's lovely," she said, "but don't leave me! I'll just lay my things off and come down with you again."

He helped her off with her hat and cape, and they went down to the living room again. Once here, seated before the fire, with Lewis beside her, her composure gradually returned. She looked about her like a cat in a new home, made joking remarks, and ran both hands through Lewis's hair just as she had been used to do. But when he said, "I'll see about some supper for us. They have theirs upstairs," and rose to his feet, she cried out again, "Don't go! I'll come with you."

They went into the kitchen and found some cold

meat and a piece of tart; Lewis put the things on a
tray and carried them into the parlour and then
started to make some coffee. Alice was sitting on the
kitchen table playing with a mincing machine which
was clamped to it.

"I ought to do that," she said, "as I'm supposed to
be here to help you." She looked at him, half doubtful and half laughing.

"Let me alone with it," he said. "I don't want you
to trouble."

He made the coffee, and they went into the parlour. All through the meal he treated her with the
attention almost of a nurse to a child: cutting up her
food for her and putting salt on it, then holding the
fork to her mouth. When he started to drink his
coffee in the large cup, she put out her hand to it to
steady it, and approached her mouth to the rim, so
that the cup see-sawed between them as they drank
alternately. They had never been like this before;
Alice had always made herself as attractive to him as
she could, and he had always shown that he considered her very attractive; but the shock of their sudden reunion had pushed them on farther in a few
hours than they had progressed in months of friendship. The sense of being entirely dependent on his
protection in this unnerving household made her cling
to him without any artifice or disguise, showing a
much humbler and more childish aspect of her affection that he had ever seen before; while the tenderness for her which this aroused in him, coupled with

the sharp, exquisite contrast she made to what he had recently been accustomed to, made him feel that he could not sufficiently cherish and worship this lovely child.

"I sleep down here on the sofa," he said. "You won't be nervous upstairs, will you? Your door has a key, so you can lock yourself in if you like, and feel quite safe till I knock you up in the morning."

"I shall be all right," she said, not very confidently. "But you won't be comfortable down here," she added, with wide-open eyes.

"Yes, I shall," he said firmly. He disclosed a pile of blankets behind the sofa cushions, and began to make up a bed on the couch, handily enough. Alice watched, laughing. "How nicely you do things," she said.

"I'm handy about the house," he answered. "You won't find me much trouble. Dear Alice, it is so good of you to come and help me."

He kissed her quietly, not at all as he had done that afternoon; then he escorted her upstairs and saw her lock herself into the blue bedroom. She was suddenly so tired that she could hardly undress and fall into bed before she was sound asleep.

The next morning after breakfast Lewis took her upstairs to see Harriet. The latter did not get up nowadays till towards noon, and was sitting up in bed, looking quite well. The nurse appeared to be very good to her. She was a dour, censorious-looking woman, but her expression changed when she spoke to Harriet, and she waited on her with a kind, encouraging, cheerful manner, so that Harriet was really very happy and did not think of missing her mother, as she might otherwise have done. When Lewis and Alice came into the room, Harriet's face brightened. Lewis went up to the bedside and said:

"Well, you're doing fine, ain't you?"

"Yes," she said. Then she looked towards Alice.

"Here's Alice," said Lewis, "come to make things comfortable for us downstairs till you're about again."

Harriet smiled at her pleasantly, and Alice forced herself to say, "How well you're looking! If there's anything you want me to do, you must tell me."

Harriet said: "Nurse looks after me; but you must keep Mr. Oman comfortable and not upset the house and dirty the new furniture."

Lewis patted Alice's arm. "She'll manage, you see. You'll have nothing to worry about now, Harriet."

With that he led Alice out of the room again. From this time on she saw Harriet only once a day: either visiting her in her bedroom accompanied by Lewis, or else undergoing her society when she came downstairs for a little in the middle of the day. Harriet made very few demands on anybody's attention; she liked to see Lewis once or twice a day, but otherwise she was content to depend completely on the nurse, who listened tirelessly to all her small wonderings and complaints. The woman had a peculiar sympathy for her; she was good at her business, but not clever

otherwise, and Harriet's deficiency made her feel that
the patient was her own property in a way that she
could not regard invalids who were lively and manag-
ing from their sick-beds, whatever their physical dependence might be.

Alice and Lewis meantime began a round of pleasure such as neither had ever known before, and it was
something to Lewis's credit that he did not require
coarse and sensuous delights to minister to his happiness; he did not want drink or music halls or crude
diversions of any kind; he was wholly taken up with
the pleasure of going about, with Alice as his perpetual companion. They did a great deal of sight-
seeing, it is true; Lewis liked to take her to the Tower
and Hampton Court and the waxworks; not that he
had more than a superficial interest in the places himself, but they had to have somewhere to go, out of the
house; the weather was fine and any excursion pleasant, and Alice made everything delicious by her interest and enjoyment. He felt, too, a curious satisfaction in this innocent manner of passing the time; that
no blame of any kind could possibly attach to him. In
the midst of all this it was a matter quite of secondary
importance when the child was born. They were, in
fact, out of the house at the time, and arrived home
that evening to be told that Lewis was the father of
a son. The nurse, sardonic as ever, did not even con-
gratulate him; she was capably looking after the patient, who had come through the ordeal very well,
and, but for the daily visits of the doctor, which now

began, the rest of the house would not have known
that anything had occurred. Alice was not disturbed
by the baby, which did sometimes cry during the
night, but not enough to waken so excellent a sleeper
and one worn out with being in the open air all day;
and during the day, since the weather continued fine,
they were out as usual.

After a fortnight or so, however, a change set in;
the weather became wintry, with an accumulation of
rigour in frost and sleet as if to make up for the previous unseasonable mildness, and now there was nothing to do but order the most appetizing meals that
could be thought of and sit beside a blazing fire. They
did not regret the change; they now had a whole vista
of new experiences before them in sitting indoors and
talking instead of talking as they walked about.
Alice's spirits were simply soaring; the sunless days
had no effect on her liveliness and bloom. She had now
completely gained control of her nerves; she could
defy the thought of Harriet and bask unrestrainedly
in this atmosphere of petting, luxury, and reverential
desire.

But Harriet, who was now getting strong again,
though still upstairs, had outgrown the comfortable
lethargy in which she had been on Alice's arrival. She
wanted Lewis beside her constantly; the baby itself
could not satisfy her; she was forever asking the nurse
what Lewis was about, and ordering her to go downstairs and bring her word. Lewis would sometimes go
up to her, though he did not now take Alice with

him. He would say, "Well, Harriet, do you want anything?" and when she looked piteously at him, unable to bring out that it was not any object that she wanted, but only some of his society, and a share of the happiness that she knew was going on elsewhere in the house, he would take advantage of her inability to express herself, and say:

"Well, you don't want anything, you see, after all. You ought not to bring me upstairs for nothing," and then go down again.

The nurse had been quite undeceived about Alice from the first; and had she not been of a suspicious nature, the fact that Alice, though acting as complete mistress of the house to tradespeople and the servant, never did a stroke of work herself, or even made any enquiry after the baby, would have been enough to make her so; besides, Lewis was now so happy and open-hearted in his devotion that he could not keep his hands off Alice even when there were other people in the room. He always had her by the elbow or was holding her hand; and when Alice kissed him she did not care whether anyone was passing through the kitchen or not. She had of course said nothing of this to Harriet, but Harriet, with that uncanny quickness she had in certain matters which seemed almost a compensation of nature for her slowness in others, knew as plainly as if she had seen them what sort of scenes were going on downstairs. When Lewis grew more and more obstinate about visiting her, standing by the bed and saying, "Well, here I am, Harriet. Just

say what it is you want," she took to sending notes
down to the sitting room by the hand of the nurse.
The woman often suppressed them, well knowing
they would do the poor creature no good; she could
not always do this, however, since Harriet would always question her about their delivery; in the evening, after tea, Alice was always specially elate, sitting on Lewis's knee before the fire, and laughing so
that the sound could be heard upstairs in Harriet's
room. Harriet had written a note, really illegible in its
bad handwriting and spelling and incoherence; nothing, in fact, but a scribble, with here and there a dis-
connected word. She gave it to the nurse, who felt
that some interruption of the scene in the parlour was
quite justifiable, and, knocking at the door, went in
with it. Alice was on Lewis's knee as usual, and he
was trying to dislodge her, or pretending to do so, by
bouncing her up in the air as high as he could, all of
which attempts she resisted with shrieks of delight.

They were sitting without the lamp, the fire being
so bright; on the table were the used tea things, and
a glass jar of water in which expanding flowers were
floating—sea-green, yellow, coral, and flame colour;
they had bought them in a highly coloured Chinese
packet from a hawker's tray during their afternoon
walk, and found the greatest amusement in watching
them uncurl from their round white discs and blossom out into weeds and stars and fish.

As the nurse opened the door, Alice restrained herself and sat tautly upright with her arm round

Lewis's shoulders; she did not attempt, however, to leave his knee, but sat with an expression of haughty defiance. Lewis merely looked round and said, "What is it, nurse?" The nurse approached him grimly and held out the slip of paper.

"Mrs. Oman has written this, sir," she said, "and would be glad if you'd spend a little time with her this evening." Lewis took the paper.

"You may tell her I'll be up presently," he said; when the door was shut, Alice, with her fingers dug into his shoulder, bent her head with his over the writing. The flames showed the incoherent scrawl.

"I don't think this is very clear," said Lewis. Alice snatched it from him and threw it into the fire. "Don't go yet," she said. She had come to regard Harriet absolutely in the light of a tiresome check on her own legitimate pleasures. The pure happiness she and Lewis enjoyed in each other's society made her sure that their absorption in each other was right; she did not stop to question the matter: she merely went on from day to day, strong in the instinct that what they did they were intended to do by all the forces of the universe. Harriet's helplessness and unhappiness might, despite this view, have pleaded for her and aroused a little consideration. But suffering had had the worst effect on Alice. Ideas of being refined by fire, and brought through unhappiness to larger sympathies, were quite inapplicable to her case; what she had gone through had had the result of making her morbidly impatient of any further pain for herself

and quite indifferent to its being inflicted on other
people. She did not forget those days of ravening tor-
ment in the fields, when she had wanted the earth to
cover her because she could not bear the relentless
mockery of oncoming summer; and now her happiness was so precious that nothing in earth or heaven
mattered beside the keeping of it; and anyone who
threatened it was not only an obstacle to be overcome
at all costs, but a personal enemy to be regarded with
dismay and horror. Any demonstration of Harriet's
or any open sympathy shown on her side had the result of arousing all Alice's active energies to repel it.
Whereas ordinarily she still maintained, even in the
midst of her wildest gambols with Lewis, in her very
kisses, the slightest hoar frost of reserve, just enough
to sharpen her gaiety and imperious contrariness,
whenever something had occurred in the nature of
this visit she melted utterly, clinging to him and looking up with eyes that seemed burning through un-
shed tears; but she had never shown such abandonment as she did at this moment; the pointed reminder
which had just been conveyed, the consciousness that
Harriet's seclusion would not last for very much
longer, and that presently she would be upon them, a
terrible threat to their bliss, made the present moment seem charged with urgency and significance.
Alice had now no lingering trace of fear as to what
the outside world might say; Lewis was mad for what
seemed to him now the crown of all his endeavours,
though he had never realized it as such until that in-

stant. Was the culmination of his whole life to fall
away in nothingness just as he was about to reach it?
He could only go on living through the possessing of
Alice; and so everything happened exactly as each of
them, ever since they set eyes on each other, had always intended that it should.

Alice did not communicate at all with her mother,
although living at so short a distance; and Lewis saw
no necessity to interrupt their idyllic days by calling
on other people; where was the need? Surely he could
be trusted to look after Alice; her mother might
know that she would be quite safe with him. So that
it was left to Elizabeth, on one of her visits to Mrs.
Hoppner, to come over to Laburnam Road and find
out how things were going on. Lewis was, as always,
pleased to see her; he appeared to have nothing on his
mind at all. He was alone in the parlour when she
arrived, and he gave her a glass of ale and some biscuits and sat down for a long talk all about Patrick
and the children, in whom he took a minute and
genuine interest. Elizabeth herself, he thought, did
not look well; she wore an old black stuff dress and a
dark blue jacket, with a black straw hat tilted on the
top of her head; and in contrast her face, with its
straw-coloured hair behind the ears, looked wan and
bloodless; her hands, when she took off her shabby
gloves, were noticeably roughened and swollen with
all the work she did. Still, she was Elizabeth; the tones
of her voice, her pose as she sat on the sofa, were full
of dignity and charm. Lewis felt she was a relation to

be proud of. He said, "I'm a father now, you know," but he did not offer to show her the child, nor did she ask to see it, and after a perfunctory enquiry after Harriet she allowed the conversation to return to her own family. After a quarter of an hour or so, during which time her sister's name had not been mentioned, he suddenly said, "You'll want to see Alice. She's out here," and led the way into the kitchen, afterwards leaving the room and shutting the door behind him.

Alice was bending over the table ironing; she looked up as Elizabeth entered, and presented a face that was both flushed and daunted and yet full of an angry defiance. Elizabeth saw at once that all, and more than all, Alice's pristine elegance had come back; her lovely, round, dark head was smoother and silkier than ever; she wore a pea-green merino skirt that Elizabeth remembered, but over it was a bodice of dark green velvet, fitting from the throat to the hips as only Alice's clothes could fit, and ornamented at the neck with a narrow lace collar and a large bow of coral-coloured satin ribbon; anything like the freshness and lustre of her appearance, the softness and sleekness, Elizabeth had not seen since the days when she had wondered at Alice's skill before. She saw at the same time that Alice was prepared to fly out at a moment's notice, and she did want so much to be friends with her. She was glad Alice was happy now, and if there was anything she herself would be bound to disapprove of, she had all her mother's capac-

ity for overlooking what she did not want to see. She
said:

"Mother sends her love, Alice, and hoped I'd find
you well. You look it, I must say."

"I am," said Alice. "Never better." An involuntary
smile hovered on her lips.

"And when do you go home?" continued Elizabeth.

"Home?" said Alice, startled.

Elizabeth looked surprised in turn.

"Well," she said, "I suppose Harriet will be downstairs soon, won't she?"

Alice said nothing, but fastened her little teeth on
her lower lip and returned to her ironing. Elizabeth
moved some of the things to one side in order to make
room for herself on the only chair the kitchen contained; and then she saw for the first time what Alice
was doing. All around were spread pieces of a dress
that had been unpicked and was being pressed before
it was made up again; pieces of stiff silk, a beautiful, deep blue like a jay's wing. Elizabeth looked
away without saying anything.

X

THE nurse was to leave Harriet at the end of the month, a period now less than a week distant; Lewis had formed no plans for the immediate future; the long series of successful happenings and the luxurious happiness of the last few weeks had put a spell over his usually active and contriving brain. He moved almost as in a trance, half stupefied by the ease with which he accomplished everything to which he raised his hand, and feeling that he was borne onward by a steady flow of circumstances all tending in the direction of his desires. It was Alice who was now restless and anxious, and who urged him to take some step in their affairs, though of what nature she herself could not suggest. Harriet was up now after breakfast for the whole day, and, when Lewis and Alice came in from their daily walk or outing, they would find her and the nurse sitting on opposite sides of the parlour fire, with the baby in his bassinette between them. This sight drove Alice almost beside herself. Harriet made little claim on Lewis's attention, and hardly said anything except to the nurse and in low exclamations to the baby; now that she was able to be downstairs she seemed not to resent Lewis's intimacy with Alice any more, and altogether to be more normal, cheer-

ful, and subdued, having quite lost the nervous irrita-
bility she had shown before the child was born. All
the same, Alice could not endure her very existence;
the sight of her sitting quietly with her netting in the
firelight, occasionally pausing to look over the cradle
with some remark of wonder or gratification, affected
Alice as if Harriet had been engaged in some indecent outrage; she would dig her nails into the palms
of her hands to prevent herself from screaming with
nervous fury. Lewis was quite unmoved, and merely
bent all his energies and strength of will to getting
the unwelcome occupants of the sitting room upstairs
as soon and for as long a time as possible; there was,
happily, a small grate in the bedroom occupied by
Alice, and he had a fire kept ready laid in it for Miss
Hoppner's convenience, so that when they were
driven to it they could retire upstairs and amuse
themselves in private. As for the child, he had not the
least interest in it; he thought of it as entirely Harriet's, and had not had a single paternal impulse
towards it since its birth. It seemed a healthy little
creature, and with the assistance of the nurse Harriet
was quite handy in looking after it; her face as she
attended to it was always solemn and devout; she had
had the care of herself impressed upon her so much as
a duty from childhood that she transferred the feeling to the care of her baby, and performed the various little rites more as if they were moral obligations
towards some overseeing authority than a spontane-
ous outcome of her own affections. None the less, she

was becoming very fond of little Tommy, and she thought herself very lucky to have a real baby of her own, and that to play with him was a treat which she enjoyed by the nurse's permission. She did not seem to expect any show of interest in it from Lewis; hardly realizing perhaps that it was his as well as her own.

As the time of the nurse's departure drew near, Alice nearly fretted herself into a fever; at present, while the woman remained with them, they had no responsibility for Harriet and really saw very little of her, since she sat a great deal upstairs. But what would happen when she was left on their hands? Any sort of service or assistance to her Alice felt to be quite out of the question; she would leave Laburnam Road sooner; but even as she told herself so, her heart contracted. How could she? It was unfair and wicked that she should be driven to such a thing; as she looked at the unconscious Harriet's face, its dense expression enlivened by a complacent smile that accentuated the lines from the nose to the corners of the mouth, she felt a spasm of hatred and indignation that caused her to run out of the room. In her bedroom she looked in the glass and saw that the lovely, childlike bloom of her face was absolutely marred by vindictiveness; she was looking hard and hateful. Good God, was the creature spreading a blight that affected even her personal appearance? Alice threw herself down on the bed and bit the pillowcase; just then she heard Lewis's step on the stairs, and all at

once she became deadly calm, and lay quite motionless, like an animal in its hole; feeling very naughty
and very cautious, as she used to feel when, as a child,
she had indulged in a passion and felt that even she
had gone too far. When Lewis came in she did not
raise her head or move; he strolled up to the bedside
and said:

"What do you deserve for running away like
that?"

Alice muttered something unintelligible.

"You are very naughty indeed," he went on, "and
I've a great mind not to tell you my news." Alice
looked up.

"That's all very well," said Lewis, "but I don't
think I shall tell you now."

Alice started up and threw her arms round his
neck. "Is it something good?" she cried. "I'm sure it
is! You're laughing! If you don't tell me, I'll wrench
your ear out."

"Well," he said, sitting down beside her on the bed,
"I've been thinking that, when nurse goes, it won't
do to leave Harriet to look after the baby. So I'm going to ask Patrick if he will take them both as paying guests for a month or two. The country air——"
But he got no further, for Alice was stifling him with
kisses.

"When does she go?" she said at last.

"Nurse leaves at the end of the week," he answered.
"I'll write to Patrick at once; I daresay she'd be off
in a fortnight from now."

"But that would leave a week here just with us," said Alice doubtfully.

"You can go to your mother's for that time, if you had rather," said Lewis; his tone was not unpleasant, but it had altered, and she did not like it. Before she could speak he went on: "In fact, it's what I think you'd better do, all things considered. I must get her into a good frame of mind so as she won't give them trouble down there. I think you'd better be out of the way for a little."

Alice felt bound hand and foot; once Lewis would not have spoken in that firm way, in case she should resent it and fling away from him; now things were different, and she could not even pretend to turn him off; she was overwhelmed with dismay at the thought of being banished for a week. She rested her head against his shoulder, gazing with troubled, anxious eyes. Lewis was imperturbable in his affection as well as in his determination; where Patrick would have cowed a person with a burst of alarming temper, Lewis grinned amiably and went on to expound details. He shifted his arm round Alice's waist so that she was supported comfortably and said:

"I shall be coming over to see you ever so often; it's only for a week or ten days, you know."

"You said a week," implored Alice. "Don't go and make it ten days! It'll be a month, for all you care."

"Darling Alice," he said, "you don't know what nonsense you're talking——"

"Oh, I daresay——" she interposed.

"I can't tell you what it means to have my sweetheart out of the house, even for that little while. But I'm doing it so that we can both be happy. Once I've got Harriet safely down there, we shan't have anything to worry about till she comes back. Now, tell me, is your mother going to worry you when you get home?"

"Good gracious, no," said Alice, in such an astonished voice as quite reassured him.

"Because I fear that Lizzie was a little distressed——" he said.

"Oh, *her*," said Alice. "But I've always gone my own way. I don't want people interfering in *my* business."

He stroked her hair, amused at her petulance like that of a little cat. He had been afraid that when she came to face the outside world again she would be frightened and ashamed, for he suspected that, though she was so self-willed, she was not very brave. Nor was she; but the fact was that she really knew very few people outside her family circle; she had plenty of acquaintances, but none that she would be obliged to see if she did not want to; in all probability no soul among them had any idea of her visit to Laburnam Road or of its nature, so that she had no front of curious and censorious society to encounter.

Going home was very distasteful, but only because it meant parting with Lewis; she was perfectly confident now; and when she came to think about it, there was something to be said for having time to one's self to repair one's wardrobe; Miss Croker was now at work on the lilac crêpe, and it would need many fittings; Alice never trusted to the dressmaker's having her measurements; and when they were thus temporarily parted, what a passionate excitement Lewis's visits would be! Alice was, for all her simple greediness, sufficiently an epicure in sensations to feel that she would enjoy a special pleasure in the situation. This did not prevent her, as the hour of her leave-taking approached, from being haughty and pouting, and expressing great surprise at Lewis's attempting to kiss her, since he was clearly tired of her. She could not quite keep away a dimple from the corner of her mouth as she said this, however. Lewis saw it; he was forged, riveted in his infatuation.

Its effect on him was not enervating, but quite the contrary. He had arranged with Patrick that Harriet and the baby should remain at Cudham for an indefinite period, and that the household should be paid one pound a week for their keep. This would, he knew, be very welcome to Elizabeth; at the same time, seeing that he had received three thousand pounds with his wife and was going at some future date to get two thousand more, his conscience acquitted him of any undue extravagance. Harriet herself would need no money during her stay—there would be nothing she would need, nor, for that matter, anywhere that she could buy it if there were. Altogether it seemed a very happy arrangement; it only remained to get Harriet's consent to it. To this end Lewis now bent

all his energies. His air of unruffled, pleasant determination could not but have a great effect on Harriet's mentality; he treated the matter as settled from
the beginning, but he took pains to be very attentive
to her. He had, unknown to Alice—who, had she
known it, would have resented her banishment as unnecessary—kept the nurse for one further week. Since
Miss Hoppner had to go home, he said, he did not
think his wife could be left quite alone to manage the
baby; the nurse would oblige him greatly if she could
stay with them till Mrs. Oman went down to the
country to stay with their sister-in-law; then she
would be quite all right, as Mrs. Patrick Oman was
not only devoted to her, but had young children of
her own. The nurse had no objection, and was, in
fact, somewhat mollified by the alteration of Lewis's
behaviour now that that brazen little minx was out
of the house; being ready, in the most natural way
in the world, to attach the greater part of the blame
to the member of her own sex.

Lewis now remained with Harriet for several hours
during the day; in the mornings he went out for
walks, often calling for Alice on his way; but he always returned to midday dinner; in the afternoons he
was also free, as Harriet took an after-dinner rest upstairs; but the evenings he gave up to her entirely,
despite the supplications and reproaches to which
Alice often treated him on the subject. She did really
think it very hard to be left by herself every evening! But Lewis was adamant. From after tea on-

wards he would sit beside Harriet in the parlour, she quite content to let him read the newspaper, or remain absorbed in his calculations. His behaviour with regard to the child was peculiar, although she had not the wit to see it. He was perfectly considerate about it, but he treated it exactly as if it were a little girl's doll, to be admired and talked of so as to please the owner. To Harriet herself he was consistently kind and obliging; and quite often he felt no difficulty in this, for she was on her part always good-humoured, and quieter than she had ever been; indeed, there were times when, with the nurse employed in the kitchen, and Harriet peacefully rocking the baby by the fire, Lewis felt as if he were an ordinarily married man. But much more often, the mere sight of her, or some nasal, half-articulated word, sent his thoughts racing to that exquisitely blooming head and those shrill, silvery cascades of talk and laughter; then he would hold himself rigid in his chair and endure until the clock on the mantelpiece said nine, and Harriet went upstairs to bed.

He took pains to talk to her, and this flattered her very much; she seemed utterly to have forgotten that she had ever had a grievance in his neglect. When he said, "You'll be ever so happy with Patrick and Elizabeth," she said, "I rather stay here, dear," but in a tone of complete submission to his will.

"Elizabeth will be such a help to you with the baby," he went on.

"Yes," she answered dejectedly.

"And," he urged, "I shall come and see you, you know."

Then her face lit up. "Often?" she said.

"Of course," he answered. "I wouldn't like not to see a lot of you, would I?"

He found himself able to pat her affectionately, with only a little more repugnance than he would have felt for some strange animal. He was able now to view her with complete detachment, and his own treatment of her, as if he were standing aside and watching a replica of himself. He inwardly blessed the fact of her having a child; it prevented her making any further claims on him, at any rate, for the present; Lewis was in that ominous frame of mind in which the next few steps to be taken are seen with brilliant clarity, but beyond them the future is a dense screen of fog. His present duty, to himself and to Alice, required the steady, persistent sacrifice of time and inclination he was now undergoing; and he made it so faithfully that in the end Harriet was not only willing to go with her baby down to the country for a few weeks, she would have found pleasure in walking into the fire at his request.

The nurse had by now been almost reconciled to Lewis, and the arrangements at Cudham on which he harped so frequently sounded to her exactly suitable to her patient's requirements. She was very good-natured in helping Harriet to pack all her clothes and in getting up all the baby's little things in readiness. "He's a stout little fellow," she thought; "it's to be

hoped he's his father's boy more than his mother's."
She gave Harriet many, many last injunctions and
reminders as to what she was to do for him, all of
which Harriet seemed quite surprised to be thought
in need of. "It's ten to one the poor dear'll lose it all
as soon as she's away from me," thought the nurse.
"What a good thing her sister-in-law has babies. It's
quite the best thing Mr. Oman could do, sending her
down there, and I hope he'll let her stay as long as
may be." She offered, in her goodwill, to accompany
Harriet down to Cudham, but Lewis said, no; he
would of course be going down with her himself, and
he did not think another person necessary.

Harriet had been so much soothed by the kindness
she had lately received that she looked forward to the
journey to be made in Lewis's company. She said
good-bye to the nurse, but with Lewis beside her she
could not feel as much regret as might have been expected from her. The nurse left on the same morning
that they were to go down to Cudham, and Harriet,
standing in the parlour as she took leave of her, looked
quite dignified and imposing, nicely dressed in dark
green cashmere trimmed with bands of black satin,
and ornamented with all her brooches, chains, and
rings. She did occasionally, as in the present instance,
assume an air of stateliness and condescension; it was
the result of her mother's upbringing: having been
treated always with great consideration herself, and
made to feel that no one was quite as important as
rich ladies like herself and her mama. The nurse was

momentarily quite awed; she had been accustomed to call Harriet "dear," but now she said, "Good-bye, ma'am. I'm sure I hope you'll be comfortable where you're going; and little master Tommy, bless him!"

Lewis put his arm round Harriet's waist. "Of course they'll be comfortable," he said. "Good-bye, nurse, and thank you for all you've done for us. I'm afraid, as Mrs. Oman will be down in Kent, it's of no use hoping you'll give us a call now and then."

"Perhaps I can run in when she's back," said the nurse. "I'm one who likes to keep up with my ladies."

"Certainly," said Lewis amiably, "and who knows, you know, when we mightn't want you again?" Altogether the nurse departed in a satisfactory state of mind which anyone who had received her confidence during the early part of her stay would hardly have thought possible.

Harriet and Lewis left by an early afternoon train, Harriet carrying the baby with a most serious and occupied demeanour, and Lewis taking the bassinette under his arm; all the other things, both for herself and the baby, were compressed into one of her trunks.

"Elizabeth won't have much room for baggage," he had said. "Besides, where's the use of your taking so much when it's only a visit?" This argument had appealed to Harriet; she allowed Lewis to lay out the dresses she should take, delighted at his helping her, and did not think of asking for any others; she took it for granted that they were all there in the wardrobe on the landing, and would be safe, with the dear house, till she came back.

She was a little surprised when they arrived at the Woodlands to find the house so very much in the country; the fly which had brought them from the station had not allowed her to see much of the prospect, and in any case, she had been occupied with nursing the baby, who had become rather restless. When they went in, no one was in the living room but Elizabeth; she looked nervous and stately, but she kissed Lewis warmly and welcomed Harriet with another kiss which might have been given from the lips of a statue; Harriet, however, detected no lack of warmth; the formal gesture satisfied her, and Elizabeth made them sit down at once to a little tea which looked cosy and inviting under the light of the circular lamp; they put the baby at once into his crib, which Lewis stood on the hearth.

"Harriet'll like to see her room," said Elizabeth presently. "Won't you go and find Patrick, Lewis, while I take her upstairs?"

"Won't I!" exclaimed Lewis.

"He's in the workroom," said Elizabeth, smiling.

Lewis hurried across the passage and collided at the door with Patrick, who had heard him coming. They caught hold of each other to steady themselves and staggered about, laughing and shoving like a pair of schoolboys. Behind them, round-eyed, was Alfred, who had never seen his father behave in such a manner.

"Sit down," cried Patrick, forcing Lewis onto a wooden chair without a back. Lewis found himself sitting in front of the easel and made a pass with a brush at the unfinished picture. Alfred, seeing him do this, said, "You mustn't touch Papa's picture."

"Mustn't I?" said Lewis, and, taking up two brushes, he feigned a terrific onslaught with both hands at once; whereupon Alfred began to cry.

"Alfred! Alfred!" cried Lewis beseechingly. "Don't cry, sonny. Look, I've not hurt Papa's picture."

"Don't be silly, Alfred," said Patrick kindly. "I have to be rather strict in here," he added in explanation.

"What a fine youngster he is," said Lewis in a low voice, drawing Alfred towards him by his pinafore. His admiration was genuine: Alfred had his father's dark hair, but a pair of solemn blue eyes, the deeper in colour for his pale little face, which recalled Elizabeth. He stood now rubbing his knuckles in his eyes; Lewis brought sixpence out of his waistcoat pocket and put it down the back of Alfred's neck. Alfred at once gave a piping little laugh and squirmed and wriggled, enjoying the joke immensely, though he had no idea of what a sixpence was, and put it into the pocket of his pinafore when his father had extracted it, just because it was small and bright and a good sort of thing to play with. He then looked up at Uncle Lewis with one of his long, wondering stares.

"You'll know me next time, won't you, son?"

asked Lewis with his peculiar, flashing smile. Alfred
did not say anything; his expression became doubtful. Then he ran out of the room.

Harriet meanwhile had been ushered upstairs to
the second bedroom containing the curtainless fourposter and the row of pegs, which Clara and Alfred
had been occupying. As they went in, Elizabeth noticed more particularly the fineness and good quality
of Harriet's attire, the sober and handsome green and
black; her sister-in-law's whole person showed a
groomed and cared-for appearance which made a
great contrast with her own, although she herself was
neither dirty nor untidy. The shabby, barely furnished room did look—there was no denying it—very
unsuitable to Harriet's accommodation.

"I am afraid you'll find us very simple, dear, after
what you have been accustomed to," she said. "But
we'll do our best to look after you and make you
comfortable. And the air here is so good. It'll do you
all the good in the world till you get quite strong
again."

Harriet smiled graciously.

"I have things," she said. "I unpack soon. This is
not so good as dear Lewis's house, but you can't help
that. It'll be very comfortable, I'm sure."

"Your trunk can stand over there," said Elizabeth
eagerly. "You could keep most of the things in it,
couldn't you, except dresses. They can hang on these
pegs."

Harriet looked about her, her genial acceptance

quite undiminished by everything she saw. Elizabeth felt, "She's really good-natured. Goodness knows, she might have complained! It won't be so bad once everyone's used to her. And then the money! Oh, Patrick, darling Patrick! Anything, everything, to give you food and boots." She pulled in her wandering thoughts and conducted Harriet downstairs again, where Clara had brought Julia into the sitting room and was holding her over the bassinette to make the two babies acquainted with each other.

"This is Clara," said Elizabeth, "who helps with the children. She'll do anything you want. Clara, this is Mrs. Oman; you must do everything you can to make her comfortable."

Clara gave a ducking curtsey. She had heard, no one exactly knew how, that Mrs. Lewis Oman was not quite right in the head, and had been looking forward to her visit with fearful curiosity and eagerness. She had not been able to make up her mind just what to expect; sometimes she had dwelt on the idea of a maniac, growling and grinning through unkempt hair; sometimes she had pictured her as vacant and slobbering, like the village idiots she was familiar with by description. At first she was disappointed in the appearance of this genteelly dressed lady who stood quietly beside Elizabeth; but a moment later she realized that Elizabeth's manner to the visitor was not quite ordinary; then she noticed that the lady's expression was peculiar. She looked away, for her furtive, unwholesome curiosity made her acutely self-conscious, but she was profoundly excited, and felt that things were livening up and no mistake.

"Will you," said Patrick softly in the shelter of the workroom, "go away while they're upstairs? I'll walk back to the station with you, you know." Lewis shook his head.

"She's too cute for that," he said. "You'd have no end of a to-do. She understands everything, you'll find."

"All right," said Patrick, "so much the better, I'm sure. I say, though, I do wish you didn't have to go back tonight."

Lewis had made this arrangement partly because there was no sleeping accommodation for him at the Woodlands unless he shared a room with Harriet, and an inn was a considerable distance away; and partly because, genuinely happy to see Patrick as he was, he did not want to waste time sleeping down at Cudham; his restless spirit could only be eased by speeding back through the dark to London, nearer and nearer to Alice with every minute. He gripped Patrick's elbow, however, and said:

"You must take a week up at Laburnam Road as soon as possible."

"I must finish this commission first," interrupted Patrick. "But then I'll come, you may depend on it."

"Well," said Lewis, "I'd better go and get it over, I suppose." They went into the living room, where Harriet, divested of her bonnet, sat in the one easy chair and looked already quite at home; the beautiful workbox stood on the ground beside her, with her netting half out of it, but at present she was watching while Elizabeth gave Alfred his supper. Elizabeth started up as he came in, and said:

"Lewis, you'll take a drop of soup before you go? You'll be back too late for dinner, I know. I've got it all ready in the kitchen."

"Thanks, Lizzie," he said. "I think I've time. Why, here's my missus quite settled in already." He bestowed a smile on Harriet and followed Elizabeth into the kitchen.

"Lizzie," he said, as she poured the broth from a little saucepan into a bowl, "this is so kind of you. I can't tell you what a relief to my mind it all is. The money will be paid regular, dear, and I hope you'll find it of use."

"It's everything to us, Lewis," said Elizabeth simply. "You may be sure I'll do my best, and thank you for the chance."

"I really think you'll find her no trouble," he said. "You see, old Patrick is such a good hand at this sort of thing. He's far better at it than I am, he is indeed. I'm so soft, I can't be firm even when it would be a kindness to the other person. But Patrick——"

"Yes, indeed," said Elizabeth. "But, all the same, I hope he'll make time to visit you, Lewis. It would cheer him up: he's sadly out of spirits at times; he works so hard."

Lewis nodded sympathetically as he drank his soup. Elizabeth had her back to him at the dresser and said rather hesitatingly:

"You'll be seeing Alice, I daresay, won't you? Give her my love."

Lewis was about to reply when Patrick came in and said:

"If we're to walk, Lewis, we must be off."

"Right," said Lewis, getting up hurriedly.

"Oh, Patrick!" said Elizabeth, "you ought to have had some soup as well—you've got the walk there and back!"

Patrick made some hasty and unintelligible answer. It was characteristic of his nervously energetic temperament that he undertook bouts of exertion without troubling about food, and was impatient of having it urged on him. He went off to put on a scarf; he had no overcoat, but he did not feel it as a privation; he burned with heat and welcomed cold airs on his body. Lewis walked up to Harriet and kissed her.

"Good-bye, my love," he said. "Look after little Tommy and do everything nurse told you. I'll be down soon to see you, so mind you don't forget me!"

She put her arms round his neck and said:

"Good-bye, my own darling."

Lewis fairly bolted out of the room, and the next moment he and Patrick were swinging down the lane arm in arm, excited almost to madness by each other's nearness and the ring of their feet on the frosty ground.

Lewis caught the 12.10 to London Bridge, and it was nearly two by the time he got home to Laburnam Road. He did not go to bed at once, however. The fire in the kitchen range still glowed, sending a red reflection onto the hearthstones immediately underneath it. Lewis foraged for himself and made a large basin of cocoa; Harriet was fond of cocoa, and it had been got for her to drink the last thing at night; Lewis gave no thought to her, however; he tipped out what remained in the tin and stirred it up with boiling milk; then he went back to the fire, and sat before it in stockinged feet with the basin between his knees, with no other light in the kitchen than what came through the bars of the grate. He sat so long that it was almost light before he went to bed.

He slept profoundly, and when he at last awoke, late in the morning, he remembered an appointment he had made to go and look at a horse and trap that he thought of keeping at the Half Moon stables for his special use, to drive out in every day. Alice, he knew, would have expected him early; but he was in such a state of vibrant satisfaction with all the affairs of life that he felt he would enjoy her reproaches almost as much as her kisses which he would get afterwards. He walked into the yard of the Half Moon with the demeanour of a cock; critical and sophisticated observers might have found something rather ludicrous in his deportment allied with the shortness of his person and his oversmartness of the lower middle class; but had they looked down upon him for this, they would have been mistaken in their estimate. Not so the groom and the stable boys who came hurrying up to him. They recognized instinctively that, though Lewis was ignorant of horseflesh, he was a customer worth pleasing. He was so obviously a man of means and might that his perfect good-humour and plainness of manner created an atmosphere of great amiability. The question of hiring the trap had been gone through before, and it only remained for Lewis to inspect the horse and clinch the matter. The groom felt, and showed in his manner that he felt, that there was a lady in the case; when the horse, a sweet little cob with white stockings, was led out, he said with sympathetic knowingness, "That's a classy little turn-out, sir. Wouldn't do you for heavy work, but for taking a lady about it's just what you'd find you required."

The stable boy fondled the cob's nose, and he, his companion, and the groom all forgot for the moment the presence of the customer in their professional admiration of the pretty animal. It gave Lewis a delicious thrill of power to break in on this, asserting his own possession of the admired creature, by saying carelessly:

"Right. I'll hire by the week, and mind you don't let him out to nobody else, otherwise it's all off. I don't want other people interfering with what I use; besides, I don't know when I may be wanting it, and if I find——"

"Lord bless you, sir," interrupted the groom, "that

ain't the ways of the Half Moon. That horse'll be as right and tight here till you want him as if we was your own stables, and the trap your own carriage. As indeed it is while you jobs it with us. You'll find we knows how to treat a gentleman when we deal with one."

"Right," said Lewis once more; he said good-day and strolled out of the yard, with its romantic smells of hay and straw and dung and the lovely reek of horses. It hardly seemed possible that this time last year he had regarded an afternoon's drive as almost a semi-annual pleasure; and now he was ordering a trap to be ready for him whenever he wished it. He would wish it pretty often, too, he thought, already in imagination seeing himself spinning along to the ring of hoofs, Alice, in one of her small tilted hats, beside him.

He turned his steps towards Mrs. Hoppner's, but, it being now nearly three, he stopped on the way to have a chop and some bread and cheese; Alice would have plenty to say to him for not coming till tea-time! When he arrived, however, he was not met by the expected hailstorm of reproaches, pelting and melting. Alice had been anxiously on the lookout all day, but at this moment she had forgoten to look for him; she had just put on the lilac dress and come down carefully to the parlour, where she was standing under the gas chandelier. As Lewis came into the room, she turned her head towards him with the arch, sweet smile of a woman demanding admiration which she knows cannot be withheld. The dress was made entirely of crêpe, the dim mauve of lilac or heliotrope flowers; the bodice and sleeves were tight to Alice's beautiful slenderness; all the elaboration and art had been directed to the skirt, which, looped up in front over an underskirt of the same material, was gathered over a small bustle at the back, caught up beneath it in many, many unsuspected yards of fullness, and then swept downwards and outwards in a peacock-shaped train to the floor. The voluminous wreathings and loopings and gatherings of the crêpe, which whispered with every movement, gave a solid but aërial appearance to the lower part of the dress, like heavy evening cloud. The strange off-shade was quite unrelieved, with one exception; Alice had meant to have it entirely so, with perhaps a black velvet ribbon; but another customer of Miss Croker's had had an evening dress of bright silk in sunset pink, and, a piece of the silk happening to lie near the heaps of dim crêpe, the contrast had struck them both, and so the lining of every bow that fastened the skirt behind, the minute piping and ruching that went above the hem in front, the little buttons on the front of the bodice, and the small flat bow at the throat, were all made of silk in the flamy rose. Miss Croker had executed the theft without any qualms, her conscience as an artist was so completely satisfied by the result.

The result was, indeed, much more beautiful than Alice, in conceiving it, had been able to foresee; when she put it on, she was amazed, vain as she was, at the mysterious beauty of her own appearance. It seemed as if the resource and intelligence and taste and determination which had been developing all her life had reached their zenith in creating this; her charm had reached its full perfection; and she was awed by the spectacle of herself. As she stood with the light of the chandelier revealing her, gazing at Lewis, her smile had in it something almost rapt and solemn, as if she were the vestal guardian of her own loveliness. Lewis, of course, understood nothing of this, but he saw that Alice had on a new dress and was looking devilish pretty; he went forward to take her in his arms, but she put up her hand in a gesture of defense, and the word that came to her lips was "Hush!"—as if she were conscious of his threatening a spell, instead of, "Mind, you'll crush me!" which was what she would have said in the ordinary way. Then she turned her long neck to look down at the train, and, moving a little away with a crisp, creeping murmur, she looked up again, this time with her usual challenging smile, though her voice was still hushed as she said, "How do you like my new dress?"

"It's wonderful," said Lewis earnestly. He turned to Mrs. Hoppner. "Doesn't she look a treat?" he asked. Mrs. Hoppner had been so struck with admiration that her usual front of resigned displeasure was quite overcome; she always admired Alice and sympathized with her absorption in matters of dress, though in other ways she had a settled conviction that if she didn't take care she would come to no good at last, which prevented her from giving way to any enthusiasm with regard to her. But this *toilette* had, as she put it to herself, struck her all of a heap. Alice and Miss Croker together had outdone themselves, and she remembered that when she was a girl she too had had very tasteful ideas about dress, though, not being so determined and clever as Alice, she had never achieved exactly what she wanted. She answered Lewis briefly but with feeling. "It suits her all right," she said. "I've never seen her look better. She can wear that shade. It's queer it should be so fashionable, for it can't suit many; but dark hair and pink cheeks it's just right for."

"You're a beauty, Alice," said Lewis; he took her face between his hands and kissed it.

"Handsome is as handsome does," remarked Mrs. Hoppner, going out for the teakettle. Alice's half mystic mood had evaporated, and as she sat down she was now any young lady keeping a lover at a reasonable distance from a new dress. The great success of the *toilette* united the party in a spirit of celebration, as if someone had received an important appointment or won a big lottery prize, and Alice was treated by both her mother and Lewis as if she had been very fortunate or very meritorious. The conversation at tea was largely about the cob and trap, which was waiting to take Alice for a drive whenever she would like to go. Mrs. Hoppner was much impressed by this arrangement, which exalted her by proxy almost to the dignity of a carriage lady; and when Lewis said casually, "When can you spare Alice to come and look after me a bit, now I'm all alone?" she said, "Hold your nonsense, Lewis. Alice can't come to you now there's no one in the house. But why don't you come and stop along of us till Harriet comes back?"

Alice clung to his arm and said: "I should say you'd better, Lewis. I mean to keep my eye on you, old boy. I believe you've got somebody else in some corner. I'm sure *we* never see anything of you now!"

Lewis said: "It's uncommon kind of you, Mrs. Hoppner. I'll make it all right about board and lodging, you know."

"You're very thoughtful," said Mrs. Hoppner amiably.

"And," said Lewis, stretching out his legs comfortably, "there's a matter of business I'd like your advice on presently. We'll wait till Alice is out of the way, and then you and me can talk a little sense."

Alice pinched him, and in self-defense he got up and helped Mrs. Hoppner to clear away the tea things, carrying them out into the back kitchen. Then he made up the fire and trimmed the lamp. He certainly was a very pleasant man to have about the house.

❦ XI ❧

THE STRIP of bedroom overlooking the woods was now Harriet's domain, and by the time the baby's bassinette was standing beside the bed and her box under the small window there was little room in it; it could not accommodate a washstand, even if the Omans had possessed one other than that in the double bedroom; whoever slept in it, therefore, had to come down to the scullery to wash. Clara Smith, in the next-door bedroom, had to do the same, and there hung on a nail behind the scullery door a tin receptacle containing a flannel and a piece of soap. Clara herself used the cold water in the scullery tap, but it was understood that some should be boiled for Harriet as soon as the kitchen fire was lit. Though this arrangement was not a great hardship to an ordinary person bent on cleanliness, it was rather an undertaking for Harriet, who had always had everything done for her, and been accustomed to the privacy of her own bedroom with a thick, soft bath mat, ample towels, and cans of hot water at any time of day. However, at first she undertook it all bravely; she knew she ought to wash herself all over every day, and, though the stone scullery was an uncomfortable place to stand about in while one did so, she managed, with the kettle of hot water provided for her, to keep up her routine at first.

But one morning she was startled by Patrick's walking past outside the window as he went for an early ramble, and this gave her a deep aversion to washing in the scullery. It seemed better to dress upstairs and just wash one's face and hands when one came down; that was all Clara did, apparently; but the relinquishing of this lifelong habit made her at first very uncomfortable, and even when she had become used to the sensation of dressing straight from her bed, she retained a sense of guilt, as if someone—she did not quite grasp who—would be angry with her for not doing as she ought. Still, no one reproached her for it, and she was the more scrupulous in her care of little Tommy; she used to bring him downstairs in the bassinette at breakfast-time, and wash and dress him afterwards while Elizabeth and Clara did the household tasks. Harriet had called him Tommy from the beginning; her stepfather's little nephew was called that, and it was the only name for a little boy she could think of at the time. She was sitting one afternoon with her baby in her lap, talking to it, and saying over and over again, "Little Tommy will have a horse and carriage, a horse and carriage and dogs and pussies for little Tommy!" when Patrick, who had been at the other end of the room stretching a canvas, said abruptly:

"Have you had that child christened?" Harriet looked up, surprised. Patrick saw that he was not quite understood, and his face became dark in his effort to keep down a tide of irritation. "Have you been to church with him and had a name given to him?" he repeated.

"I not been to church since I was married to dear Lewis," said Harriet. She stopped. She had been used to go to church regularly with her mama, but when she transferred herself and her obedience to Lewis, she had unquestioningly adopted his ways, and, since these had not included church going, she had never once thought of it. Now she became thoughtful, but Patrick interrupted her dim cogitations.

"He must be christened," he said, getting up. He looked so darkly determined that Harriet clutched the child to her breast in a gesture of protest and defence, and it set up a loud cry. Patrick was in one of his nervous moods, and the noise exasperated him. He stood over Harriet, cowering in her chair, and said:

"I won't have an unchristened child under my roof!"

"Patrick," exclaimed Elizabeth, who had come in behind him, "don't take on so! We can take the child over to——"

"Hold your tongue," shouted Patrick. He strode into the scullery, where Clara and Alfred were blowing bubbles over the sink, and returned with a slop basin full of water. Clara and Alfred, amazed at his appearance, left their occupation and came after him to the doorway of the sitting room to see what was going to happen. Elizabeth stood by in silence; meanwhile Patrick, having slammed the brimming bowl on the table, attempted to take the child from Harriet's arms. She gazed at him in stupefaction and held it all the tighter; Patrick was, for some reason, beside himself; Harriet's grasp was strong, but he was stronger. He literally wrenched the baby from her and held it in the crook of one arm, while its screams became horrifying. Its face was flushed a dark purple. In the middle of its paroxysm, a dash of icy water on its mottled, throbbing scalp suspended its breath, and in the lull Patrick pronounced:

"Thomas, I baptise thee in the name of the Father, the Son and the Holy Ghost." He looked round with the lost air of a man relaxing tension after a great effort, and if Elizabeth had not been at his elbow to take the child, he would perhaps have dropped it on the hearth. He walked slowly to the door, across the passage and into his studio, oblivious of the scene he had left behind him. He stood with his hands in his pockets, looking through the window, his chin jutting and his head thrown back, as he focused the distant edge of the coppice above the dun fields. Elizabeth, quite pale, came softly to the door, and paused, fascinated by the rigid, inflexible shape, sharp as bronze against the fading afternoon light; she quite forgot what she had been going to say: she no longer heard the noises in the room across the way. She stole up to him and put her arms round his waist. For a moment his head turned over his shoulder towards her cheek; the eyelids drooped, giving him the look that Alfred wore when he was sleepy, and she noticed the faint, peach-like down that covered his under eyelids and projecting cheek-bones. The next instant he had pushed her off good-humouredly, and was asking for the lamp to be brought in; with it and the last of the daylight he thought he could just make out enough to finish his picture of Autumn Tints.

Harriet managed to pacify her baby at last, and sat rocking him to and fro, but her complacency had received a rude shock, and when, some time afterwards, she raised her head and saw Clara standing in the doorway, devouring her with avid curiosity, she started forward out of her chair and shouted:

"You're a bad, wicked girl! Get along with you!"

Clara vanished precipitately and ran into Elizabeth, who had come out to warm up a scone for Patrick's tea.

"For pity's sake, Clara!" she exclaimed impatiently. "What are you doing to Mrs. Oman?"

Clara at once burst into loud sobs, the outcome of previous emotional debauch, and grief at being spoken to with such unprecedented sharpness. "I done nothing at all," she wailed.

Elizabeth felt as if her head would split. She pressed her lips together until they vanished in a line, and her chin trembled. She took Clara by the shoulders, and, opening the side door, pushed her out on to the frosty, twilight path. "You don't come in till you've done making that noise," she said, and clapped to the door.

"What's wrong with *you*, Alfred?" she asked, feeling a tug at her skirt.

"I love you," said Alfred.

"That's a good boy," she said, relieved that that was all. "Now, if you're very careful you can help me carry in Papa's tea."

Alfred jumped about at such a splendid prospect. The noise of his little shoes on the flags made a happy sound in her ears, such as more romantically minded people find in the notes of larks and nightingales. She felt, "We're all so happy when nothing puts us out. It's a shame other people try Patrick so."

The fact was that, in Clara, familiarity was breeding contempt; when Harriet had first appeared she had had quite a fear of being found looking at her, in case she gave offense, and was thought by other people to be as naughty as she felt herself to be. But as day succeeded day and Harriet was established as a quiet inmate, with but little extra respect or consideration, Clara became as tame as inquisitive birds round a scarecrow. She rapidly became used to Harriet's ordinary deficiencies of speech and comprehension, noticing them far less than a more intelligent observer would have done; but every now and again Harriet gave some peculiar demonstration, or said something really unintelligible, and this was a treat keenly to be savoured. Clara would stare and listen, all eyes and ears, until the outbreak had subsided, and for half an hour afterwards she would still eye Harriet as a curiosity. Harriet had hardly noticed her, ex-

cept as someone who was there to help, and who did
Tommy's washing, but after the commotion of the
christening, when she caught Clara looking at her
through the door she seemed to feel, as never before
in her shielded life, that she was pointed at as being
different from other people. This consciousness began
gradually to invade her and made her fall farther and
farther behind the standard of ordinary competence.

Her *toilette*, which used to be one of the main interests of her life, was somewhat neglected now. Her
box had had a few garments—an odd skirt, a jacket,
a shawl, and a few articles of underclothing—removed from it, and had then been moved downstairs
and deposited in an outhouse. It did not much distress
Harriet that she put on the same dress day after day,
because dressing at all was a wearisome business now.
Her hair, too, was so difficult to arrange in all its plaits
and coils when her fingers were numb on a cold morning. When she arrived, her coiffure was made by her
own hair plaited over a false chignon; and this, at
home, had always been brushed separately when it
was taken off at night. Harriet did not do this now,
and her hair began to look like a bird's nest. Elizabeth
noticed it particularly one morning at breakfast. Patrick had been in a benevolent humour of late, playing
a great deal with Alfred and allowing her to make
much more of them both than was at all usual with
him. The baby Julia was filling out and becoming
sleek and pretty; their household, in spite of hardships, was gracious and happy, except that wherever

she turned her eyes she saw Harriet or her child, a perpetual irritation. Harriet's appearance of being better dressed and cared for than the rest of them was not noticeable now; there was nothing now to atone for the unsightliness of her person and manner; and the sight of her disordered, neglected hair drove Elizabeth to say sharply, "You shouldn't come to table with your hair like that, Harriet! Why in the world don't you keep it decent? Go and brush it after breakfast."

Harriet said nothing, but she looked stupid and sad. Clara had at first listened with delight to her getting a talking to; but then a little impulse of pity stirred in her, and after breakfast she said with the blunt good-nature of her kind, "You come upstairs with me; I'll brush your hair nice and tidy."

In the shabby little room she found Harriet's brush and comb and did her hair for her, not in the elaborate way it used to be done, but quite simply and neatly. Harriet said, "Thank you. That's a good girl," and from this time onward Clara felt a strange pleasurable instinct of protection towards her. She liked looking after creatures more helpless than herself—the fowls, and Alfred and Julia; and she little by little adopted Harriet as her care as well as little Tommy.

Harriet became very grateful to her as the days went by, for no one else said anything kind to her, or spoke in a general, pleasant way to her now, and she began deeply to miss the voice of sympathy and encouragement; still, she was very good and patient;

Lewis had wished her to be here, and she would stay quietly till he came to fetch her; she never doubted that he would come, just as she had always felt sure that he would come and take her away from her mother. She and Clara and the children had some quite happy times together, but it was very hard not to be important any more; never to have anything specially nice to eat, or pleasant things arranged for her. All her handsome dresses and her trinkets, and her piles of flannel and calico underclothes, and her dozens of pairs of stockings had gone too; she did not like to ask where they were, in case Elizabeth or Patrick should be angry with her. Sometimes she quite forgot to miss them, for Clara kept a change of clothes ready washed for her; but sometimes, particularly when she put on the same pair of boots day after day, getting now so worn and scratched and dull, she would remember the row of smart boots and slippers she had once had, and feel very lost and melancholy.

One morning, however, everything seemed changed and joyful. Patrick said to Elizabeth at breakfast, "Have you told Harriet?" and Elizabeth said, "Harriet, Lewis is coming to pay you a visit today. But you must mind and do everything he says and not worry him, or else he won't come and see you again for ever so long." Harriet said nothing, but her face looked elated and sensible; she sat nodding her head to herself, her lips moving as if she were holding some important and delightful conversation. They had hardly drunk their tea when she said in her old imperious way:

"Come upstairs and do my hair, Clara." Clara was nothing loth; she did not resent the change in Harriet's manner, as she was always stimulated rather than otherwise by being ordered about.

When Lewis arrived, she did not see him till he had been there for an hour or so; this was because he had walked up and down the lane outside talking with Patrick before he came into the house. When he did come in, Harriet came to meet him with every sign of joy; she was neat and tidy in her appearance, but she looked shabby, and, as she sat in the window seat, he saw with repulsion that her cheek around the ear and jawbone had become flaccid and leathery, which he had never noticed before; but straight from Alice's heavenly smoothness, that combined the qualities both of silk and porcelain, he could not but be struck by it. He had not been in her company ten minutes before the attitude of mind which had been gradually developing ever since Harriet's removal to the Woodlands crystallized, hard and distinct; he had come down in a state of uncertainty that he himself had deliberately refrained from exploring; come to ask Patrick's advice, as he thought; but now he knew that his mind was quite made up. That Harriet should ever live with him again was completely shut off from possibility; he had ceased, since his entry into the sitting room, even to consider it; now, every atom of his formidable strength of mind was directed to the aim of her living apart from him, as entirely separate from his existence as two balls from each other when they are rolled in opposite directions.

He sat near her with the others around them, for Patrick and Elizabeth had too much tact to leave them to themselves, and kept up a general conversation in which she was included, but could make no direct appeal to him, or have the opportunity of saying anything except answers to questions, such as whether Tommy was well, or if she had been out yesterday, or had one of the fowl's eggs for breakfast, before the subject was swiftly changed and swept from comprehension. He was to go back in the afternoon, but he avoided anything in the nature of a scene by saying, "Well, Harriet, you and me must go up to London very soon. There's something I want you to do, my dear."

Harriet's face betokened eager acquiescence.

"It's this," said Lewis; there was a shade of hoarseness in his voice, but his eyes rested on her with their ferocious amiability, and she noticed nothing else. "I want you to come before some gentleman in London and sign a paper to say that you want me to be able to use that two thousand pounds of yours that you're to have when your aunt is dead." Harriet looked surprised.

"Is aunt dead?" she asked.

"No," said Lewis, "she ain't. But you see, Harriet, I can arrange with somebody who wants to do us a good turn to let me have the money now, and him to have the money when your aunt is dead. He won't mind waiting; it's all the same to him. But I thought that if we had the money now, there'd be no end of use for it."

Harriet did not in the least object to this; in fact, she thought it a very clever arrangement, and much better than anything her mama had ever been able to do for her; but what chiefly occupied her was the thought that if she said yes, she would go up to London with Lewis, and after that perhaps she would go home. So she nodded her head very vigorously and said, "We do that. Whenever you want."

"That's very sensible, Harriet," said Lewis approvingly, and she preened herself in satisfaction.

"But there's one thing," he went on. "The gentlemen will ask you if you quite understand what you're about, you know, saying you want me to have the use of the money. You'll tell them that we want it to do things to the house with, won't you? And to make a gentleman of Tommy."

Harriet nodded again, and looked very stately, as if she were perfectly equal to standing up to the whole board of Commissioners for taking the Acknowledgments of Married Women on Lewis's behalf. She was so taken up with the prospect of the excursion that she said good-bye calmly, as if she were going to see him again in an hour or two. Lewis took a more lengthy farewell of Patrick outside the house.

"I think I'll close with Mrs. Chevenix," he said at last. "There can't be any hitch now."

"No," said Patrick, "not if you're quite sure the property will suit you."

"It'll be near you, my dear fellow, for one thing," said Lewis affectionately, "and, all things considered, I believe I really can't do better. I'm quite decided on leaving town; give me a bit of land, that's what I say. There's nothing like it for making you feel your own master; and, then, it's a pretty little house; as to the dairy part of the concern, we shan't have anything to do with that; but the man who runs it now for Mrs. Chevenix is very trustworthy, very trustworthy indeed, and I've no doubt he'll stay. I don't really think anything could suit us better."

Patrick did not for a moment misunderstand his brother's "us."

"How'll you manage Mrs. Hoppner?" he said.

Lewis shrugged his shoulders. "I may have to bring Lizzie into it a bit," he said; "you won't object to that? Make out that she's stopping along of you; once we get down here there'll be no trouble. We shall be Mr. and Mrs. Oman, you know. Nobody'll be a penny the wiser round about here."

"It ought to do," said Patrick thoughtfully.

"I can't tell you how grateful I am to you and Lizzie," said Lewis earnestly. "I can never repay you. What a lovely family party we shall be down here, shan't we? Only twenty minutes' walk away, you know."

Patrick grasped his shoulder affectionately. "Of course," he said, "it'll mean keeping Harriet pretty close, with you so near and all. Still, you can trust me."

"I know I can," said Lewis simply.

Behind the stretch of wood, and about half a mile distant from Patrick's house, was a small property consisting of a comfortable little eighteenth-century dwelling house, to which had later been added a small byre and dairy, the cows of which pastured on what had once once been the pleasure grounds of the house. The house was of red brick, square and elegant, with a concealed roof and oblong sash windows. Its accommodation was not extensive, consisting of two good-sized front rooms and roomy kitchens on the ground floor, and four small bedrooms, with an apple loft, above. The garden had all been turned into pasturage, but two or three apple trees stood before the front windows and it was backed by trees gradually deepening into the copse. The whole was known as Sirenwood, and Mrs. Chevenix wanted two thousand five hundred pounds for it. The house was rather well furnished, including the kitchen and all the dairy appliances and fourteen cows; and was supposed to carry with it quite a pleasant little income, since it supplied all the milk, cream, and butter to the neighbourhood. The dairy was in good working order, and, provided Lewis could retain the services of Andrew Waggett, who managed it at present, he could live on the premises without a care. He looked forward to it already as an existence in which all the mundane pleasures of life would be enjoyed against a background of the Garden of Eden. He did not, of course, analyze his impressions in such terms; he merely retained a sense that it was a desirable little property on which he and his girl would be uncommonly snug.

He tried to explain to Alice what the estate was like when he got back that evening. Alice was feeling a little out of sorts and did not conceal the fact; at first she was exasperatingly cool and flighty, asking what it had to do with her? She did not suppose she should ever see the place!

"There are fourteen cows," Lewis said.

"Goodness!" said Alice, "I didn't know you were as fond of cows as all that!" She opened her green eyes to their fullest extent. "What are their names?" she asked.

"Then there are apple trees in front of the windows," went on Lewis imperturbably. "They don't look much now, but there'll be blossom on them soon. Very pretty, that'll look."

Alice remembered the white thorn thicket against the dark woodside; an involuntary shudder passed over her. She clung round Lewis's neck, shivering and sobbing like a child; Lewis gathered her in his arms and said soothingly:

"Why, I thought you'd like to hear all about it, sweetheart! I mean my girl to be so happy down there!"

"Yes," said Alice, laying her head on his shoulder.

Lewis turned as Mrs. Hoppner came in, and said, "She seems a bit low."

"Oh," said Mrs. Hoppner, "she's been under the weather all day. You'd better go to bed with a hot drink, Alice. She'll be all right in the morning."

"I shan't go to bed—not yet, at least," said Alice impatiently, "just as Lewis comes in. And what's the name of your wonderful property, Lewis?"

"It's called Sirenwood," said Lewis.

"What a queer name," said Alice. "What is it all about?"

"Why, you know what sirens are," said Lewis.

"Yes, whistles for workmen."

Lewis pinched her ear. "They were women," he said, "who sat on the rocks and sang so sweetly that the sailors rowed onto the reefs and got shipwrecked."

"Good Lord," said Alice, "what a silly tale!"

"I don't know about that," said Mrs. Hoppner unexpectedly; "there's a good deal in these old ideas, when you come to figure them out."

Alice raised her head. "What with Lewis's fourteen cows, and you with your women singing on the rocks, I've had enough for one evening," she said. She moved away, and paused at the door, looking back to say good-night. Tears did not disfigure Alice; they made her eyelids purple and her eyes overbrilliant, and gave an unconscious droop to her mouth even though she smiled, but her face was no more impaired by them than a rose drenched with chill, sparkling rain. Lewis kissed her and could feel that she was still tremulous, although she had stopped crying. As she disappeared up the dark staircase, he felt as though all the force of his being were carrying him along like a straw on a current, into the heart of Sirenwood, where Alice stood in all the radiance of her youth behind the apple trees.

⊰ XII ⊱

LEWIS had by him enough ready money to complete
the purchase of Sirenwood, but when that should be
done there would be very little left over for current
expenses, and to secure the remaining two thousand
pounds was a matter of some urgency; not that he
would obtain the whole of that sum; he had agreed to
sell the reversionary interest of the two thousand for
one thousand two hundred, and everything was in
order for the transfer except his wife's signature. He
arranged to take possession of Sirenwood on an early
date in April, and to accompany Harriet to London
on the day after.

He had now cut himself adrift from his previous
life in a manner that gave him, it is true, increasing
satisfaction, but satisfaction with a keen, disturbing
edge of exhilaration, and here and there a faint rustle
of terror. He could now no longer, should he be called
upon to do so, explain himself creditably. He was in
process of disposing of the house in Laburnam Road,
so that Harriet was homeless; he had not the slightest
intention of telling her so, and had no actual fear of
her getting to know it through other means, but still,
the position would, considering all the circumstances
—the money he had had with her and the violent

manner in which he had removed her from her friends
—expose him to some very unsympathetic criticism.
Then, too, he had formally arranged with Alice that
she was to join him at Sirenwood and pass as Mrs.
Lewis Oman; her mother could be hoodwinked, or
persuaded to hoodwink herself, which amounted to
the same thing; Alice herself was his heart and soul,
and he had the strong support of the family at the
Woodlands; but supposing that fact also were to be
known, it would be impossible to explain it away.
Lewis was not haunted by any sensation of guilt or
awkward struggles of remorse; as the perfectly
healthy body is one of which the owner is unaware,
perhaps the perfectly healthy conscience is one that
gives no trouble; and if so, by this rule Lewis's conscience was remarkably sound and thriving; but he
was vaguely troubled and alarmed by the fact that
he had piled up against himself, as it were, a cloud
bank of disapproval and protest, separating him from
the rest of men; and that if his doings were to be
brought to common knowledge, flame and thunder
would burst from the cloud; not justly, for he was
doing nothing that he himself did not approve and
find good reasons for, but none the less in a manner
to make him shrink. He despised clergymen and old
women and interferers with his peace as a whole; but
he feared and hated the forces of public censure
which they represented. He felt that all about him
was an unsympathetic world, and he bore a sense of
ill usage, knowing the criticism it would have ut-

tered had it been rather more up to snuff than it actually was.

All this had the effect of making him live intensely in the present; he had always been the reverse of dreamy and speculative, having a firm grip of his own existence and great powers of sensuous enjoyment; but now he threw himself completely into every plan and every trivial scheme of pleasure. Alice was sometimes surprised by the tenacity with which he carried through their arrangements. If she expressed a wish to go anywhere, or to have anything done about the house, and difficulties arose, Lewis would overcome them with dogged energy. "It doesn't matter, darling!" she would exclaim, and he would say, "It does. We'll do it." Such fierce determination over things which, even if she had suggested, she did not much care about, made her feel that he was enjoying something even above and beyond herself. The intense relish with which he would speak of their going down to Sirenwood at times almost startled her. She was very much in love with him, according to her lights; but, now that she was sure of him, it was his eligibility, his money, in fact, and the physical attraction he exercised over her, which placed her altogether in his power. In her circumstances, he was the most valuable man she could catch; even now, if a nobleman with thirty thousand pounds a year were to come her way, she would have been capable of stifling her feelings and going off with him; whereas Elizabeth could not have left her husband to be made a grand duchess in her own right. Alice did not realize this, since no one capable of superseding Lewis ever appeared on her horizon; and she prepared to go down to Cudham, ostensibly on a visit to Elizabeth, in an extraordinary mixture of curiosity and timidity and happiness.

In the meantime Lewis had walked over to the Woodlands to fetch Harriet and drive with her to the station. Elizabeth had taken pains to produce her looking respectably dressed and as became a woman about to endow her husband with a large sum of money. Harriet's boots had been cleaned and her hair carefully done, not without some distaste, by Elizabeth herself. The dark green dress she wore, after a shaking and brushing, still looked good; her jacket had been little worn since she came down, so that was more than presentable; gloves were found, and Clara brought out Harriet's hat from behind the curtain. Elizabeth took it, and then paused, considering. It was unfortunate that there should be a bruise on Harriet's cheek under the right eye. Elizabeth went into her room and returned with a bonnet of her own, which had a black fall attached to it.

"You may wear my bonnet, if you like, Harriet," she said. "It'll make you look much more dignified than a hat. You want the gentlemen to see that you're a person of property, accustomed to manage things for yourself, don't you?"

Harriet would much rather have worn her hat, but she could not help being influenced by what Elizabeth said. While she hesitated, Elizabeth put the bonnet on her, and Clara, with her offensive readiness, began at once to say how grand she looked in it. Harriet looked mollified and gradually broke into a smile; she was looking forward already to returning home, and so she did not trouble to ask that her box should be brought back to her bedroom so that she could choose grander things to wear. These did for the present; all she wanted was to get to London as soon as possible.

The solicitor who had managed Harriet's affairs on her marriage, handing over the three thousand pounds to Lewis, had also arranged the matter of selling the reversionary interest of the two thousand, and it was at his office that the Commissioners for taking the Acknowledgments of Married Women had appointed to meet Harriet. She was shown into a big room on the first floor, while Lewis remained downstairs with Mr. Sloane, the solicitor. Six gentlemen looked narrowly at Harriet as she came in, and one of them requested her to put back the fall of her bonnet. When she had done this, she sat at the end of the table, looking so proud and pleased with herself that they felt there was no need to be at all suspicious on her behalf. Still, they asked her with very particular care and slowness whether she quite understood what she was doing, and Harriet said to everything, "Yes, I understand. Yes, I want that. We want the money for our house and for my baby." So Lewis's sufferings were not intolerably prolonged; at the end of half an hour he received his lady once more, saw the document in the solicitor's possession, partook of the sherry and cake which the office provided for its clients, and went off gaily with Harriet on his arm.

He had some difficulty in persuading her to return peaceably to Cudham with him; Harriet had thought, when she came up in the morning, that it was more than possible they would go back to Laburnam Road immediately afterwards, and send for Tommy, perhaps by Elizabeth. She was not altogether downset by the disappointment, but she began to waver in her submission to Lewis, and to feel very definitely that she had been at the Woodlands long enough, and that he ought now to take her home. Lewis said that they would certainly go home soon, and that she should only stay a little longer, to please him. They were saying good-bye in the Woodlands parlour, and Harriet's eager, nervous determination robbed her farewell of any appealing or tearful nature. She said once or twice very emphatically, "You come for me soon, Lewis," and then she said, "You miss your train. You have to stay here all night." Lewis had forgotten that, though he was really only taking a half-hour's walk across the fields, Harriet was expecting him to return to town; he had not realized either that she would have remembered enough of his previous visits to know when he ought to be leaving for the station. Patrick came to his rescue and said:

"I can take you a short cut, Lewis. But you'd best be coming along."

Outside, Lewis said, "She's getting sharper, if you

ask me. There'd be a rare set-out if she came upon Alice down here."

"She won't do that," Patrick promised him grimly.

Harriet felt after this that everyone was angry with her for having said that she wanted to go home; she thought that perhaps Patrick and Elizabeth were hurt because she had made them feel that their house was not so nice as hers; she was sorry about this, and she was beginning also to be very much afraid of annoying Patrick. So she was especially humble and conciliatory with them, but it did not seem to make things any better. Elizabeth never spoke to her now when she could help it, and Patrick only to order her about. Clara was so busy with the growing needs of the children that she had not time to wash out things for Harriet or to do her hair for her; and though essentially she was kindly disposed towards her, she was too weak and impressionable to resist the prevailing atmosphere of gloomy dislike with which the others regarded her. Harriet began to miss Lewis very sorely, in a way she had never done before, when she had felt that his return to fetch her was a glorious certainty of which only the day itself was uncertain. Now she wanted him so much, deprived as she was of all other kindness and affection, that she determined to attempt the difficult task of writing him a letter. There were a box of notepaper and a penny bottle of ink in Patrick's workroom, and one day she ventured to go in there, and, touching the stationery as it lay on the window seat, she said to Patrick, "I write a letter?" "You can if you like," he said, thinking, "After all, what's the odds? It won't go to post." So Harriet sat down contentedly, and after a long time she wrote out:

My own Darling:

I hope you come down soon. When you come please bring me a pees ribon for my coulor and sleevs. I have not had clean flanel for a month. It is time I should be at home. My boots is wore out. Your loving wife,

Harriet.

When she had folded it up and addressed it, she looked timidly towards Patrick.

"Give it here, Harriet," said Patrick. "It's to Lewis, ain't it? I'll see he gets it."

Harriet said, "Thank you *very* much," and walked out of the room, nodding her head to herself with a cheerful little air. An hour or so later Patrick took the note out of his pocket and gave it to his brother, as the latter stood driving nails for pictures into the wall above the fireplace at Sirenwood. Lewis gave it half a glance, then gave a smothered, half-humorous exclamation and pushed it behind the looking glass.

Clara was not good company for Harriet nowadays, and so the latter, when she went for a walk, would go by herself. The summer of this year was relentlessly wet and cheerless, and with the grey skies overhead the wood looked more like autumn than midsummer. Harriet one afternoon walked out of the house, getting sadly draggled with mud as she crossed the field, but finding the ground better once she left the clayey earth and got onto the firm, moss-covered paths of the wood. She walked along her solitary way, feeling a pleasure in the gentle motion, although there was no sun, until she came to a shallow dip in the ground, which was here covered with brushwood on either side of the path. The hollow was spanned by a sort of bridge, made by throwing a broken old five-barred gate across it. Harriet stood still, hesitating. A working man in corduroy trousers and a glazed hat, who was taking a short cut through the wood to a neighboring farm, came up with her and was about to pass the time of day and wait for her to go across before going himself, when he was struck by the forlornness of her appearance and by something not quite at home in the glance she gave him. He said cheerily:

"Shall I give you a hand across, missus?" Then he added, "But happen you're just on a little walk? Would you be wanting to come back this way? Because, you see, I wouldn't be there when you wanted to come back, and per'aps you'd be finding yourself in a fix with no one else coming along this way."

Harriet did not quite follow all he said, but she recognized the accent of kindness, and a smile of comfort overspread her face. She said slowly, "Thank you. I go back now."

"Then I'll just help you through these brambles," said the man. "Nasty things for a lady's skirts they are." He pushed aside the creeping brushwood through which she had just come, and, taking her by the elbow, he steered her through them onto the upper path. "There now," he said, "you'll find your way all right now. Do you know where you are?"

"Oh, yes," said Harriet. "Thank you. Thank you very much."

The man touched his hat and walked off, saying to himself, "No call to thank me that way. Poor soul, I hope they're good to her at home." He was quite glad to be out of the wood with its sombre green, and to get into such light as was afforded by the open fields.

Alice was now installed as mistress of Sirenwood, to do as she liked with Lewis and the house, though Andrew Waggett was very surly if she put her nose inside the dairy. Alice saw no reason why she shouldn't step in there to fetch cream or extra butter if they felt they would like some, but Andrew Waggett was so plainly disposed to think otherwise that she gave up these marauding incursions. Mr. Waggett was every bit her match in peevishness, sullenness, and self-will; so she retired before him and contented herself with ordering about his niece, who came daily to do housework and cooking for them.

Alice had always, at home and in Elizabeth's house, been decidedly undomestic; she was no longer a slave to housework; but now that she was mistress of a house, full of pretty furniture, with a maid to wait on her, and Lewis with nothing to do but amuse and

please her all day long, she showed an interest and
delight in home of which she had not known herself
capable. She liked to walk about from one parlour
to the other, sometimes even dusting the china ornaments on the mantelpiece; in the lovely dustless air
of the country the business of cleaning was so very
slight. She had sometimes thought that she would be
dull in the country in spite of Lewis's society; but,
for the present, at least, she was more than contented.
Under the sophistication of her appearance she had,
perhaps, something of Elizabeth's capacity for valu-
ing peace and silence as a background for emotional
happiness. The damp summer had at least had the
effect of keeping fresh the landscape; everywhere was
luminous, bewildering, endless green, and the front
parlour was papered with a Chinese wall paper of ash-
pink roses on a green ground; the windows of this
room were half smothered with a growth of jasmine
and honeysuckle, and barricaded at a little distance
by the apple trees in full leaf; so that the pale light
came in with a watery hue, and Alice sometimes had
the feeling, as she paused here, that she was asleep and
would never wake up. A year ago such an atmosphere
might have depressed and bored her to the point of
exasperation, but it was different now; Lewis's love-
making was so fervent that she often relapsed into
long spells of languor, in which she moved about as in
a dream, and the small occupations and interests of
their secluded life were all the stimulus she needed.
Although she was so worldly and elegant, she never

had had much pleasure in promiscuous society: she
was too secretive and cat-like to be generally sociable;
and now she would have avoided much company in
any case. She felt herself to have altered so much as to
be hardly, at present, quite self-possessed and able to
present a firm and confident front to strangers. Lewis's passion, now that it was quite unrestrained, made
her almost nervous, although actually she felt quite
safe in all their greenery and quiet. She had become,
when they were quite alone together, much more ten-
der in her manner to him, dropping altogether, even
when she was commanding him, the imperious tone
that had been so characteristic of her; she would say,
"Don't, sweetheart," or "No, darling," in the gentle
undertone of someone talking in their sleep. She sometimes felt that she had never known Lewis, he was so
different in his free-and-easy, careless, loving, and yet
humble ways from the dapper and energetic admirer
he had been in London. There were, of course, times
when nothing was at all strange or mysterious between them; in the evenings, when the weather made
ample excuse for a fire, she would sit on his knee as
she had done in Laburnam Road, and they would be
as riotously gay and festive as ever, glorying as they
looked around them at the elegant little parlour, or
voyaging gaily into the kitchen to make themselves
tea in the smart china left behind by Mrs. Chevenix.
Alice had never felt the least self-consciousness in
passing off as Lewis's wife to the tradespeople and the
servant and to Andrew Waggett. She felt as poised

and secure as if she had been married to Lewis for
fifteen years, as far as her outward position went; in
fact, when she sat opposite to him pouring out his tea,
or appeared before Andrew Waggett or a cowman
who asked for him when he was out, it is doubtful if
she even remembered that she was not Mrs. Oman.
When she was called upon to meet someone from the
outside world, her confidence asserted itself and she
appeared unusually brisk and self-possessed; it was
only inwardly that she was conscious of this new,
tremulous uncertainty, which she described to herself
as feeling as weak as a kitten. One morning she heard
a stir on the path below and the voices of her brother-
in-law and a man she did not know. She stood behind
the window curtain, hoping she would not be called
down, and presently she saw a labourer whom she remembered having seen about the Woodlands going
off down the path. It then occurred to her that Lewis
was out in the byre, for, though he did not interfere
in the management of the dairy, he liked, as he put it,
to keep an eye on things, and though there was no
love lost between him and Andrew Waggett, there
was something about Lewis which made the latter
tolerate his presence with surly acquiescence; and,
Lewis being out there at the present moment, Alice
supposed she ought to go down and see what Patrick
wanted. When she got downstairs she saw him standing beside a trunk.

"Whatever is that, Patrick?" she asked.

"Oh," he said, "it's a box we've had in our outhouse. It clutters us up rather, and Lewis said I'd best bring it over here."

"Upon my word!" thought Alice, "using us as a rubbish-heap! Whatever next! I'll teach Lewis to say anything of the kind!" Aloud she said, "Oh, indeed!" in no very agreeable voice. Just then Lewis came in from the back of the house, and she went sulkily upstairs again, leaving them together. She was sorting out Lewis's clothes which had come up from being washed, and presently, when he called her to come down, she found he was alone; she said at once, "Whatever did you let Patrick bring that great thing over here for?" Lewis said:

"I thought you'd like it."

"You thought *I'd* like it—a great, useless——"

Lewis kissed her. "Yes, you've got to take charge of it," he said.

"I won't go near it," exclaimed Alice, her determination weakening as she sidled towards it.

"Why!" she cried a moment later, and dropped on her knees beside it as he threw back the lid.

"Wait," he said, "and let them carry it upstairs to the bedroom before you unpack it. That'll be the best way."

Upstairs, Alice plunged her arms up to the elbows in the contents, disordering what had been so carefully packed, in a riot of excitement. Three or four dresses smothered the double bed, piles of snowy, fleecy underclothing lay about the floor, balls of stockings rolled hither and thither, a small snowstorm of pocket handkerchiefs and laces strewed the carpet beside the trunk, and Alice, with a small beaver muff pushed up one arm, was kneeling, holding up a long chain studded with fragments of turquoise matrix, now tangled into thick knots. She looked so serious and intent, so vivid in her lovely enthusiasm, that Lewis, who had come into the bedroom again, paused to watch her passionately. It was a wonderful sight to see Alice keen on something! There was so much go and spirit about her; she was like nobody and nothing in the world. He could not help taking the smooth, flushed face between his hands and kissing it while she said, "There's ever so much more I haven't got down to yet!" She knew, of course, to whom the box belonged; but in the ecstasy of turning out the contents she really had not, after the first second, given it one thought. Now, as Lewis stood above her, and they both looked at the scattered clothes and ornaments, it came home to Alice that he was watching her rifle the possessions of his wife. For one second she was disconcerted; but only for a second. She had not forgotten that once she had sat up in bed in the transparent gold light of the moon, enduring a wild, unbelievable misery, so lost and strangered in her woe that that serene, unearthly face looking at her through the window might have been the presence into which she had been called, being dead. Although she was so happy now, the memory still caused her to feel outraged that such suffering should have been inflicted on *her*. She rose to her feet, with a dark, resentful flush, and as she pulled the muff off her arm she felt a defiant pleasure; she was glad, consciously and determinedly glad, that these fine, expensive things had been brought to her. It was right she should have them; she would not use them all just as they were, her thoughts went on; most of them would need altering, of course, but all that would provide delicious occupation. Lewis interrupted her by saying:

"Sweetheart, the landlady has called in, on her way, to see how we're getting on. I said I'd see if you could see her. She won't stop above a minute; her phaëton's waiting at the gate."

Alice said, "All right." Before she left the room, however, she twisted the turquoise chain, still partially tangled, round her neck.

Mrs. Chevenix, who was, as Lewis had said, paying a friendly call, limited to the time her horses would stand, surveyed Alice with some astonishment. This lovely young creature was not at all what she had expected to see. She had imagined Mrs. Oman as a capable woman, used to country life, and rather older than Lewis himself, caught, perhaps, as women nearing middle age so often were, by the fascination of a young husband, and willing to overlook complete lack of means and inferior social status on the score of good looks, which Lewis undoubtedly had. ("Not that I admire 'em myself," thought Mrs. Chevenix.) Still, she was very civil and good-humoured with the young pair; as she saw that Mrs. Oman also was, in spite of her attractions, of the same walk of life as her husband, she dropped into an easy and patronizing manner that had nothing offensive in it. She hoped they found themselves comfortable, and applauded their decision to keep on Andrew Waggett, who, she said, was the most trustworthy and capable old bear imaginable and had always run the place like clockwork; and if he did respect the cows more than his employers, she herself had never objected to that, and if she had, she would have had no means of supplanting Daisy and Sorrel and Maggy in his regard. Lewis faced up to all this sprightly conversation with perfect *sang-froid;* he stood in a negligent and gallant attitude, flashing his white teeth and feeling that he understood how to talk to a handsome woman as well as anyone. Alice rather hung back, looking haughty and suspicious; Mrs. Chevenix glanced at her repeatedly with an interest she was at no pains to conceal. When Lewis had conducted her down the path and handed her into the phaëton, she drove away, her thoughts busy with the surprising apparition of young Mrs. Oman. At first she could not make out why she had been so much surprised; there was no reason why her vague expectations of what her successor's wife would look like should not have turned out quite wrong; she was not one of those women who pride themselves on having premonitions of great accuracy. The girl's attractiveness was surprising, certainly, and would have been so anywhere; so young and slender and sulky—and then it occurred to Mrs. Chevenix what the root of her surprise had been. The girl did not look like money. She understood that Mr. Oman's fortune had come to him with his wife; well, she might be mistaken, of course, but she did not believe that that girl had had anything to do with a fortune, except perhaps to spend it. She'd do that to the manner born, no doubt.

⊰ XIII ⊱

MRS. OGILVY had schooled herself into a long period
of resignation in which some slight resentment was
mixed; in the months that followed her visit to Harriet in Laburnam Road, and the letter sent at Lewis's
dictation, she settled down into feeling that Harriet
had made her bed and must lie on it; and the complete manner in which she herself had been thrown
off after all the years of intimacy and affection had
paralyzed her and deprived her active spirit of all resource. As time went by, however, her maternal
instincts reasserted themselves, and she began to feel
once more the old protective impulse, and to wonder
with more and more urgency whether they were
being good to Hatty. As the time at which she had
last seen her receded into the distance, everything became dimmed except the fact that Harriet was much
loved, and that she distrusted the Omans and Hoppners, every man Jack of them.

At last she heard from a roundabout source,
through the gossip of one of her maids with the
family of the woman who had worked for the Omans
in Laburnam Road, that Harriet had had a child. At
first the indignation and dismay which she felt at
Harriet's never having told her such a piece of news

overcame every other feeling; but this was not for long. A strong anxiety, the more urgent for having been repressed, took possession of her; and when, on visiting Laburnam Road, she found the house dismantled and a board up announcing it for sale, she became determined with the resolution of a person who fears a real danger; she went in person to visit Mrs. Hoppner, and swore to herself that she'd get the truth out of her.

This, however, was easier said than done. In spite of Mrs. Ogilvy's determination, Mrs. Hoppner presented her usual front of apathetic sourness. No, she did not know where Lewis was, exactly, except that she believed he now had an estate in the country near his brother.

"Is Alice at home?" said Mrs. Ogilvy with sudden sharpness.

Alice, said Mrs. Hoppner, was on a visit to her sister, she did not know for how long. Mrs. Ogilvy had no actual suspicion; but she did not like the idea of Elizabeth, Patrick, Lewis, and Alice all gathered together in Harriet's neighbourhood like a flock of carrion crows. She asked Mrs. Hoppner whether she had seen the baby, and Mrs. Hoppner said no. Mrs. Ogilvy would not ask for any news of it; she could not bear to show before Mrs. Hoppner that she herself was utterly ignorant of the whole business, and had only the word of the servants that the child was a boy. She went away, therefore, very little wiser than she had come; but the attitude of enforced resignation behind which her seething anxiety had been kept in check had been broken up; she determined that she must investigate further, even at the risk of causing trouble in Harriet's home. Mr. Ogilvy quite agreed with her, and thought that someone should go down to Cudham and demand information from Patrick Oman, whose house at least was known. While this was being decided, however, Lewis, who had been up in town seeing to the last of the business of disposing of the house in Laburnam Road, had called in on Mrs. Hoppner and heard of Mrs. Ogilvy's visit. The next morning Mrs. Ogilvy received a letter which said:

MRS. OGILVY:

I hear from Mrs. Hoppner that you called wishing to spy on my whereabouts. I only wish I had been there. Now I tell you, once for all, after your brutal and unnatural conduct your daughter never wishes to see you again, nor would I allow her to do so. In fact, while you live, she considers she is in danger of her life. If I have any more trouble from you, I will take care that your neighbours know your true character. Yours,

LEWIS OMAN.

When his wife gave him this, Mr. Ogilvy became definitely alarmed; he viewed it as being more ominous than she herself was at first inclined to do. She was, of course, distressed. "He's poisoned her mind against me," she exclaimed; but Mr. Ogilvy did not think so; he thought from the tone of the letter that Harriet had had nothing to do with it whatever, and therefore that if Lewis were writing this sort of thing without her connivance or knowledge, the indications pointed to something serious indeed. He did not want to increase his wife's alarm, but he advised her to go down to Cudham without delay, and offered to go with her. She refused this, with her usual independence, so he said that when she had found out what there was to be discovered, he would then take the next steps. Mrs. Ogilvy meant to go to Cudham the following day, but the next morning she woke up in the throes of a violent cold in the head. She was subject to this ailment; her colds always took her the same way, with a touch of fever for the first twenty-four hours and then nothing but a heavy catarrh; she knew it was no use trying to get the better of it till it had run its course, so she put off her journey till the next day but one; loth to do so, but feeling that after all a couple of days after so much time would not make a great difference. When she was up and about on the afternoon of the second day, it occurred to her that she did not know which was the nearest station to Cudham; it was either Bromley or Orpington, she thought, but she wanted to make quite sure, for it was a long drive even from the nearest station, she knew that, and she didn't want to spend half the day rattling about Kent in a musty station cab. The fact that she had been forced to postpone her journey made her restless and eager, and she thought she might as well drive over to Mrs. Hoppner's to find out the correct destination for the morrow, and also to see if further news could be gleaned, since Lewis was obviously in communication with her. She had a cab called, therefore, and towards six o'clock she alighted at the door of Mrs. Hoppner's house. She got no farther than the door, however; for, as she was about to knock, it opened, and upon the threshold appeared, dressed for a journey and with a valise in her hand, Alice. The totally unexpected apparition of Mrs. Ogilvy petrified her; and each stood gazing at the other in a second's silence. Alice had little courage and consequently but small presence of mind; a few words of casual greeting such as befitted so slight an acquaintance, a remark about catching a train, and a graceful exit, would have tided her over this awkward moment, but this was just what she had not the calmness to do. She stood looking angry and aghast, and then attempted to hurry past Mrs. Ogilvy without a word. The latter put her hand on her breast to stop her, and in doing so she noticed something which acted as a searchlight suddenly turned onto the shrouded, unexplored confusion in her mind. Alice wore, pinned at the neck of her dress and revealed by the cape that she wore unfastened on her shoulders, a garnet brooch as familiar to Mrs. Ogilvy as her own watch and chain. It had been a favourite trinket of Harriet's, and one which she wore more often than any other. She exclaimed, "I see you have my daughter's brooch!" Alice turned quite white under her lovely impossible glow of paint.

"She gave it to me," she said in a strangled gasp. "After I'd nursed her when the baby was born!"

Mrs. Ogilvy gave her a long, searching look; the mention of the baby, however, shook her; she said in a pleasant, conciliatory tone, "Well, I'd be very glad of some news of them; we had words, as I daresay you know, but I hope that's all over. I want to see Harriet very much; in fact, I am going down to Cudham to-morrow——"

"She's not there!" Alice exclaimed wildly.

"Where is she then?"

"I think," said Alice, with a desperate slowness, feeling terror leaping in every vein and drumming with sickening insistence inside her head. "I think that she and Lewis are at Brighton." The name came into her head because she had been urging Lewis to take her there for a week's sea air.

"Oh," said Mrs. Ogilvy. "Perhaps you can give me her address!"

"I can't," said Alice, with mad emphasis. "But perhaps my sister, if you wrote——"

"Then tell me this," said Mrs. Ogilvy; "which is the station for Cudham? I might come down and see your sister; she would probably tell me more than you can."

"It's Halstead," said Alice; she added, with a sickly vivacity that was almost servile, "Harriet got over the baby very well, you know. You should see her playing with him. It's great fun." A shade passed over Mrs. Ogilvy's face, and chilled Alice anew, like the shadow cast from some colossal granite head whose expression of solemnity belongs to something quite outside the traveller's experience. She saw that she had made a mistake, and this increased her anxiety to get away as soon as might be. She said, "Well, you must excuse me. I have to catch a train." Her voice, always high pitched, was like the squeal of a frightened rabbit. She hurried past Mrs. Ogilvy and made for the gate, walking swiftly down the road. Mrs. Ogilvy watched her a moment; it did not occur to her now to go in and see Mrs. Hoppner; she got quickly into the waiting cab again and told the driver to take her back as fast as possible.

Harriet's mind was becoming very dark now; she still looked after the baby, although she did not wash it, leaving that to Clara, when the latter could or would make time to do it; hardly anyone spoke to her nowadays, and when she tried to go out for walks by herself Patrick threatened her and made her go back into the house again. She went out one morning without her hat and jacket, for she could not find them, and came upon Patrick talking to a labourer at the gate. Patrick rounded on her and said, "I've got a policeman here, Harriet, and he'll run you in if you ain't away." The forlorn creature stood a moment uncertain, and then went back into the house. The labourer thought it must be a joke, and gave a laugh in which Patrick joined. When Harriet was indoors, it occurred to her that if she could dress herself properly in her hat and jacket, it would be allowable for her to go out. She said to Clara:

"Where are my outdoor things? You find my things!"

Clara made a face of dramatic caution, and said:

"Mr. Patrick's got them. Don't you ask for *them*."

After that Harriet gave up all thought of going out, and presently the desire to do so left her also. She began to feel towards the house as an animal may feel towards its den; she was conscious of shelter and society, although she was hardly spoken to. She always liked to be where the greatest number of people were, which was as a rule in the sitting room. Elizabeth, with her children by her, and Patrick in and out, felt her peace and comfort utterly destroyed by the continual presence of the figure crouching over the worn wicker cradle or occasionally bursting out into irrepressible, half unintelligible speech. She would try to stop Harriet when she began one of these loud-voiced rambling harangues, but Harriet would take no notice: it was only when Patrick swore at her or struck her over the mouth that she was reduced to inaudible muttering. Once he drove her upstairs to her bedroom, and then the relief of her absence was so exquisite that it was inevitable that Elizabeth should long and pant for it again; and so she got into the way of sending Clara upstairs with the breakfast for her and the child, and of saying peremptorily at

about seven in the evening, "It's time you went upstairs now, Harriet." She had got to the pitch at
which it cost her a hard effort to speak to Harriet at
all; sometimes, when she was out walking with Alfred
or half asleep with Patrick in her arms, she would
think, "It would be better if I could break the ice
with myself; once I started talking to her it wouldn't
be so hard to go on." Then the next day she would
stand over Harriet and say, slowly and distinctly:
"You had better wash Tommy this morning, Harriet," or "I am going out, so you can sit quietly in the
sitting room with Clara and not disturb Mr. Patrick."
If Harriet had responded, this would have led the
way to something better; but when all she received
was a vacant stare, or some remark which, when it
did come forth, was almost lost in the accompany-
ing muttering and humming noise which was now
much more frequent in Harriet's utterance, Elizabeth began to feel that she was hardly human, and,
once this stage was reached, her attitude, and her behaviour too, underwent a subtle but profound
change. Harriet, meanwhile, her thoughts turned in
upon herself, spent much time merely in apathetic
wretchedness, and sometimes in spells of lucid recol-
lection; she would have liked very much to see again
the kind man who had spoken to her in the wood: as
he was the last person who had treated her with kindness, his image sometimes overlaid that of her mother,
which had become dim, though she often recalled it
with a heavy heart. She was not sufficiently used to

the hardship of her lot to have become dulled to it; the pillowcases and sheets had been removed from her bed to be washed, but no one had provided her with any more, and the ever more dingy pillows and blankets filled her with a yearning homesickness, more poignant than the desertion of Lewis. The baby, who was now getting on for nine months old, a long-limbed scraggy child with an extraordinary tenacity of life, had long ago outgrown its little first clothes, and was wrapped day and night in Harriet's large woollen shawl; the bedclothes of its cradle had sunk to the bottom of the crib, a wrinkled, indistinguishable mass of grey, and the covering used was a piece of old blanket come from nobody knew where. The child itself looked so odd and weazen, with its flesh a yellowish leaden colour, more like that of a plucked chicken than a human infant, that one could hardly feel for it the sympathy and natural kindness aroused by an ordinary baby; it was more as if Harriet carried about some mummy or antique doll in which none but herself had any interest.

She fed it with a mixture of condensed milk and water; tins of the former were a great stand-by in the household, and Harriet herself was very fond of the stuff; it was the only thing she had to eat which was sweet and rich, and at the actual moment of eating, it satisfied all her wandering longings for the delicious food she used once to have, the buttered crumpets and plum cake, the honeycomb and chocolate and jam. When the ecstasy was over, she found herself scraping with her finger inside a jagged tin, in the, midst of shabbiness and coldness and desolation.

The pound a week which Lewis provided, Elizabeth was always meaning to do something definite with, which might include Harriet in being to the general advantage; but every week some pressing claim presented itself—boots for Patrick, clothes for Alfred or the baby, cod-liver oil, or curtains for one of the rooms. If they had not had the money they would have realized that all these things *might* be done without; but their lack would be a considerable privation, and as Elizabeth had the money to hand, how could she do anything but use it? The sacred rights of her husband and children to whatever they could get were paramount with her; she realized in the abstract that Harriet had claims on her too, both legal and humane; but these were as a difficult lesson, while the others were a joy and a deep satisfaction, absorbing, and natural to fulfil as drawing breath. As days went on, Elizabeth found it harder and harder to wrench her mind round to the idea that she ought to be different in her treatment to Harriet; the struggles were fainter and fainter, and at last were made no more. She had always felt, and quite truly, that so long as Patrick and the children were happy she really did not care how she was, what she ate or wore. But now she was suddenly alive to the fact that she had hardly a presentable garment in the world; she knew it annoyed Patrick to see her shabby beyond a certain limit; and as she had about thirty shillings in hand that she had saved, and the pound for the coming week, it seemed sensible, indeed inevitable, that she should go to Canterbury and buy a hat and some gloves and stockings, and a length of material to make a new bodice to the skirt she was turning. The children had been so sweet and dear of late that she indulged herself in the rare pleasure of buying toys: some celluloid balls, quartered in pink and white, and a box of lead soldiers. Alfred was so much struck by these that for a long time after the parcel was unwrapped he could not say anything at all; then he hid his face on her knee, and she had quite to coax him to play with them, as if they had been medicine.

Her thoughts had begun to take a new direction, now that everyone had settled down under the new régime. She had been so little in Alice's confidence, and Alice's affair with Lewis had been of such a tacit order—everyone's understanding it and nobody's mentioning it—that to one of Elizabeth's temperament it had been impossible to ignore it and to be wilfully blind to its full significance. She had even at times told herself that it was possible that Alice was not Lewis's mistress in the full sense of the word, that they loved each other's company, and naturally Lewis liked kissing her and romping with her, but the open manner in which they conducted their gambols was a sign that they were actually innocent. Elizabeth was no fool, nor was she ignorant of the world, but the curious construction of her mind allowed her at times to believe what nothing but the grossest

credulity and most contemptible simplicity could
have lent an ear to; and therefore the forcing home
of truth to her reluctant understanding came in a
series of shocks that made the pulse beat in her throat
and sent from it the dull, strange red of the woman
to whom blushing is not natural. The sight of Lewis's
and Alice's night clothes on the same bed, one morning when she had gone upstairs to look for Alice and
the maid had been late in doing the room, spoke
hardly more clearly to her than Lewis's tone as he
greeted Alice on her return from a shopping expedition. They had been awaiting her in the parlour, and
Lewis had been, to all appearances, passing the time
very pleasantly with his sister-in-law, but when Alice
came in and kissed his forehead, he said in a tone of
repressed yearning, "I thought you were being a thousand years!" Alice walked airily about the room, de-
positing her purchases and talking with unusual
cheerfulness to them both, while Elizabeth looked
down, feeling shaken and sick and yet with some
weight of stifling sweetness that made her not want
to do away the cause in spite of the pain it gave her.
These, however, were momentary sensations. When
even she had accepted the fact that Lewis and Alice
must be sleeping with each other, it began to take on
a different perspective. She did not regret the connection; it all seemed so inevitable, so natural, so right;
but she did begin to feel it most important that the
connection should be legalized. While she was entertaining her fantastic, childish delusions, she was con-

scious of great constraint with Patrick in regard to
the matter. So long as anyone showed a disposition to
be in doubt, Patrick, for his brother's sake, refused to
discuss the question; if Elizabeth had said, "What is
the position, really?" Patrick would have refused to
answer her; but now that she was undeceived he
could talk coolly though slightly with her, and she
was herself no longer someone to be put off in the
matter. She was now, in all the dignity of an elder
married sister and a disillusioned woman of the world,
a party to be reckoned with, as the natural guardian
of her young sister's interests. She spoke boldly to
Patrick of the state of affairs, and said that it was a
thousand pities that things could not be made right.
Patrick agreed with her; and now on her visits to
Sirenwood she made it quite clear that she understood
the whole, and, when Alice happened to be absent,
she talked about her to Lewis in the anxious tone of
one who discusses the illness of a relation. Elizabeth's
new, rational attitude had its effect on Alice too; the
latter now often dropped in at the Woodlands in an
airy, cheerful manner, and sometimes she saw Harriet.

The first time this happened Alice felt merely a
sensation of curiosity and surprise. "How changed
she is!" she thought. Harriet had lost the solid, rather
muscular appearance she used to have; she was so
shabby, and her hair was such a tangle of dust-
coloured rubbish, that at first it appeared almost as
if she must have dressed up to look like that. She saw,

but did not appear to take in, Alice's presence, and, crossing the room, she went into the kitchen; Alice stole to the door to look at her and saw that she was standing in front of the dresser, looking in a searching, curious manner all over it, almost nosing it. Alice thought, "Just like a dog looking for something to eat." Presently she came dragging back again through the sitting room and went out without noticing or seeming to expect notice. "Where is she going?" whispered Alice. "Oh," said Elizabeth, "she'll be off upstairs, I daresay. I wish she'd stop there! She gets more and more foolish; and as to her clothes—she won't wash or do a thing for herself. Downright obstinate she is." Alice said nothing; her round eyes, deep and cloudy as chrysoprase, stared for one moment into space. Then she said abruptly, "Have you any jam pots? We're going to make some apple jelly."

When she got home that night she repeated to Lewis what Elizabeth had said. Lewis made some slight reply, and she was perfectly content to abandon the subject and sit down to playing draughts with him at the parlour hearth; he sat beside instead of opposite to her, with his left arm round her waist, and sometimes he played her move for her when he saw how to do it better than she did. But next day, when Patrick strolled over before their bread-and-cheese lunch, Lewis took him out into the pasture and walked up and down with him, too far off for anyone in the house or byre to catch a word of what they said.

"I should say there was no doubt of it," said Patrick. "She doesn't take in half of what she did. And then she won't look after herself either." Lewis was silent for a little, then he said with an uncomfortable air:

"I do feel this is very hard on dear Lizzie."

"Well," said Patrick, "I suppose so. But we don't mind the inconvenience if your mind is at rest." Lewis gave a grateful pressure to the arm linked in his; then he said:

"I don't feel that she should be about the house, you know. Why don't you keep her upstairs? She and the child would do very well up there."

"Very well," said Patrick, brightening. "That would make things simpler, certainly. The child doesn't look to me as if it would last long."

"Don't it, though?" said Lewis. "Well, perhaps it would be the best thing that could happen, really." They walked on in silence. Then Patrick said:

"I shouldn't wonder if Harriet didn't take a turn for the worse one of these days. She alters so much; she's still as stubborn as they make 'em, and she has a temper like fury; still, in other ways she don't seem as if she——" He paused.

"Really," said Lewis. "Well, I'm sure I can never be grateful enough to you and dear Lizzie for all your care and trouble."

They retraced their steps and went back into the parlour, where Alice was arranging the bread platter and the triangular cheese dish on the table. The green plush tablecloth she had covered diamond-wise with a crochet lace afternoon teacloth. She hardly ever took the trouble to make a definite display of house-keeping, and when she did it was always with something which her mother and sister would have thought unsuitable. Not so Lewis, however; if he admired a lace tablecloth, he admired it as much at half-past twelve in the morning as he did at afternoon tea-time, and, as he sat down to the meal and watched Alice's small yet long and narrow hands reaching for this and that, he felt himself to be rioting in luxury and happiness.

"The country suits Alice, don't you think?" he said. "She's not looking quite so plain as when she came down here first."

"Certainly," said Patrick sedately, "Alice looks very well." Alice pouted; safe in the adoring protection of Lewis, she didn't care who knew her opinion of her brother-in-law.

⊂⅏ XIV ⅏⊃

WHEN Patrick returned he had a conversation with
Elizabeth; she adored these rare interludes in which
he bestowed all his confidence upon her and seemed
to be depending on her with perfect abandonment
and trust. She was always willing to do what she knew
he wanted, but at those times she lost all sense of what
the actual command implied, and walked as if
through a labyrinth holding his hand. Patrick now
said that Lewis suggested Harriet's being kept altogether upstairs, and Elizabeth's eyes dilated as she listened. There were two reasons why the idea was exquisitely acceptable: the first, that it would remove
the perpetual infliction of seeing Harriet about: the
second, that it would avoid the risk of anybody else's
seeing her. Lately Elizabeth had begun to dread, on
Alice's behalf, the possibility of any outside person's
seeing Harriet and remotely guessing her identity.
Alice was recognized by the few visiting tradesmen
and by Mrs. Chevenix as Mrs. Lewis Oman, and the
idea of public disgrace, consequent upon the discovery of Harriet's presence, gave Elizabeth a sensation of dread coupled with aggressive defensiveness.
She did not think that Harriet had been seen by anyone outside the house except once or twice. There was

the workman who had seen her at the gate, and once the baker's boy had brought his basket into the kitchen where she was seated by the fire with Tommy in her lap; but otherwise Elizabeth felt they had kept her well; they would go on doing so, and now with the consciousness that it was for Alice's sake as much as Lewis's.

Harriet had been accustomed to creep about the rooms, though so quietly that people had got into the way of not noticing her presence for hours at a time —everyone, that is to say, except Elizabeth. She no longer had her meals with them; Clara would take her a plate and mug upstairs after the others had done, and she had got into the way of going upstairs, when the others sat down to table, and waiting, like an animal who recognizes the approach of feeding time. But Elizabeth, in her eagerness to be rid of her, ordering her upstairs in the middle of the afternoon when Harriet's instinct told her there would be nothing to eat, aroused in her the long dormant spirit of rebellion. She faced about from where she had been drawing her finger over the outside of the dresser drawers, and said, "I won't go upstairs. I stay down here long as I want to." She shook a good deal as she spoke, and twitched her dilapidated clothing round her; her hair stood out round her head like the straw coiffure of a scarecrow. A curious change came over Elizabeth: she became all of a sudden bold and hard; she spoke in a voice quite unlike her own, more like that of a man. "Go on up with you," she exclaimed, and started forward, shaking her skirts. Harriet faltered, turned, and stumbled up the narrow stairs. "After all," thought Elizabeth, "it isn't as if she felt anything——" From that time onward, having taken the first step, she found it easy to be firm and rough. It wasn't, after all, as if Harriet felt anything.

But unfortunately the attempts to deprive her of even the small amount of liberty she had formerly enjoyed seemed to have revived Harriet's sense of personal injury. She roused up from her previous passiveness, and when she did manage to get downstairs, she was constantly jabbering; it was really impossible to disregard her or tolerate her presence. Elizabeth, by ordering, and Clara, by coaxing, managed to shepherd her out of Patrick's way for some time, but at times she eluded their vigilance, and Elizabeth was terrified of the storm she knew would burst upon their heads. Harriet had been passively indifferent to their presence for a long while, but now she seemed crazily desirous of being in the midst of things; she did not want the society of one person, but the noise of the family all together in one room drew her irresistibly. She was always trying to creep down of an evening; sometimes she would not venture to the bottom of the staircase, but would crouch on the middle stairs, listening. Clara usually found her here, and would persuade her upstairs, back into her bedroom, light a candle for her, and shut the door upon her; though she did sometimes wonder what the poor thing did with herself, alone with the wizened baby between those four bare walls. One day, however, when they were all at midday dinner, Harriet came halfway down the stairs and called out some inarticulate word. Elizabeth, with the roughness of apprehension, called out, "Go upstairs, Harriet, we don't want you here." Harriet came farther down and said, "I will come down in spite of you all." At this Patrick rose from the table and shouted, "Get upstairs, you damned cat, or I'll break your back," and she hurried, stumbling, upstairs again. A deadly silence reigned over the dinner table, in which shuffling about upstairs was audible. At last Clara said, "Shall I take her plate up, ma'am?" "No," said Elizabeth shortly, "let her wait."

When the others had finished and Clara was carrying out the dishes, Elizabeth put some food on a plate, and Patrick, watching, said, "Are you giving her meat?" Elizabeth looked up, questioning. "There is no need to do that," said Patrick. "If you feed her up like a fighting cock you must expect trouble." Elizabeth did not feel that he was being quite reasonable; still, there seemed no reason why Harriet should have meat; they had little enough themselves, if it came to that. So from henceforward no meat was taken upstairs. This did not, however, reduce Harriet's spirit, as might have been expected. She still escaped downstairs when she could, and once she made such a commotion in the kitchen with Elizabeth that Patrick was disturbed in the workroom. He came in, carrying in his hands a plaster cast which he had brought back from Canterbury and was in process of unwrapping. He laid it down on the kitchen table, and Harriet's attention was immediately attracted to it; but Patrick seized her roughly by the shoulder, and Elizabeth heard her own voice, as if coming from very far away, saying, "Don't kill her."

When Harriet was in her own room again, one image seemed to hover in her mind above the darkness and pain: the pale plaster head of an angel with haloing wings that she had seen on the kitchen table.

❦ XV ❦

LONDON is so vast that when chance meetings occur in its area they always seem a hundredfold surprising, though actually they may be hardly more unlikely than if they took place in a small country town. At least, Mrs. Ogilvy received a start of exultation and surprise when, on arriving at London Bridge station, she saw Patrick Oman leaving the barrier. He wore a battered billycock hat and carried a portfolio under his arm. She knew him immediately from having once met him at Mrs. Hoppner's, and, leaving her assiduous porter to follow in her wake, she swept through the intervening passengers and placed herself in his path. Patrick gave a single quiver of surprise and then stood dead still, his face unnaturally white against the background of the hurrying, animated crowd.

"Mr. Oman," said Mrs. Ogilvy, "I should be obliged to you to tell me where my daughter is." Patrick did not meet the situation with Lewis's ferocious gaiety; he was silent, with a pallid, vindictive air, as if he would have liked to do something dreadful but was powerless before so many witnesses. Mrs. Ogilvy, raising her voice, repeated the question, and even in that commotion her tones were loud enough to draw the attention of the passers-by nearest to them.

Patrick was exasperated by the sensation of being watched.

"I don't know where your daughter is," he said in a rasping voice.

"I don't believe you," cried Mrs. Ogilvy. "I insist on your telling me where I can find her."

"I tell you I don't know where your daughter is," he answered savagely. "Damn your daughter!" And, hoisting his portfolio on his hip, he strode past her and was lost to view. Mrs. Ogilvy found herself trembling, a sensation she never used to know. The porter was at her elbow.

"Get me a corner seat," she said, and pulled down the veil in front of her bonnet. Something in Patrick's manner had horrified her deeply. She had been tactless, no doubt, but he had shown himself the very incarnation of evil. It was better he should be out of the way; she would make her enquiries of Elizabeth and force the truth out of her more easily in his absence. As the train bore her into Kent her warm and lively imagination soothed itself by determining that she would bring Hatty home with her that very night. It would not take five minutes to get her old room ready, and she lost herself in the pleasing consideration of all the details she would carry out: the fire—for, though not yet actually necessary, a fire in the bedroom was so comfortable! And the bed made up in a jiffy, with perhaps a hot brick in it, and a nice little supper brought up on a tray. "Not a minute it'll take, once we get home," she thought, her lips moving; and afterwards it would be time enough to see about the future. Hatty would want to go back to her husband, no doubt, but her mother would see to it that she was more comfortably settled than she had been in that poky, dingy house in Laburnam Road! While she was at home, being made a fuss of, and having a bit of spoiling once more, she herself would look into the question of her comfort generally. The old habit of affectionate domineering was so strong that Mrs. Ogilvy did not stop to consider the fact that Harriet's last communication with her had been a request that they should remain apart.

When she alighted at Halstead she was momentarily at a loss how to proceed in a neighbourhood entirely unfamiliar to her. However, the sight of so substantial and handsome a lady standing on the platform of a small country station at once commanded attention. A trap was called out, and meantime Mrs. Ogilvy talked to the stationmaster. She wanted, she said, to find the house of Mr. Oman. Did he know the name?

"Let's see," said the stationmaster. "There's the Patrick Omans at the Woodlands——" Mrs. Ogilvy was about to interrupt him when he went on: "And then there's Mr. and Mrs. Lewis Oman at Sirenwood." Mrs. Ogilvy could hardly have concealed her start, and did not attempt to do so. She did not care who knew she was looking for her daughter; there was no furtiveness or concealment on *her* side of the question.

"Mrs. Lewis Oman!" she exclaimed. "That's my daughter! I've hardly seen her since she was married, and quite lost track of her since they came into the country. Things weren't very pleasant with my son-in-law, but I thought now I'd just come down and see how they were getting on."

"Ah, dear, just so," said the stationmaster, full of ready sympathy for this grand and pleasant lady. The trap driving up, he helped her into it with great courtesy and, slamming the door, said, "Sirenwood, George. This lady's come to see Mrs. Lewis Oman." As the trap drove off, a small phaëton drawn by two horses bowled into the station yard. Mrs. Chevenix, going up to town, had some little time to wait for the train, and the stationmaster was delighted to regale her with a small piece of news. Mrs. Chevenix had the true landowner's interest in local gossip, and sitting in her carriage, as more comfortable than the station waiting room, until the train should be signalled, she was more than ready to listen to anything. She had seen the outgoing trap and noticed Mrs. Ogilvy, so that when the stationmaster, leaning forward confidentially, told her that the lady was going to see Mrs. Lewis Oman at Sirenwood, she turned round as if to catch the last glimpse of her.

"Some friend, I suppose," said Mrs. Chevenix.

"No, ma'am," replied the stationmaster. "Mrs. Oman's mother."

"Mother!" repeated Mrs. Chevenix. Well, to be sure, there was no reason why she should not be, ex-

cept that in the glimpse Mrs. Chevenix had had of
portly worth and heavy black moiré silk, the lady
had not looked like the mother of that lovely, slightly
sinister young creature whom she had been so surprised to see as Mrs. Lewis Oman. Her train being
signalled, however, she got out of the carriage and
went into the station.

The trap took some half-hour of brisk driving to
accomplish the distance, and at the end of that time
turned into the lane over whose hedge the front of
the house could be seen. Everything looked very pleasant—the tanned brick of the house itself, and the surrounding foliage and fields, still luxuriant but
touched with bronze and rust. Half a dozen cows
strayed comfortably in the silent field.

"Wait here for me," said Mrs. Ogilvy, descending
at the small gate behind the apple trees. She rustled up
the path to the front door, and George, hitching the
reins to the gatepost, followed discreetly after, and
stood, half concealed, by the slight porch.

As Mrs. Ogilvy approached the front door, she saw
through the window to the right the back view of a
woman seated in the parlour; at the sound of steps on
the gravel, she turned round, showing a pale face
with a quantity of loose fair hair under her black hat.
Elizabeth rose to her feet and came towards the window, then turned sharply round, as if speaking to
someone inside. Lewis darted from the room to the
stairs and called softly, "Alice?" A voice answered
from upstairs. "Stay where you are," he called in

low, urgent tones. At that instant a loud knock was heard on the front door. Bracing himself, and deriving comfort from the fact that Lizzie stood in the doorway of the parlour, he pulled open the front door. The sight of Mrs. Ogilvy's ponderous figure so absolutely close to him gave him a shock of dismay which for an instant he was unable to conceal. Then his powers came back, his spirit of determination sprang to his eyes like a ferret rounding on an attack. Mrs. Ogilvy's eyes were all over the hall, her ear strained for the least sound of what she wanted to hear, but all that met her beyond Lewis's shoulder was Elizabeth, standing motionless in the doorway. Mrs. Ogilvy advanced, and Lewis could not but give back a step.

"Lewis," she said, "I have come to see my daughter." She pressed on, and made her way into the green and flowery papered parlour, where a workbox, not Harriet's, stood in the window, and the remains of a cold lunch on the table. She searched the room with her eyes, then turned and confronted Lewis and Elizabeth. She repeated, "I want to see my daughter." Elizabeth, conscious above all of Alice arranging her hair upstairs, forced herself to say with great calmness:

"You cannot see her."

Mrs. Ogilvy drew herself up and said haughtily, "I know of no possible right which you have to speak in this matter, Elizabeth Oman. I insist, Lewis, on seeing my daughter."

Lewis's moment of uncertainty had passed now. He gathered himself together like a wild creature about to spring.

"You shall not see her," he shouted. His violence aroused Mrs. Ogilvy's own; she became crimson, and her eyes sparkled; she fought for words, and, as she did so, the absolute silence of the house came over her —silence, stillness, and in the dim light of the parlour two faces watching her fixedly. Her jaw dropped, and, with her voice unnaturally high she cried:

"I believe you've put her in a lunatic asylum!"

The opportunity of truthfully denying an accusation made Elizabeth warm and eager in her reply. "We have not!" she exclaimed, and added, "I have had dinner with her today."

Mrs. Ogilvy turned to her impulsively, saying, "If you will only let me hear her voice or see her hand on the banister, I shall go away content." Her eye caught that unknown workbox again. "I shall know that she is in her proper place with her husband," she said.

Lewis turned livid; he leant over the table and clutched the handle of the bread knife; it was merely a gesture, but Elizabeth flung her arms round his shoulders.

"Don't," she gasped, "don't hit her."

"Get out of here, you dirty old bitch!" yelled Lewis, relinquishing the knife and starting towards Mrs. Ogilvy. Elizabeth, to whose anxiety was joined a terror of what Lewis might do, seized Mrs. Ogilvy by the arm, and together they rushed her out to the doorstep and slammed and bolted the front door.

At the sound of the commotion inside, George had hastened to the gate, so he was already unfastening the horse when Mrs. Ogilvy came down the path.

"I shall go straight to the constabulary," she exclaimed, as much to herself as him, but he took it as a direction and said:

"There ain't one nearer than Bromley."

"Then go to Bromley," she said; "or stay: I will go back to Halstead first." They returned to the station, and the stationmaster, seeing them, hurried out. "I can get no news of my daughter," said Mrs. Ogilvy hoarsely. "I want to go to a magistrate—the police."

The man kindly recommended her going on the next stopping train to Bromley, and in the meantime hadn't she better have something to eat? There was no refreshment room in so small a station, but he sent a boy to the inn, and presently she partook of sherry and sandwiches in the ladies' waiting room. The stationmaster was sincerely concerned about her, but at the back of his mind was the thought that he'd have something to tell Mrs. Chevenix when she came back. He mentioned Mrs. Chevenix as the landlady of Sirenwood who had driven into the station just as Mrs. Ogilvy had left it that morning. Mrs. Ogilvy paused over her sherry. "Indeed!" she exclaimed. "Now, would you be able to give her a message from me?" The stationmaster was all attention, and when Mrs. Ogilvy had finished her sandwich he took her to his office and gave her a pen and ink. Mrs. Ogilvy wrote down her name and address and gave it to him. "You'll mention to her that I'm anxious for news of my daughter," she said, "and that, if she hears or knows anything, I'll be very grateful if she'll send me word." The stationmaster was delighted to promise. "I shall go on to Bromley and inform the police as well," she said finally.

At the Bromley police station she stated her case, and the inspector was attentive but without any of the stationmaster's agreeable partisanship. Had she positive reason to fear her daughter was ill used? No, she couldn't say she had, but she thought it very likely. Had she had an open disagreement with her son-in-law? She had, naturally, over the marriage. So that it was hardly to be wondered at if he were unwilling for her connection with the household to be renewed. And now, as regards the daughter. Did she think her daughter was trying to see her and being prevented from doing so? She thought it very probable. Indeed! What had been the last communication she had received from her daughter? Well, actually it had been a letter forbidding her the house, but she thought this had been written at the dictation of her son-in-law. The inspector exchanged glances with the other officer, but Mrs. Ogilvy's appearance was too impressive to allow of her being brushed aside as a hysterical female who carried problems to the police with which they were by nature unable to deal. He was not encouraging, but he was perfectly civil and open-minded; he said he would put a man on duty outside Sirenwood and also the Woodlands, and if anyone answering to the description of her daughter was seen, they would communicate with her immediately. He gave her the address of the local magistrate, and before she went to bed that night Mrs. Ogilvy had yet once more set forth her story, this time on paper, and posted it to Mr. Mortlock of Halstead Priors. She now felt that she had got out of the inaction so fretting to her vigorous nature and that she had set things in the right direction; once she had admitted this she relaxed her mind and gave way to the great fatigue she had been incurring all through the day. She had the comforting sense that things were never so bad while something could be done about them.

ELIZABETH was a surprise to herself in these days. She did not come home trembling after Mrs. Ogilvy's visit as she would have expected to do; she was, in fact, calmer than Lewis. She was filled with determination and actually with a sense of righteous protectiveness towards Lewis. It was not only convenient, it was right, to lie to Mrs. Ogilvy; if the latter knew that her daughter was being kept out of the way she would of course have made an outcry and, seeing things from her own narrow point of view, would have misjudged the whole. Elizabeth had, with the full approval of her own conscience, summoned up all her forces of deception and resistance in order to protect something which was in itself completely justifiable: of that she felt sure.

The feeling that Alice must marry Lewis was growing within her every day. Her own inborn sense of the sanctity of married life and the strong respectability of her class urged on her the necessity of the step; she knew that men, even good men, did not feel quite in the same way about these matters, and that though both Patrick and Lewis—and especially, of course, the latter—had Alice's welfare at heart, it was from her that the strongest influence must some.

Her complete subjection to her husband did not prevent her from feeling at times that, as a woman, she had an insight, an instinct, for what was good and holy beyond what could be expected of him. She did not plume herself on her virtue, but she consciously exerted all her strength in the interests of morality.

As for Alice, she regarded herself as married already. She had the fresh, keen passions of the ordinary girl, but once these were satisfied, she was not essentially voluptuous; Lewis fulfilled all her wants, and at first she had not looked beyond the present moment; but now that she was so entirely his and he hers, she was waking out of the delirium of her bliss to the calm, happy consciousness of a lifetime to be spent with him. She had behaved like a young child in the abandonment with which she had left all responsibilities, all arrangements, to him, taking herself no thought for anything, careless in the complete protection of his love; but now, though only a few months had passed, she was older. She felt no undue impatience about the matter, but she saw that the marriage ceremony would be very useful to them. They would want, some time, to come out into the world; Lewis had not the unworldly interests of Patrick; she herself was no slave to a household like Elizabeth; vague visions of the future began to form themselves in the mists of her dreamlike happiness. As she sat at the dressing table, a towel pinned round her shoulders while she brushed out the dark silk of her hair that flew round her face, delicate in its natural pallor, her eyes had a far-seeing expression. She brushed slowly, slowly, and thought how much, how much she loved him, and how dear and precious he was to her as a companion, although she did not now feel the wild excitement which she still seemed able to arouse in him. At moments like these she was steeped in a heavenly quietness; and this had the effect of making her, in her contact with the outside world, sharper, more aggressive, more determined to achieve the outer state of perfection of which she already felt the inner calm.

She and Lewis now made a habit of going over to dinner at the Woodlands every Sunday; always taking with them some contribution—a cheese or some cream from the dairy, a shoulder of veal, a bottle of brandy, or a stack of walnuts from the old tree that stood halfway down the meadow, marking the boundary of what had once been the garden of Sirenwood. At these gatherings Alice felt, nowadays, a new sense of respectability and importance. Patrick, though taciturn, was always particularly civil to her, and Elizabeth now confided freely to her all the little matters which might be supposed to be of interest between one married sister and another. Formerly she had always felt that Alice was neither a suitable confidante nor an interested one; but now Alice seemed not only to have increased in dignity but to meet her sister halfway in a discussion of her affairs. There had never been such sympathy between them, even in childhood.

One Sunday morning the two brothers were walking up and down outside while Alice helped Elizabeth to lay the table for the midday dinner. In the scullery, Clara, rather pale and silent, was helping a strange-looking object to wipe its face and hands on a damp cloth. Elizabeth came to the scullery door with a cullender of vegetables to drain them in the sink, and saw through the scullery window Lewis and Patrick pausing in their walking to exchange a word with a man whom she knew vaguely by sight as the inhabitant of the house round the bend of the lane. The trio had their faces in the direction of the Woodlands, and as they were about to part, Patrick and Lewis returning to the house, the neighbour in making his final remark took a step in their direction. Elizabeth swung round on Clara.

"Take her upstairs," she said peremptorily.

"I can't, ma'am," said Clara uneasily. "She seemed set on coming down to wash this morning!"

"I've told you," said Elizabeth angrily, "she is not to be about when anyone may see her! You've no business to let her down at this time of day."

"She would wash, ma'am," repeated Clara in a fearful tone. "I didn't like to say not."

Harriet meanwhile stood as if oblivious of their conversation, making motions with the rag as if washing, though hardly touching her face. Suddenly she straightened herself and said, "I'll have dinner now. I won't go upstairs today."

Alice had now come to the scullery door and saw

that Lewis, with Patrick, was approaching the house. In an instant's panic she gazed at Elizabeth, not daring to speak lest Harriet should catch her meaning and look out of the window; in her anxiety to conceal the nearness of Lewis she pressed her hand over her mouth, her eyes above it wide with consternation. Elizabeth mouthed something which Alice seemed to understand; quick as thought she was out of the side door, down the garden path, and clinging, breathless, to Lewis's arm, turning him round again while Patrick strode on into the house. Elizabeth, however, had managed to get Harriet to the foot of the stairs, and it only needed Patrick's appearance at the threshold to drive her up out of sight.

At the dinner table everyone relaxed into gaiety again, but while they sat over the walnuts, Clara, when she had taken the children out to play in the parlour, came back and said hesitantly, "Shall you give me Mrs. Oman's dinner to take up to her now?" and Elizabeth said sharply, "No, let her wait." Clara went out again.

Patrick, cracking shells, said coolly, "That was a near go before dinner!"

"Yes, indeed," exclaimed Alice, leaning up against Lewis's shoulder. "If it hadn't been for me, darling, just think what would have happened to you!"

Lewis sat with a fond, contented smile on his face while she fondled his ear and asked him whose baby he was.

Elizabeth said, after a discreet interval:

"One never knows what may happen; of course, she hasn't the least idea of Lewis's being in the neighbourhood, but I'm always terrified of her coming down when he's here; or even seeing him through the bedroom window, though of course that does look out the other way from your path up here."

She stopped, looking pale and harassed. Patrick said: "We can stop that all right, at least."

He left the table and, fetching some tools and boards from the outhouse, went upstairs; a noise of hammering succeeded, and then the heavy slam of a door. When he came downstairs, the table was cleared and the party sitting cosily round the kitchen fire. Lewis looked up interrogatively as he came in again from putting the tool basket away.

"I've boarded up the window," he said, taking his seat in the circle.

"Is it dark, then?" said Alice, in the tone of a curious child.

"Oh dear, no," he said; "plenty of light comes through the top."

They all stretched out their feet to the comforting glow; the afternoons were drawing in fast, and the firelight turned them in their afternoon drowsiness to Egyptian-like figures, ruddy and black. Alice half slept, her head on Lewis's breast; when she became fully roused again the room was too dark for her to see Elizabeth, but she felt Lewis's voice vibrating in his chest; he and Patrick were talking, but, as it seemed to her dulled ears, tonelessly and like machines.

"It wouldn't need that," Lewis was saying.

"No," Patrick answered. "Just not going out of our way, as far as I can see."

"Does she often do this? It ought to be possible to make her keep upstairs."

"It ought," said Patrick, "but you know what the women are: careless, or soft; she's quite often down for one thing or another, though if I appear she's off in double-quick time."

"I hate to feel that you and dear Lizzie have so much bother."

"Well, to tell you the truth, it does rile me more than I can say. I feel that one more of these scenes and I can't be responsible!"

"I leave the whole thing in your hands," said Lewis.

Alice drifted off into slumber again. When she awoke, the lamp was lit and the kettle hissing, and everyone twitted her on having slept so long. She said nothing, but pushed back her hair with a languid, joyous air. When she and Lewis were walking homeward through the dusk, she felt so gay and light-hearted that she frolicked about him as she had done in the mad hilarity of their first days together. Lewis was delighted; his spirits were always like tinder to the fire of hers, and they stopped to exchange so many kisses on the way that it was only the coldness of the night air which drove them in at last.

As Christmas approached, Patrick went to stay in

town for a week; he had to visit a picture dealer, and also to interview a client, an old friend of his father's, who had the benevolent fancy to have his portrait painted. Patrick undertook to do it in four sittings, and put up meanwhile at a commercial hotel in the Euston Road, where he was known. Lewis suggested that they should all go up and have a day's amusement and bring him home; they would take Alfred to Astley's, and, though Julia was too young to appreciate the spectacle, she was such a good baby, she would be sure to sit quietly on Elizabeth's knee and give no trouble, and Elizabeth did not like to leave her in the sole guardianship of Clara. Clara herself looked so doleful when it was explained to her that she would stay behind that Elizabeth was about to promise her a present when the girl said something about not liking to be left alone to manage. Elizabeth was nonplussed for the moment; something restrained her from positively commanding Clara in the matter; perhaps it was the unrealized knowledge that Clara would not, in the outside world, be so insignificant a member of their family now. A decided quarrel with Clara might be something to avoid. At all events, she said kindly, "Come, come, Clara! It's only for the day. We shall be back on the nine o'clock." Clara was mollified by the tone, and said, could she have in the girls from up the lane to stop along with her? She shouldn't mind with a bit of company. The girls were the cook and nursemaid from the house the owner of which was known to Elizabeth by sight. Clara had a slight acquaintance with them, and Elizabeth saw no objection to having them in the house, provided the remaining occupant kept upstairs. The door of the bedroom could not very well be locked, because the room contained no conveniences of any kind; but there had been one or two scenes lately, and Elizabeth felt tolerably certain that now Harriet could be controlled by a word of command from anybody. So she said, "Very well, but remember, they are not to go upstairs, and you must see to it that——"

"Oh dear, yes," interrupted Clara, with her old enthusiasm. Now that the nightmare of solitude was removed from her she almost looked forward to the importance of responsibility.

Susan Hathersage, the nurserymaid, had the half day off, so she came to the Woodlands early in the afternoon; Jane Burrows could not get off till after dinner, as she had to dish up, but as the family dined at half-past five, she was with the other two by just after six. It was dark at that hour, and the fields on the other side of the hedge were a trackless sheet of adhesive mud; where the starved hedges broke down, the tide of liquefying soil seemed to have spread into the lane.

"I'm glad I'll have you to go back with, Susan," Jane was saying, as she spread her stockinged feet out before the fire, while Clara put her boots to dry before attempting to remove the mud with a bone scraper. "We'll flounder along fine, I can tell you! There isn't a even a star."

"Dear now, how good of you to come and all," said Clara. She busied herself with getting the new-comer a cup of tea; she and Susan had had theirs some time ago, and they now made buttered toast for Jane while she drank and gossiped; she was the merry one, and always had some inspiriting observation to make on things in general, or something droll and caustic to say about her employers. Clara was proud of her position as hostess, and bustled about attentively, while Jane, balancing her steaming cup of tea on her lap, regaled them with an account of how things were between her mistress and that lady's sister-in-law. "There's no love lost there," she wound up. Clara sat enthralled; it was just the sort of conversation her soul thirsted after. She and Susan were sitting on the hearthrug while Jane occupied the rocking-chair. Suddenly the latter suspended her swinging to and fro, and said, "What's that?" They all sat motionless. From above their heads, in the direction of the staircase, came a hesitating, dragging sound, a slow, slithering step. Clara sprang to her feet and advanced to the foot of the stairs.

"Go back, ma'am!" she exclaimed. As she stood there, the blood pounding in her ears, she felt the excitement and uncertainty of someone who performs a conjuring trick before a critical audience being slightly uncertain of his own powers. The trick seemed to work this time, however. After a second's pause, the curious step was heard again, retreating. Clara, looking conscious and important, came back to the fire again.

"Lor'!" said Susan. "Is that how you speak to a lady?"

Jane's anecdotes, and her own successful demonstration of authority, had gone to Clara's head. She was wrought up to be dramatic.

"Pooh!" she said, "that's no lady! She's Mr. Patrick's sister-in-law."

Jane leaned forward, obviously scenting a mystery; Susan, at her elbow, was round-eyed with awe, and Clara had had no confidante since she came to Cudham. Gathering her skirts round her knees, she forthwith told them, under thrilling pledges of secrecy, all she knew; she was surprised herself to find out how much that was.

❧ XVII ❧

THE MAIDS were required to be in by half-past nine, and, owing to the impassable nature of the lane, they felt they must start out at nine o'clock. Clara knew the family would be at home shortly afterwards and was not afraid of being left, and, furthermore, a sense of having been exceedingly indiscreet made her anxious to get rid of the guests, certainly to have them well out of sight before the arrival of Patrick and Elizabeth.

The latter, Patrick carrying Alfred, and Elizabeth Julia, arrived unaccompanied; Alice and Lewis had thought it too late to do anything but go home, for they all kept country hours. They all seemed quite worn out with the day's pleasuring and were up very late next morning. As Clara crossed the scullery to throw out the cinders, Elizabeth, who was busy at the sink, said casually, "Did you get on all right yesterday evening?" "Oh dear, yes," said Clara. She was so relieved that there was no possible way of Elizabeth's finding out how indiscreet she had been that she toyed wantonly with the situation. "I thought once," she said, "that she was coming downstairs, but I went to the foot of the stairs, and she went back again. They didn't notice anything." Clara was so impressionable that when Elizabeth appeared to repose any confidence in her, she was all on Elizabeth's side and identified her interests with her own; but when left to herself she now felt strangely uneasy and troubled about the situation upstairs. At first these moods of disquiet were fleeting and would leave her feeling that what Patrick and Elizabeth did must be right; that the creature, being a natural, couldn't feel anything like ordinary people, and that she was, in a way, guilty, because her existence was against the interests of Mr. Lewis.

But Clara, though flighty and ignorant, was at bottom a normal little human being, and one, moreover, not blinded by morbid love, by perverted passion, by avarice, selfishness, or lust; she was in this respect, for all her weakness and silliness, much more of a responsible creature than any of her elders. At one time the peculiar goings-on had been keen pleasure to her, supplying the food her sensational temperament hungered for; but while her unsatisfied appetite was sharp, it did not take more than a certain amount to quench it. She saw Patrick some days later carrying out to the ash-bin a pile of rusty, tattered cloth, with a mouldering stocking depending from it, and watched him uneasily as he stuffed the armful into the bin and put the lid on again. When she went upstairs with a plate of rice that evening, she found Harriet wearing nothing but a nightgown, with the old shawl wrapped round her waist. Clara put the plate down on the bed and looked at Harriet, wanting very much at that moment to say something kind, but she could not think of a single word; so at last she said, "Eat your dinner, dear." Harriet came up to the bed and looked at the plate and looked all round it to see if there were nothing else, and then began to eat, oblivious of her presence. Clara glanced at the wicker cradle, then went nearer and looked right in; she had not seen the child close to for weeks, and now it seemed, so far from growing, to have become much smaller; it had bread and milk twice a day, brought up with Harriet's own food, but it didn't seem to be doing it much good; perhaps it wouldn't eat it, for Clara saw remains of the food all round its mouth and on the wrapper over its chest, as if it had been fed with difficulty. It was so quiet, it was hard to tell if it moved at all until you had looked at it for some minutes.

When she went downstairs she was feeling very strange and unhappy and not quite knowing what she ought to think; but a few days later she was left no more in doubt. The child's stupor seemed to have vanished; it woke up into a thin wailing cry, and never stopped; the high, penetrating sound filled the house and lacerated them. Clara, standing by Elizabeth in the kitchen, said boldly, "It's hungry," and then hung her head in fear. Elizabeth said impatiently, "It has as much food as it can eat. It won't eat!" Patrick, trying to work downstairs, flung down his brush and dashed upstairs time and again; but, though a commotion was always the result, the noise never stopped; it was heard above all other sounds, and went on after he had come downstairs again.

Lewis and Alice now kept away from the Woodlands altogether; but one morning Lewis was seen by Clara standing outside the gate. She went to tell Elizabeth, not knowing if the latter had seen him, but Elizabeth came out of her bedroom with her hat and jacket on and said, "Yes. We are going to take the child to London, to Guy's Hospital."

Clara went downstairs again, and presently Elizabeth went out to join Lewis, carrying a wrapped-up bundle, quite silent now. Clara watched them depart with thankfulness; not to hear that dreadful sound was so much. She gave Alfred and Julia a special washing and combing that morning.

But the calm that succeeded the removing of the baby was short-lived; Clara felt that she would give anything now to be back again as they had been. She really couldn't think what had got into Patrick; even if Harriet did answer up now and keep on saying she wanted something to eat, he might have let her alone. She didn't come downstairs any more, though she would sit huddled up on the very top step. Patrick need not have made such a to-do when he passed her there on the way to his bedroom. Alfred went quietly by her a dozen times a day with no more notice than if she had been the newel post of the stair; and once or twice, when his ball had rolled through the open door of her bedroom, he had gone in after it and come out again as quiet as you please. But Patrick seemed possessed of a devil, and the worst of it was that his rages seemed to raise a response in Harriet; for weeks she had been listless and apathetic, without a word for anyone, saying nothing when the child was taken or making any sign that she missed it; and yet now she was as noisy as ever she had been before, always clamouring; and then it struck Clara what was happening. Nobody had a great deal to eat in the house —hardly ever so much but that they would not at any time have been pleased with a bite of something—and Clara knew that very much did not go up to Harriet, for, though she did not always carry it up herself, she usually saw it put out. But she had taken it for granted that she would want less than the rest of them. Once the idea had struck her, however, she was thoroughly frightened. When she next had to go upstairs with a small piece of bread and some vegetables, she gave the plate to Harriet, who was crouching on the floor, and whispered slowly and distinctly: "Are you hungry?" Harriet was stretching out her hands for the plate, not answering, but Clara, not intending any cruelty, felt she must know, and, withholding the plate, said again, urgently and low, "Are you hungry?" Harriet fixed her eyes on her, understanding her words, and answered with frightful eagerness, but without saying anything. Clara put down the plate beside her, feeling sick, and ran downstairs again.

That evening she busied herself with amusing Alfred: entering into his game with the soldiers as earnestly as he, for she did not want to think about anything except what was immediately in front of her; and in the glow of the hearth, trying to make the soldiers stand upright on the uneven flags—for they had rolled back the rag mat—she really forgot. Elizabeth was bathing Julia on the other side of the fire, and singing a low song as she did so; every time she paused, Alfred would look up and ask why she was stopping, and then she would go on again. In the pauses of her voice there was not a sound except the light clink of the soldiers' tin pedestals on the stones; till at last Clara said sharply, "What are you scratching for, you bad boy?" Alfred stopped at once, but the next moment he was at it again, and so persistently that at last Clara took him to the lamp and held his head sideways under it. Elizabeth had carried Julia upstairs, and they were alone in the kitchen; but Clara did not need anyone to tell her what that was. Lice.

She could not give a very clear account of the days that followed that discovery; there seemed to be a tacit conspiracy between Alfred, Elizabeth, and herself that nothing should be mentioned which might hurt. Alfred, very composed, very pale, went about exactly as usual; if there was a noise or disturbance, he never showed, by so much as raising his eyes, that he heard it. He played by himself, so quietly, so serenely, he might have been one of the children immune in the fiery furnace. Elizabeth said very little, and nothing at all about Harriet; Patrick took up everything that was to go upstairs now; and when anything was heard, she and Clara averted their eyes by mutual consent. When Elizabeth lay in bed at night, her eyes were often hot and wakeful, and as she turned from side to side she felt she had a thorny path to tread and wished that it were all over. Patrick slept like the dead.

The weather continued wild and wet well into the new year, and the land outside the door was one smooth sheet of liquid clay, catching a faint gleam in the tempestuous twilight. One evening Clara came to the door, and looked out, flushed and desperate; she was resolved to go up the lane to the house, there, and fetch help—tell everything she knew; she put one foot over the threshold, but instantly it sank almost ankle deep, and at the same time she heard the wind rising in the copse. It was almost dark—what could she do? Behind her was the warm kitchen full of light, and Elizabeth, gracious and homely, bending over the teakettle; at that moment she looked up and called to Clara to shut the door. Her manner was peremptory yet motherly. Clara closed the door and came creeping back.

Although the evening set in cloudy and wet, by the time the moon rose the sky had cleared except for fleeing wrack. The policeman who had been detailed to watch the neighbourhood of the Woodlands for the last months stood on the lower road from where the roof could be seen and saw the wet slates burn with a blush of silver. Everything was silent as the grave. High overhead the remaining clouds raced, and higher still, in a field of transparent aquamarine, the polished silver moon poured out floods of light; the purity and calmness of the universe seemed altogether free of any stain of human grief, a serene, radiant repudiation of pain and misery.

☞ XVIII ☜

"ALICE," said Lewis, coming in one afternoon just at tea-time, "we must go over tomorrow and help Lizzie." Alice, toasting bread before the parlour fire, looked up enquiringly. Lewis sat down and went on: "Harriet's on the move, dear." Alice sat back on her heels, staring at him; then, as she grasped the meaning of his words, she frowned and said:

"What have *we* got to do?"

"We think of taking her over to Penge," said Lewis, "to say we got the best doctor's advice and so on."

"But," objected Alice eagerly, "she will die anyway?" Lewis nodded. "Then," said Alice, "why not leave her where she is?"

"Listen, dear," said Lewis gently. "Before you can bury anyone you have to get a doctor's certificate to say what they died of. We don't want any doctor poking his nose round the Woodlands, do we?" Alice was kneeling in front of him, her arms on his knees.

"No," she said presently.

"So," he went on, "the simplest thing will be to go over to Penge. It will look very well too. We want everything aboveboard and so on." He ran his hand through her curls. "How will you like yourself as

Mrs. Lewis Oman, eh?" he asked. Alice tossed her head.

"I won't be any different from what I am now," she said pertly, "except that I shall nag you, Lewis."

"What do you do now?" cried Lewis. But in a moment he was grave again. "See here, dear," he said, putting his hands round her shoulders and drawing her close to him. "If any questions are asked, we must all say the same thing, d'you see?"

"No one must ask *me* questions!" cried Alice sharply. Lewis was very patient, however, and between coaxing and firmness he got her to accept the fact that, whatever might come, she must take her share in it. He then told her, slowly and distinctly, that Patrick had been housing Harriet for some months because she and Lewis had separated by mutual consent, that they had seen each other frequently, and that two days ago Harriet had begun to complain of a feeling of drowsiness and of a disinclination to eat; and that, as they were not satisfied with the local doctor, Dr. Deering, who had, in fact, attended Alfred on one or two occasions, they were bringing her to Penge for better advice. He spoke as if teaching a child a lesson, but Alice's quickness more than reassured him; she said nothing, but he could see by her eyes that every syllable went home. He was unwilling to begin tea till he had said everything he had to say, so he went on, "We'll go over tomorrow morning, and Lizzie wants you to take over a set of clothes—you know. So will you look them out this evening, darling?"

Alice nodded. Now that the first reluctance to being put upon in any way was over, she was perfectly prepared to be Lewis's instrument. Not that she leapt to do his bidding, and further his wishes almost before he expressed them; but she was instinctively passive and obedient: there was nothing else to do! The sense of being irresistibly committed to some course was new and oppressive to her, and all that evening she was taciturn. Lewis did not say much either, but he sat beside her, holding her elbow loosely in both his hands while she made an attempt to sew.

Next morning, however, he was full of vigour, and as they set out to walk to the Woodlands through the dank morning mist, Lewis carrying in a bundle a complete set of garments from the store upstairs, Alice felt her spirits rising, not in joy, but in a painful, thrilling excitement. She was glad now—yes, glad— that something was going to be done. She had not heretofore wanted anything but to be left to enjoy her idyllic quiet; but now she felt she could never go back to that again until the coming moment of action had been battled through. When they got to the Woodlands the children were out of the way, and, in the kitchen, Clara was boiling a fowl—for an early lunch, it seemed. Elizabeth, pale as marble, came downstairs to them; she greeted them with pleasure, but not with any smile; rather with a lighting up of the eyes, which were deeply sunken and ringed. Alice unclasped her cape and sat down, trying to look and feel at ease, and Lewis put his hand on her shoulder and said with quiet courage:

"Now, Lizzie, we're all here, dear. You sit down a bit. We shan't be making a move till after lunch, and you look fit to drop."

Elizabeth smiled now, and looked the more ghastly for it. Still, she sat down, and they discussed their arrangements, although everything had been settled beforehand. Patrick was out ordering a trap to be round after lunch to take them to Halstead station. When he came in he greeted them calmly, and proposed a cup of tea. The suggestion was eagerly seized upon, and Alice, glad now of something to do, moved to the dresser to set out the china and put the kettle on to boil. Clara had done all that was necessary to the fowl, and had gone out of the kitchen, leaving it to cook.

The morning was passed away in strained idleness till twelve o'clock, when Clara came in to get the lunch, and then Elizabeth said:

"We ought to get her ready."

She glanced at Alice, and Lewis said:

"Go and help Lizzie, darling."

But Alice flushed crimson and stood speechless with dismay. Patrick turned round as if to remonstrate angrily, but Elizabeth was going resignedly upstairs by herself with the bundle, when Lewis said:

"Take Clara, Lizzie. Alice'll finish getting the lunch ready."

So Clara laid down the pile of plates and went up-stairs after Elizabeth.

Alice had finished laying the table and had dished up the fowl before they came downstairs again. They all sat down and had lunch, and then Elizabeth said:

"Hadn't you better bring her down, Patrick?"

Whereupon Patrick went upstairs, and Elizabeth began cutting up some fowl on a plate. Patrick came down with a figure in his arms which he put in the rocking chair, and, really, it was not so very frightening. Harriet was dressed with what seemed to them all, by contrast, extraordinary splendour. She wore a handsome dress of dark woollen material faced with velvet, and as she lay inert in the chair the frills and hems of lawn and flannel petticoats could be seen beneath the skirt. She had a hat and a face-cloth pelisse, and gloves of which all the fingers had not been fitted on before they were secured at the wrist. Her face was a dark bronze colour, and her eyes were closed all but a slit, which showed the eyeballs of an odd yellowish tint. Her head was sunk right back and to one side, and she did not move or make a sound; she appeared quite peaceful. Elizabeth had screwed a pair of her own earrings into her ears.

Patrick came forward with the plate of fowl and held a morsel on a fork to her mouth, but, without opening her eyes, she seemed to refuse it.

"Can't you let her sleep?" said Lewis.

"If she goes to sleep now it's my opinion she won't wake up again," said Patrick, but he put the plate back on the table again. Elizabeth was putting eggs and some tea and butter into a hand basket.

"Alice," she said, "fasten this up while I put my things on. The trap'll be here in a few minutes."

While Alice did as she was asked, Patrick went to the door and looked about. "We don't want any damned loiterers from up the lane spying about," he said. But the coast seemed clear, and a few minutes later, when the trap drove up, they all went out, the two men carrying Harriet between them, and Alice and Elizabeth placing themselves on each side of her once she was on the seat.

At the station Lewis led the way to a first-class carriage. Alice had never been in one before, and was occupied in examining the upholstery and lace antimacassars while Patrick and Elizabeth settled their burden and Lewis stood at the window to prevent any possible intrusion before the train started. They did not have to change on the short run to Penge, and, once there, Alice felt their difficulties must soon be at an end, as they summoned a cab and hoisted Harriet into it. But the others did not think so; as she was being lifted in, Harriet raised her arm and moaned, and Elizabeth said quickly, "All right, dear, you shall have your supper very soon now"; but the cabman had heard, and two or three people stopped to look. She and the two men felt the ordeal of casual observation.

It was a relief to get to the lodgings in Hound Street, which Patrick had secured two days ago. He

had told the landlady his sister-in-law was coming
for medical advice, and therefore she was not altogether surprised at the lady's seeming too weak to
walk and being put to bed immediately. The husband,
a very pleasant-spoken gentleman, asked for the address of the district nurse, and upon Mrs. Morpeth's
offering to fetch her, for she lived only in the next
street, he said not just now. Perhaps in the evening:
they would see how things went on.

Upstairs, Elizabeth and Alice worked like the possessed; the latter's reluctance vanished like straw in
the furnace draught of their necessity. Lewis was in
the next room, which gave them some comfort; they
got off the clothes which had been put on that morning and laid them on a chair; and over the nightgown that had been worn for so long they huddled on
a clean one from the basket. They managed to lay the
figure in bed, and then hurriedly pulled up the sheet
to the chin. The earrings caught Alice's eye, and she
pulled out the one nearest to her; then her courage
failed, so the other one was left.

By mutual consent they hastened into the next
room, where Lewis and Patrick were side by side on
the sofa; Lewis held out his arms for Alice to come to
his knee, while Elizabeth said breathlessly:

"We'd better ask Mrs. Morpeth to make some tea
and to boil one of the eggs. And I think someone had
better go for the doctor." Patrick rose immediately.

"I'll go," he said; "and I'll give the nurse a call at
the same time. I think they might both come now."

On his way downstairs he sent the landlady up to them.

Elizabeth received Mrs. Morpeth with all her dignity and grace of demeanour, a little marred, and naturally, by anxiety. Alice and Lewis went away and left the two for a really comfortable talk about symptoms, such as landladies are known always to enjoy. Her sister-in-law, Elizabeth said, had always been difficult—stubborn, one might say—and wouldn't attend to keeping herself nice; though they were all fond of her and couldn't bear to think that this mysterious illness was being neglected because it was outside the experience of the country doctor. Her refusal to eat was the most worrying feature of the case, and if they could now have one of their own country eggs, which they had brought with them, lightly boiled, and brought up with some thin bread and butter and a pot of tea, she and her sister would try Mrs. Oman with it and perhaps get her to take a little. Mrs. Morpeth departed, full of zeal, and presently Patrick returned, saying the doctor was out, but he had left a message at the surgery. The nurse would be with them in about half an hour.

He looked with some anxiety at Elizabeth, but her unnatural paleness had vanished; she was now so busy in her rôle of sick nurse, and supporter to the other three, that her death-like rigidity had relaxed, allowing the blood to flow normally, eagerly, and show a little in her cheek. Patrick laid his hand about her shoulders with a glance of enquiry at her, and she smiled and stroked his hair quite playfully; then she was at the door, receiving the tea tray from the landlady.

When Lewis and Alice came in from their brief stroll to the end of the street and back once or twice, and they were all sitting round the sitting-room table, by tacit understanding they began to speak as if it were a genuine patient next door. Not that they risked their own composure so far as to express any sympathy for her; but they gravely and anxiously discussed her state, and debated as to whether they would try to find another doctor who might be at liberty to come to them at once. They were completely in the mood of people attending a sister-in-law who is gravely ill: the men troubled and helpless, the women finding relief in small journeying to the sick-room and back and short conversations with the sympathetic landlady.

Towards supper time the nurse was shown upstairs, and went into the bedroom with Elizabeth, who left her there after a whispered word or two and returned to the others. Presently the woman came out and said: "I think I'd try to get Dr. Horsham now, and if he's still out, you could try——" Here she gave them two other addresses. Alice, who had been growing more and more wrought up, here started to her feet and said she would put on her hat and jacket and go for him once more. Lewis was about to say he would accompany her, when Patrick stepped forward authoritatively and said, "I'll go with her. You'll want to stay, Lewis." Lewis instantly recollected himself, with a thrill of gratitude, and said, "Why, yes, yes, I had rather, certainly."

Patrick and Alice hastened through the dusk and arrived at the surgery just as Dr. Horsham was swallowing a cup of coffee before turning out again in response to their message. Alice realized that Patrick expected her to do all the talking, and her nervous, agitated manner of speech passed well for anxiety; she could tell that, even while she smiled at the doctor and put her hands over her heart to try to make it beat more quietly, for it felt as if it would shake her to pieces.

"But," said the doctor, when she had described the symptoms they had agreed upon, "have you not had your own doctor to attend to her?"

"Oh, yes," said Alice, "but he didn't seem—my brother-in-law thought——"

"We were not altogether satisfied," put in Patrick.

"I see," said Dr. Horsham. "Well, I'll come round. But I had better have the name of your own medical man."

Alice felt their case was immeasurably strengthened by every atom of truth they could introduce.

"Dr. Deering," she gasped, "Dr. Deering of Brastead."

"Very well," said the doctor. "Now, if you're ready, we'll come along." He looked at her kindly, and she felt a glow of reassurance. "I think we'd better take a cab," he said. "You seem done up."

When they got back to the lodgings, they left the doctor with the nurse, and joined Lewis and Elizabeth in the sitting room. When the doctor came out, he was met by four pale, anxious faces.

"I'm sorry," he said gently. "I'm afraid there is not much to be done. Absolute quiet is essential, and I've given the nurse directions about beef tea. She'll know how to make it. I'll call first thing tomorrow morning."

To the nurse he had said, "It seems like apoplexy; in any case, I don't think it's more than a matter of hours. She may last the night, but you must be prepared for it any moment."

Patrick had not engaged any rooms except the two, and he and Lewis had planned to sleep at the station hotel while the women sat up. Patrick accordingly took himself off soon after supper, but Lewis said he would remain to keep the others company. Alice lay down in her clothes on the sofa and was soon in an uneasy doze; Elizabeth sat upright by the fire her hands curled over the arms of the chair, so still that nothing moved about her except the shifting firelight on the drooping masses of her hair. Lewis prowled noiselessly up and down the room for some time, then came and sat in the light of the hearth, where Elizabeth could see him through the falling shade of her hair. The expression of his face absorbed and fascinated her, and frightened her through her inability to understand it. Lewis was feeling as if his veins ran liquid fire; more than once, since he had begun this adventure what seemed so long ago, he had felt himself approaching some crisis, and hardly able to contain his bursting heart, as some invisible force swept him up to the crest of a towering wave. But now the feeling was upon him a hundredfold; it was almost agony to exist, as that swirling torrent of excitement, rapid as a mill-race and sharper than a harrow, poured through his veins. The force of his tremendous experience made him feel, as he crouched before the fire in the quiet room, that every time the clock above him chimed the quarter he had become æons older in self-knowledge; that the tide of time was carrying him out and away, where at every turn he could see farther and farther, gather more and more to his breast of the length of that clue which suddenly would lead up to the heart of the mystery; in another second the secret of creation would be spread before him like a map.

The small clock chimed again, and Elizabeth shifted in her seat and pushed back her chair with a gesture that reminded him—of whom? Of course, there was Alice, asleep on the sofa. There was a sound in the next room, and Lewis got to his feet; his face was ashen, and, without knowing what he did, he took Elizabeth's hand in both his and looked down into her dear, loving face raised to his. At that moment the door opened, and the nurse, coming softly in, said:

"If you want to say good-bye to her, sir, you'd better come. I think she's going."

Lewis uttered a suppressed sound and stood stock-still, and Elizabeth, clasping his hand with both her own, said reprovingly:

"Pray don't, nurse. You worry him so!"

Nevertheless, a moment or two afterwards she herself went into the bedroom and saw the nurse bending over the bed. She went up and met the woman's glance. The shock of pure happiness and relief was almost too much for her, and she returned to the sitting room so shaken and tearful that the nurse did her best to comfort her, and Alice, waking up cold and stiff, found her head pressed against Lewis's breast for one stolen second of ecstasy while the nurse was leaning over Elizabeth.

When Patrick rejoined them at an early hour, the one thought in all their minds was to get away as soon as possible. Lewis interviewed the nurse and asked her to communicate with the undertaker and to do everything that was necessary in the way of preparation beforehand. He engaged the room from Mrs. Morpeth for the two days during which the body must remain in it, and, having paid down the necessary money, he suggested to the others that, as they could not catch a train for another hour, they should first have coffee at the station hotel and then refresh their cramped limbs by walking up and down the neighbouring streets. It seemed quite perfect that whereas the preceding days had been damp and foggy, this morning the sun was bright and clear and the air windless.

THE PENGE district nurse came round to Dr. Hor-sham's surgery on the afternoon following the death of the lady at Mrs. Morpeth's lodgings and asked to see him. The doctor, who was extremely busy, replied that he had already filled in the death certificate as: primary cause, cerebral disease, and secondary cause, apoplexy; and he did not see what further he had to do with the matter. But the nurse asked him whether he would not come round, now that she had begun to lay the body out, and just take a look at it? When he had done so, he thought it necessary to send over to Brastead for Dr. Deering, whose name had been given him as the lady's medical adviser.

"But," said Dr. Deering in astonishment, "I have never attended Mrs. Lewis Oman!" Nevertheless, when he had accompanied Dr. Horsham to Mrs. Morpeth's lodgings, he agreed that something must be done; on his return he stopped at Halstead and paid a call on Mr. Mortlock, the magistrate.

"Indeed!" said Mr. Mortlock. "I know the police had a communication from the lady's mother some time ago. We had better have the inspector up, if you can spare the time, doctor."

The inspector, on arrival at Halstead Priors, agreed

that the burial must be stopped until Mrs. Ogilvy had been communicated with, and went off to send her a telegram right away, summoning her to Penge.

"It will be a very dreadful thing," said the magistrate. "Poor creature! I wonder, now, if Mrs. Chevenix would help us? If she would go with the inspector to meet this poor woman at Penge, it might be of great use and comfort."

Mrs. Chevenix's bounteous good-nature was relied upon by the whole neighbourhood, and with justice, as on this occasion; and if a strong spice of curiosity was mingled with her sympathy and protectiveness, it did not make her the less effective and soothing in her support of Mrs. Ogilvy.

Ever since the party had got home to the Woodlands and Sirenwood, they had abstained from visiting each other and been, in their own homes, very silent; it was as if, after great storms, they were now becalmed, motionless; their very movements were slow, as if weights hung on them. Elizabeth had her usual round of occupations to follow, and pursued it as in a dream; but Alice was quite idle, and even Lewis wore an expression that was almost awestruck. When he held Alice in his arms, he looked beyond her, as if she were a symbol of something he had attained and her actual face meant nothing to him; yet they kept close together, almost always hand in hand, and Alice felt, "Soon all this will clear away, and we shall be as we were before, but all will be better." But Lewis was hardly looking forward to the future; he was con-

scious of anxiety, like a severe pain in his head, which
grew worse as the hours went on, and took the pleasure out of every sense of touch, taste, and sight. He
dared not seek comfort of Patrick; he feared lest, if
he put the thing into words, he might give it tangible
form; so he hung about the house, alone although
Alice was beside him, and for the first time in his life
he really suffered. Things he had endured before—
thwarted ambition, raging lust—all seemed to have
been pleasures under another name compared with
this grim, deadening affliction that seemed to be a
long-drawn-out death. And so, when the next morning a stifled scream from Alice drew him to the bedroom window, it was with a sensation something like
relief that he went downstairs and opened the door
to Sergeant Brownlea.

Very pale, grave, and courteous, he ushered him
into the parlour, and when the constable said that it
was thought better to postpone the burial for which
he had left orders, so that a few enquiries might be
made, he replied, "By all means"; he had far rather
that everyone should be satisfied. He repeated to Sergeant Brownlea the circumstances of his separation
from his wife by mutual consent, and of her sudden
illness two days before her removal. He also, as one
man of the world to another, confided to him that
while Mrs. Oman boarded with his brother, he himself had allowed his sister-in-law to pass at Sirenwood
as his wife. It was irregular, undoubtedly, but there
it was. The constable appeared quite to understand,

and presently took his leave. He was no sooner out of the house than Lewis summoned Alice, who was speechless and helpless in his hands, and hurried her off to the Woodlands. There he turned Clara and the children into the garden, and, shutting all the doors, sat down with Patrick, Elizabeth, and Alice at the table.

He was not now frightened; his deadly heaviness had vanished, and he was filled with thrilling excitement. It would all be quite easy, he assured them, and Patrick agreed with him; his confidence in Lewis to get the better of a pack of fools was unbounded. They both rehearsed the story once more, and Lewis put it forward that the chief cause of his amicable separation from Harriet had been her intemperance; Patrick amended that he had always been strictly careful to keep spirits out of her way, and that as she was deprived of them her longing seemed to decrease, and they had had every hope of her being quite cured, before she was taken ill so suddenly.

"She was quite conscious when we arrived at Penge, I take it?" said Lewis, glancing round the table.

"Oh, yes," cried Alice, "she undressed herself and took out her own earrings!"

They were all so ardent, they almost lost the sense of danger; it was all so simple, and their immense solidarity in the face of a world not related to them or bound by their interests, and therefore of inferior creation and without their rights, gave them a feeling of deep confidence and courage.

"There's only one thing," said Lewis at last. "We may all have to say this in front of a magistrate, so you'd better see that Clara knows what to do." Patrick undertook to see to that, but it gave Lewis rather more satisfaction when Elizabeth said she, too, would talk to her. "So really," he said at last, "there is nothing more to do at present. I don't think we need disturb ourselves." His face wore an almost wolfish smile as he looked at them all; Alice clung to his arm and would not let him go; but his other hand was in Patrick's. Elizabeth, calm, graceful, resigned, expressed complete agreement with all that was said, but whereas she bore herself with the dreadful gentleness of a martyr, Patrick was cocksure and defiant, proud of Lewis's dependence on him and ready to lay down his life, only of course it would not come to that!

And when, the day following, Sergeant Brownlea arrived to take their depositions, they underwent no change of attitude. He saw them one by one in the parlour of the Woodlands, and wrote down on sheets of foolscap their answers to the questions he put, afterwards reading the whole aloud to them and making them initial it, page by page. Then it appeared that they must all five, including Clara, attend the coroner's inquest at Penge, and Mrs. Hoppner was sent for hurriedly, and, without receiving any precise information as to what was happening, made to understand that she must take Alfred and Julia to London with her for the present while the Woodlands was locked up and the family given rooms at the Park Tavern in Penge.

The coroner's court was held in the banqueting room of the Park Tavern, a large and lofty apartment with four tall staring windows, and faded, elaborate gilt and plaster on the walls. The coroner sat at the head of a large mahogany table and the jury at a trestle table on his left hand. Alice and Lewis, and Patrick and Elizabeth, all well dressed, modest and quiet in their bearing, sat on four chairs together at the right of the bottom of the table. Between them and the coroner sat gentlemen with papers, most of whom they did not recognize; but Dr. Deering and Dr. Horsham and Sergeant Brownlea were among them.

It was some little time before all four of them realized that Clara was no longer with them; it was not till after the opening of the proceedings they learnt that the day before, when they had all attested their depositions, Clara had afterwards gone up to the coroner and said:

"None of that is true. They made me say it."

The newspapers meanwhile had been busy, and it was in fact from them, no kinder source, that Mrs. Hoppner learnt for the first time what was the matter; read the facts as far as they had been ascertained; and, having put the children to bed, sent out for the evening edition and learned that Patrick, Lewis, and Elizabeth Oman and Alice Hoppner had been found guilty by the coroner's jury of the wilful murder of

Harriet Oman and were to go before the grand jury.

Alice and Elizabeth were lodged in one cell in Maidstone Gaol, and Patrick and Lewis in another. The room, small as it was, contained two camp beds furnished with unbleached linen sheets and coarse, dark brown blankets; but the brothers did not lie down. Seated side by side on Patrick's bed, their arms round each other, they whispered into each other's ears all night long. It was the conclusion of all the midnight conversations they had held as children, when, side by side in the double bed, they had whispered under the clothes so as not to be heard next door. The darkness was the same; it was the same surrounding silence. Patrick had pulled up the blankets round their shoulders, and their breath was warm and damp on each other's cheeks just as it had ever been; and the confidence was the same—the unreserve they had never achieved with women, or with anyone in the world except each other.

The window of the cell gave into a passage, so that the morning light which they had expected to warn them was delayed; and Lewis fell into a heavy sleep just half an hour before a warder entered the cell and told them to wash and be ready for breakfast. When Lewis opened his eyes, roused by the noise, he saw Patrick pouring out water from the tin jug into the bowl, and at the sight of him a flood of thankfulness and relief welled up in him. He got off the bed and, going up to him, slapped him gaily on the back; Patrick turned round with a brilliant smile, and each felt that the other was the best and truest and most precious friend the whole world could offer.

Neither of them had given more than a passing thought to the women; but now they met them again, as all four were to drive, with one constable beside them and one on the box, to the magistrate's court. Elizabeth looked much as usual, except that she had a dreadful look in her sunken eyes. Patrick drew her arm within his, and then she looked so stately that the constables gazed in astonishment at her unconscious face. Directly Alice saw Lewis, she gave a little sob and clung to him, and he patted her arm kindly, as if she were an importunate child.

The blinds of the carriage windows were down and prevented any glimpse of the streets through which they passed; but presently Patrick asked the constable if they were nearly there, and was told it would be a matter of ten minutes or so. Elizabeth and Alice sat on one seat, and Patrick, Lewis, and the constable facing them; Alice had wanted dreadfully to sit beside Lewis, but the constable had somehow marshalled them in that position, and she had not dared to say anything. Her face was white, for she had not with her the means of painting it, and she looked in her natural state much younger, quite a child, Lewis thought dispassionately, watching her. Suddenly she raised her head with a puzzled gaze: there was a curious noise, which the others did not seem to notice, and which sounded at first as if it came from among the wheels of the carriage, but then forced itself on everyone's notice as it grew louder and seemed to fill the air about them. In response to her look, Lewis turned to the constable beside him and asked him what it was. The man looked at him oddly, and turned away again without saying anything.

At the moment the carriage stopped, and their guard pulled up the blind, revealing through the window a double file of other policemen, all, it seemed, to escort them the short distance to the entrance of the court. Then, as the door was opened, the noise, in increased volume, could no longer be mistaken: over the shoulders of the policemen they saw a confused multitude of people, and all round them heard the hideous roar of execration from a thousand throats.

❦ XX ❧

THE LORD CHIEF JUSTICE of England was laid up with threatened appendicitis, and so it devolved upon the junior judge, Sir Henry Tyrell, to open the Quarter Sessions at the Old Bailey. He had taken only a cursory interest in the Penge tragedy, never having supposed that the case would come before him. However, local feeling had been so much inflamed by it that after the grand jury had found a true bill, it was decided that the case must be tried outside of Kent. It looked like being a serious business, and poor Ammersham was a little chagrined that his ill health should baulk him of so sensational a trial. Well, well, naturally enough, thought the judge pleasantly, as the usher helped him into his robes, zealously arranging the scarlet folds with their bands of miniver. There was no real reason why he should not have put on his own robes; most judges, in fact, were obliged to do so, but everybody ran about for Sir Harry Tyrell, handsome, charming, and good-natured, for many years standing counsel to the Jockey Club and ready to listen to the affairs of anybody. He was rather above middle height, with a powerful, good-humoured face and that ready, mobile turn of feature which is often seen in actors; his powers of mimicry were in fact remarkable, and his elocution consummate: but instead of that joyous, confident lift of the head of the man who is accustomed to being looked at, Sir Henry Tyrell's head had the slightly sideways poise of the man who is accustomed to looking at other people. His reputation as a criminal lawyer was truly appreciated only in his profession, for in his dealings with the world at large it was the warmth and humanity of his disposition that made the chief impression. Cruelty was not, to him, as to respectable people in general, a disagreeable and shocking thing; it was an obscene horror which almost took away his presence of mind. He had once while at Harrow come upon another boy tormenting a dog, and he could still recall the voluptuous satisfaction with which he banged the fellow's head into semi-stupefaction on the asphalt pavement. His reactions now were of a less primitive nature; whatever impulse sprang up in him now had to travel through such outworks of self-control and judgment before it reached the outer world in action; but the sensitiveness was still there; though he had not long been raised to the bench, it was getting to be known that Sir Henry Tyrell always gave the maximum penalty for any crime involving cruelty.

He was now entertaining the usher, and Tripp, his smooth-haired fox terrier, a creature who lived only in his sight.

"It was when I was on circuit in Devizes," he was saying. "I really had to complain about the condition

of the lodgings; but it gave great offense, great offense indeed; one man said: ' 'E comes 'ere complain-
ing of us, but I 'ave it for a fack, on 'is own circuit a
man was summoned for not paying the rent: which
he refused on the ground that the place was so bad,
the fleas stood up on the backs of the chairs and barked
at the people as they came in!' Ha! Ha! Ha! Ha!"

"Ha! Ha! Ha! Ha!" echoed the usher.

"Yap, yap, yap, yap, yap, yap," bellowed Tripp,
seizing one end of the scarlet robe and racing round
his lordship's legs as far as the tether would permit.

"Tripp!" besought the judge, stooping over him,
"this is contempt of court, my dear fellow!"

At last the dog was persuaded to relax his hold, and
the usher picked him up to be out of further mis-
chief, while the judge turned to put on the great full-
bottomed wig surmounted by its small cocked hat,
which, mercifully, he would be allowed to exchange
for a small tie-wig once he had made his bow to the
court. In that atmosphere, the heat and weight of the
other were an infliction, even for a few minutes.
Among other public questions, he took a great interest in elementary schools, and frequently deplored the
scandal of their bad lighting and ventilation: but he
felt, all the same, that no school-child would be asked
to add two and two in an atmosphere as fœtid and
oppressive as that in which he was required to perform the most exacting duties, requiring every ounce
of capacity and involving questions of human life and
death.

The dark panelled room with its small square windows was dim even at ten o'clock on a bright autumn morning, and appeared yet smaller than it was from the denseness of its crowding; every niche, every atom of space to far up the walls, was a close, blurred sea of faces, alive, restless, yet silent. Opposite the bench there was a small area of comparative emptiness, where the counsel sat in a kind of well; and from it rose up the dock, surrounded with spiked bars, where, in front of two warders and two wardresses, who were ranged like wooden figures, sat Lewis, Patrick, Elizabeth, and Alice, whose ordinary attempts at sitting still showed strangely restless against the immobility of the four behind them.

When the attorney general opened with his speech, giving the story of the events of the past year, explaining to the jury the relationship of all four to each other, Lewis felt an inordinate excitement, a keen relish such as he had never experienced before; the dramatic situation, the fact that his least action in his humble sphere was of breathless interest, vital importance, not only to this crowd, but to those important-looking men in front of him, and to that calm, magnificent figure in scarlet above their heads, made him, once he had got his breath and could slightly relax his attention, gaze round the court in fiendish triumph. Patrick, beside him, was nothing but eyes and ears, seized already in the grip of an agonized concentration. He had mechanically reached for Elizabeth's hand, and, now that he had it, held it unconsciously. Elizabeth's eyes were cast down in modest dignity; Alice gazed about like a newly caged bird.

As the clear, well modulated tones went on and on, the atmosphere of the court altered: from eager listening it seemed to change to a sort of frozen tension, as if hardly anyone dared blink or draw breath lest they should lose the significance of some syllable. The judge, with bent head, was calmly writing on the sheets spread out before him; the perfect mechanism of his brain was registering every point with unerring exactitude; with his impassive face he might have been some miracle of machinery; but, far away, beyond the all-absorbing present, something was transfixed in agony.

When the attorney general sat down, none of the four felt much disquiet, because they could see the four counsel who were to defend them all busy over their papers, and it gave them a sense of fresh, untried forces preparing for their aid while the first bolt against them was already shot.

The first witness was put into the box, and Lewis gazed at her with a livid hate that was obvious to everyone but her; she did not direct a single look towards the dock, and seemed all unconscious of their presence, yet, a stout, foolish, blubbered old woman in black, she dealt them blows that were staggering.

"I knew my girl was a very simple-minded girl."

"She was fond of dress and knew how to dress, and she was a very clean girl indeed, very particular about her person."

"We always treated her like a child, because she was so simple."

"When you saw her at Penge, was she in her coffin?"

"Yes, and I noticed how greatly she had changed, apart from the difference between life and death."

"Will you tell us in what the change consisted?"

Here the witness became much affected.

"She was looking very old, very much older than she really was. She looked very dirty and miserable, and I scarcely knew her."

There followed in succession what seemed to Elizabeth like apparitions, so unexpected was their appearance; some of them people seen but once or twice in the world before, some unknown altogether.

"My name is William Cartwright; I am a porter at Halstead railway station. . . . I saw the two male prisoners lifting a female out of a wagonette. I saw the female prisoners come through the booking office. The lady was got into the booking office by one man getting hold of each side of her."

"My name is George Arthington; I am one of the inspecting constables in the Kent County Constabulary. I have known the Woodlands for two years. I knew only of Mr. and Mrs. Patrick Oman, Clara Smith, and two children living there. I remember an enquiry being made by Mrs. Ogilvy. I heard her say that she was searching for her daughter. I received directions to watch the house. I watched about twenty times from the road, and from the wood at the side of the house, at different times during the day. I never saw either Mrs. Harriet Oman or her child at any time. I had no idea they were living there."

"My name is Henry Crosthwaite; I work at Eden's farm, a mile or so from the Woodlands. Mr. Patrick Oman stopped me one morning to ask if he could get any poultry food. The lady came out, and he said: 'I've got a policeman here, and he'll run you in if you don't go back.'"

"My name is Arthur Perry. I am a gamekeeper and work in the woods. I knew Mr. Patrick Oman by sight. I was not aware that Mrs. Harriet Oman was living with the Omans."

"On one occasion did you hear something from the direction of the house?"

"Yes, on the afternoon of Sunday, October 22d, at half-past three, I heard a scream."

"My name is Richard Tansley. I am a fishmonger. I went to the Woodlands about half-past ten in the morning twice a week. On one occasion I saw Mrs. Harriet Oman. She was sitting in the kitchen. She had a child in her lap. She looked very ill or else half starved. That was the only time I saw her."

Then the matron of the hospital appeared; Lewis and Elizabeth felt a growing sense of injury that circumstances so slight, scenes which had lasted only minutes, should be brought up against them in this solemn manner.

"Do you say the child was ill?"

"I told them it was rapidly sinking, and I asked Mrs. Patrick if she would stay. She said no."

"How was the child dressed?"

"Not as a child of that age should be. It was dressed like a child of a month. I took charge of it. It was very ill."

"How long did it live?"

"It died the same night."

"Suddenly?"

"It gradually sank. It was not able to take food, and it did not make any noise."

"Was anything said as to how long it had been ill?"

"I don't remember. Mrs. Patrick said its mother was unable to look after it, and she had brought it out of kindness."

"Did you notice its face?"

"Yes. It had a bruise on its left cheek."

The day passed, and the night, and the next day found them there as if the whole court had never moved. Mrs. Morpeth appeared and told the story of their coming to her lodgings, contradicted herself once or twice, was taunted and rebuked by Patrick's counsel, and disappeared again.

"My name is Ethel Hosegood. I was called in to nurse the deceased. The patient was lying as if in a fit. She never moved until she died. I tried to give her food and some medicine, but she did not swallow anything. I noticed, about half-past one, that she was dying, and I asked Lewis Oman, who was in the sitting room, if he would like to see the last of his lady, as I did not think she would last very long. Mrs. Patrick Oman, who was also in the sitting room, said, 'Don't ask him, nurse. You worry him so.' "

Elizabeth's hand was over her mouth; her eyes were glassy. Patrick pressed her other hand, but she did not feel it. The cruelty, the wickedness, of bringing up her own words to hurt Lewis, almost stunned her.

"I went to wash her, but the body was in so filthy a state I could not. Her head was alive with lice. The dirt on the body was such that I couldn't wash it off. I never saw anything like it before. It was like the bark of a tree."

What are you all staring at, you fools? How dare you sit up to pass judgment on us? What in hell has it got to do with you?

"My name is David Horsham. I am a member of the Royal College of Surgeons and practise at Penge."

"Describe the condition in which you found the invalid."

"She was perfectly insensible. The breathing was stertorous and laboured. I knew that she would not recover. I did not make an examination because the patient was so near death. I certified, from what I had heard, cerebral disease and apoplexy. I had been told she was of weak intellect and had had a fit. I heard nothing more of the matter until the nurse called upon me. . . . When I had withdrawn the certificate the coroner sent a warrant for a post-mortem examination. There were present my partner, myself, a police surgeon, and Dr. Deering on behalf of the

prisoners. . . . The body was fearfully emaciated
and filthily dirty all over, particularly the feet. The
skin of the feet was quite horny, as if from walking
without shoes for some time. There were lice all over
the body. On the head I found real hair and false hair
very much matted. We pulled the false hair off with
forceps to get to the scalp."

Alice had a glimpse of herself as she had appeared
in Dr. Horsham's surgery, lovely, trembling, breathless, delicate as wind-tugged anemone, and thought,
"He can't fasten this on *me!*"

"Have you formed any opinion of the cause of her
death?"

"Yes. Starvation—accelerated by her removal from
Cudham."

And now began the crucial struggle of the trial.
Dr. Horsham, Dr. Deering, and the police surgeon
were all examined, cross-examined, reëxamined, and
re-cross-examined; the sum of all their evidence was
the opinion that the deceased had died of starvation
and neglect. But the defense called three other doctors, one of whom had assisted at the post mortem,
who, after submitting to an equally lengthy process,
left it as their opinion that, from the condition of the
brain, the deceased had died of tubercular meningitis:
how much her end had been hastened by neglect they
were not prepared to say. They admitted beneath the
bludgeon of the attorney general that to be confined
to a small room of which half the window had been

blocked, and fireless in the depth of winter, was not the treatment they themselves would have recommended for a patient in these—or indeed in any—circumstances, but that tubercular meningitis was the cause of the death they were quite clear. For days, as it seemed to the spectators, the whole affair had become a technical discussion between six doctors: the causes of emaciation, the symptoms of diabetes, of meningitis, of Addison's disease; the swiftness and slowness of succumbing to tuberculous complaints, the circumstances liable to heighten the virulence of half a dozen diseases respectively. The prisoners and the court in general lost track of the argument and remained in passive noncomprehension. Only in the small area comprising the judge's seat, the counsels' table, and the witness box the air was alive and humming as if with an electric current.

At last, the last doctor had been released from the rattling fire of interrogation; there was a general feeling of expectancy, as if things would now be within the spectators' understanding once more, and Clara Smith stepped up into the box, her head only just appearing above the front of it. Alice and Elizabeth could hardly believe their eyes; they knew Clara would be called as a witness against them, but actually to see her, one of themselves, standing up over there while they themselves sat within spiked bars, gave them a feeling of dreamlike unreality. Clara's face was white and piteous; the sensational character of the proceedings was quite lost upon one who would in the ordinary course of things have so much appreciated it. She was conscious only of feeling very frightened and of a great desire to be sick, and an additional terror lest she should be so, in front of these stern gentlemen. She heard herself saying in absurd, squeaking tones:

"My name is Clara Smith. I was sixteen last month." As she went on, her cousins, listening to her, lost the feeling which her first appearance had given them. Alice longed, longed to be able to strike her, to tear out her hair, to put both hands round her neck and squeeze until the silly eyes should start out of her head! Elizabeth put her other hand over Patrick's hand which she already held, and with lowered eyes felt the coldness of death creeping over her.

"Her habit of grinning and screaming was the cause of many of the first blows she had. He took to keeping her so long without food that she became desperate. One night, after she had had nothing all day and nothing was put for her supper, I said, 'Shall I take Harriet some supper up?' and he said, 'No, let her wait.' When Harriet saw I had nothing for her she began to cry dreadfully. She kept moaning and begging of me to fetch her a bit of food. I could not, because it was all locked up. After a bit she seemed to go quite mad. Then she got quite insensible, and they were frightened; they tried to bring her to, but she never came round, and was quite helpless when she was moved. Patrick was always threatening what he would do if he caught me mentioning her name outside the house."

After what seemed an interminable time to the people in the dock, she was allowed to stand down. Patrick had a haughty, contemptuous smile at the corner of his mouth. Lewis was breathing deeply, with a great inflowing of relief: the defense had not failed to point out that the girl had sworn the contrary of all this before the coroner, and had come into the box a self-confessed liar.

And now who in the world were these? Two women altogether unknown to Patrick, Lewis, and Alice: but Elizabeth saw with a sinking of the heart the two servants from the house of their neighbour: it was a nightmare, this starting up of everyone with whom she had had the faintest connection, even that of acquaintance by sight, as a witness against her. As they told the story of their evening spent at the Woodlands, and of the attempt made by Harriet to come downstairs, checked by Clara, Elizabeth remembered how the girl had lied to her the morning after, and felt that it was she who should be in the dock, instead of running loose, the wicked, wicked creature, bringing trouble on people who had always been good to her. Alice clenched her hands as if she really felt Clara's throat between them.

Sergeant Brownlea came up next, and after mentioning the depositions he had taken from the prisoners, he said that while they were away he had made a thorough examination of the Woodlands, and taken note of the back bedroom, which was, he said, very dirty. Then he had gone over to Sirenwood. Here Alice flushed darkly with indignation; how had he dared to do anything of the kind? They were supposed to be criminals, and yet this was the sort of thing that was allowed to be done to them behind their backs! Sergeant Brownlea was saying: "In the parlour I found this letter tucked behind the overmantel." Alice had seen that scrap of paper every day for months, until the smoke from the fire had made it so drab as to be almost indistinguishable. It was pushed well in behind the fretwork ornamentation, and would have taken several seconds to get out, so she had always left it there. It was Harriet's letter to Lewis, saying, "My boots is wore out."

When the court adjourned for lunch, the judge repaired to the back room, where two lamb chops, a potato, and half a bottle of Lafite, with a small portion of Stilton cheese, awaited him. Mad with expectation, there was Tripp, who tore in from the passage where the kindly usher had been allowing him to stretch his legs. The judge put down his knife and fork, and said, "Well, Tripp, my little man!" At the sound of his voice, the dog stopped in mid-career, lay down with his head between his paws, and looked at his master with sick eyes.

The speeches made on behalf of each of the four prisoners occupied a day, and the strained attention of all of them relaxed as they listened without effort to the arguments of their own innocence. The medical evidence in their favour was put forth again, and the jury urged to understand that the deceased had died of tubercular meningitis, and that the condition in which her body had been found was due to the inability of a person of enfeebled intellect to take proper care of herself. Mrs. Patrick Oman had, on the evidence of the servant, several times rebuked her for not keeping her hair clean. That she ought to have had more attention than she had was unquestionable; but the deficiency arose, partly from the ignorance of the accused, and partly from the general scarcity of help and conveniences in the house. As for the condition in which the room was said to be—did anyone believe that Mrs. Patrick Oman would have allowed her own child to run in and out of it had it been as described?

On behalf of Lewis it was urged that, as he paid his brother one pound a week for the support of his wife and child, he discharged his legal obligation to provide for her keep; it might not be generous provision —no doubt the jury would think it ought never to have been made at all, inasmuch as his wife and child should have been under his own roof: still, they were not here to critize the conduct of the accused, which everyone must agree to condemn in some part, but merely to decide the single question as to whether or not murder had been committed.

As to Patrick, against whom it might be considered the gravest part of the charge rested, would they but consider the facts for one moment? He was admittedly in very needy circumstances, and his brother was paying him one pound a week to board and lodge his wife and child. Was it not in Patrick's interests to prolong the lives of his charges, rather than to do away with them? The accused had been described as committing acts of revolting cruelty; admittedly he was a man of harsh temper; they made no attempt to whitewash his character in that respect; and no doubt when roused he treated everyone who came in his way with a roughness which could not but be very shocking to ordinary people; but all this being granted, as it was fully and freely granted, what remained? The evidence of a hysterical child of sixteen, who on her own admission had already perjured herself! Finally, if the accused had, any of them, been conscious of guilt in their treatment of the deceased, would they have pursued the course which had actually been attributed to them by the prosecution? Would they have mentioned the name of their own doctor? Would they all have left the body at Penge, to be seen by the nurse and the undertaker, if they had not in their own minds been satisfied that the condition of the body, however deplorable and, indeed, shocking, it might appear, was due entirely to the disease and helplessness and obstinacy of the unfortunate woman? Surely, if they had been guilty, or even conscious of the misdemeanour of

carelessness and indifference which might not un-
justly be brought against them, would they not have
taken pains to prepare the body for inspection, instead of leaving it in the condition in which the evidence said they did actually leave it for anyone who
chose to see?

On behalf of Alice, her counsel did not propose to
detain the jury very long. He wished to point out to
them that unless a charge of murder were brought
home, his client could be convicted of nothing. The
prosecution had reminded them that persons under a
legal obligation to provide someone with the neces-
saries of life, who failed to fulfil that obligation, so
that the person died, were, if not guilty of murder,
guilty of manslaughter. But in the case of Alice
Hoppner no such charge could be brought, since she
was not liable for the discharge of any duties towards
the deceased, inasmuch as the mistress is under no
legal obligation to provide for the wife. No one would
attempt to condone the position, in which she was
passing as Lewis Oman's wife, while the real Mrs.
Oman was excluded from her own house; but they
were not here to pass judgment on that aspect of the
case. The point at issue was not adultery, but murder, and of that he denied that there was one par-
ticle of evidence against his client. That she had been
a party to concealing the whereabouts of the deceased
from her mother was readily admitted, but he would
say thus much in extenuation of her—that she was
very young, not yet twenty, that she had yielded in

an unlucky moment to the seduction of Lewis Oman, and that, having once done so, retreat was impossible and she hoped at all costs to cover up her own disgrace; the motive being an equally powerful one with her sister.

All eyes now turned upon Alice, and in a mixture of exhaustion, shame, and feeling for interesting display, she buried her face in her long, slender hands and burst into sobs. The others sat like stone.

At half-past ten on the following morning the judge began his summing up. With an interval of half an hour at midday he continued, while the light thickened and the yellow gas softly flared up, and candles were placed before him, while the jury grew whiter and more exhausted, racked in their uncomfortable seat and poisoned by foul and fouler air, yet all unconscious of these things, while through the whole court was an atmosphere of almost visible tension as the packed faces grew dimmer and more blurred and flecked with deeper and deeper shadows, and the prisoners sat, still now as the warders behind them, with dilated eyes, feeling a clutch that tightened and tightened with every gasping breath they drew, and the windows became a polished black, while here and there a stray light or hoarse call penetrated to the court from the world outside, and always the deep, thrilling voice went on and on and on: until at twenty minutes to ten at night there came a change in its tone, at which there was a rustle and a long-drawn sigh all through the room.

"And now, gentlemen, I think I have gone through the whole of the case. You and I have had an arduous, an onerous duty to perform. We can have—we ought to have—we have, but one object, to ascertain the truth. I know it is superfluous to warn you against both prejudice and sympathy; yet on the one hand you cannot help feeling sympathy for the unhappy woman who, to say the least, came to so miserable an end, and on the other hand you cannot help feeling prejudice against those—whoever they were—who brought about her death. But discard these feelings, and above all let me entreat you to leave out all consideration of the consequences of your verdict should it be against the prisoners. Your duty is solely to ascertain the truth, to declare by your verdict what you believe to be the truth, regardless of the consequences to anybody. With the consequences you have nothing to do. For them, the law, whose minister I am, is alone responsible. I entreat you therefore to let your verdict be, as I am sure it will, the expression of your honest opinion, arrived at by a calm but firm consideration of the facts that are now before you."

The entrance and exit to the dock is down through the floor, and as they went down the dimly lit stairs to the regions below, Elizabeth was half stupefied; the long strain, which had begun for her long before her coming into the dock, had told on her brain; she was not unhappy, she was merely vacant, as the wardresses gently put her into a chair. Patrick and Lewis were absolutely calm, the former with the courage of despair, the latter with a mind amused by a variety of sensations and soothed by a dreamlike feeling of being above and beyond everything that was happening to his earthly presence. Only Alice was broad awake to horror. Alice had not the sense to know that in the last resort it is not pain, but the resistance to it, that is killing; that in crises of either bodily or mental suffering, when the time for fortitude is past, the only thing to do is to remain passive and allow the tide to overwhelm one. She should have forced her mind to expect the worst, and regarded the coming preparations for her death with no more emotion than if they had been made for pulling out a tooth. Instead of the dentist's yellowish mask being put over her face, for her to draw in the sweet, stupefying fumes of oblivion, from which, alas, the patient must soon be roused again, the hangman's linen bag would be put over her head, and when they took that off she would be safe forever. They would bury her in a pit of quicklime below the prison yard, and it would not matter in the slightest; the great object of her existence would have been attained, she would have got rid of every kind of pain and trouble forever. But she could not take this easy way into peace, and she laid herself on a rack of suspense and hope from which everyone was powerless to deliver her.

It was eleven o'clock before they went upstairs again, where, by contrast, the court seemed brilliantly lighted, and the row of white-faced jurymen were already in the box. It was not until the words, "Gentlemen of the jury, have you agreed upon your verdict?" were spoken, that Lewis, livid and shining with sweat, felt the veils before his consciousness lift, and disclose him to himself in the grip of earthly agony; his hands clenched as against a spasm of physical pain, and the sharpness of suspense was like the bitterest pang of steel.

"Do you find the prisoner Lewis Oman guilty of the murder of which he stands indicted, or not guilty?"

"Guilty."

"Do you find the prisoner Patrick Oman guilty of the murder of which he stands indicted, or not guilty?"

"Guilty."

"Do you find the prisoner Elizabeth Oman guilty of the murder of which she stands indicted, or not guilty?"

"Guilty."

"Do you find the prisoner Alice Hoppner guilty of the murder of which she stands indicted, or not guilty?"

"Guilty."

At opposite ends of the dock, Lewis and Alice had no thought for each other; each was conscious only of the terror of death. But between them Patrick and Elizabeth sat with their arms round each other, as alone with each other as if the sea of faces had been a

sea in truth, washing about the bases of a high rock
on which they clung together.

The judge now had a square of black cloth over his
wig; what he said would not hurt those two, because
they had already suffered in one moment everything
that they could suffer, and listened now with a kind
of wonder.

"Lewis Oman, Patrick Oman, Elizabeth Oman,
and Alice Hoppner: after a long, patient, and anxious enquiry, you have been found guilty by a jury
of your country of a crime so black and hideous that
I believe in all the records of crime it would be difficult to find its parallel. With a barbarity almost incredible, you plotted to take away by cruel torture
the life of a poor, innocent, helpless, and outraged
woman. . . ."

This is not about us!

"It is a sad thing to see four young people standing there convicted of so cruel a murder as that of
which you are found guilty. Though you do not stand
convicted of having murdered her helpless child, I
am satisfied that not only are you guilty of the crime
of which you have been tried, but that you plotted
and brought about its death also."

*You don't understand. It is not as if anyone else
had done it—with us it was different.*

"It is incredible, to my mind at least, how you
could have carried out your design, how you could
look upon, and see sinking into her grave, the poor,
unhappy creature whom you sent to her rest."

*Are you going to put my wife and me to death be-
cause of that animal? We are warm, living human
beings. It is you who are a murderer, a hundred times
worse than we.*

"I earnestly entreat you to make the best of the
short time which remains to you here on earth to prepare to meet your Maker. Mercy belongs not to me. I
have no power to grant mercy. That belongs to a
higher authority. It remains only for me to pass on
you the dread sentence of the law which I am bound
to pass——"

Oh, it seems so strange to think of Alfred *a grown-
up man, and me not there to see him!*

"The sentence of the court upon you is that you
be severally taken back to the place from whence you
came, and thence to the common gaol of the County
of Kent, and thence to a place of execution, and that
you be each of you hanged by the neck until you be
dead, and the bodies of each of you be buried within
the precincts of the prison in which you shall have
been last confined. And may the Lord have mercy on
your souls. Amen!"

The whole court echoed the last word like a groan,
but Elizabeth and Alice did not hear it. Elizabeth's
head drooped onto Patrick's shoulder, and her knees
sank. Alice had fainted already. The wardresses raised
them both tenderly, and then Patrick turned to
Lewis, who was gazing into vacancy; he gripped his
hand, saw a faint smile come through that stupefaction.

❧ XXI ❧

THE wave of popular excitement that greeted the verdict swung high and then began to subside. The applause which had greeted Sir Henry Tyrell's brilliant conduct of the case began to be chequered with adverse criticism. The terrible *tour de force* of a ten hours' summing up, it was said, was what neither judge nor jury could stand without damage to their impartiality. It had been a display of forensic genius, but Sir Henry Tyrell had not been a judge long enough to forget that he had been a brilliant advocate. He had gone all out for a conviction in each case, and the jury, hypnotized by his powers, and influenced, as he himself had been, by the atrocious nature of the crime, had confused the issue between what was morally guilty and what could legally be proved so. The medical profession, under the leadership of Sir Hubert Stretton, complained that the evidence called for the defense had been treated in too cavalier a fashion. Altogether, though in the circumstances it could hardly be regretted that the prisoners had heard the death sentence passed upon them, the moment had arrived for a cooler consideration of the matter. The Home Secretary reopened the case, and, with the assistance of three judges, converted the death penalty to penal servitude on Lewis, Patrick, and Elizabeth, two days before the execution was to have taken place, while Alice was released forthwith.

Without her lover, deprived of luxury and pleasure, blasted with public loathing and contempt, returning to her mother's house, yet she was happy, because in the lowest types the instinct of survival is the strongest of all, and she was alive.

⚜ XXII ⚜

TWO years after these events, the governor of a gaol and the prison chaplain found themselves confronted with the painful task of telling one of the female prisoners that her husband, also serving a sentence, had died in the prison infirmary. He had developed pneumonia, and, being a man of little stamina, he had died suddenly even as arrangements were being made to bring his wife to him.

When they entered the cell, Elizabeth was expecting the arrival of the wardress with the midday meal. In the plain prison garb, with her hair tucked under a cap, she was strangely different from her old self, and had become quite stout. She received the news which the governor conveyed as gently as he could with her usual dignity of manner, and assented calmly to the chaplain's offer to stay with her and read the prayers for the dead. But it was with relief that she saw him at last close his prayer book and prepare to go, because she knew it was past her dinner time and that his presence was delaying the bringing in of her food; and food, though plain, was so delicious; looking forward to it, and receiving it and then eating it, was the pleasure and interest of her uneventful life; and the sure knowledge that at certain hours it would come was the support of her existence.

AFTERWORD

✳✳✳✳✳✳✳✳

Only one photograph is known to exist of Harriet Staunton, née Richardson: it was taken to mark the occasion of her engagement to a hard-up auctioneer's clerk, Louis Staunton, in 1874. At first glance, she looks like any other woman of her time and class. Her dress is modestly high-necked; her toque, worn stylishly forward, is lavishly trimmed; her hair, drawn back to reveal the ears, ends in a confection of prettily coiled plaits (these would have been made of 'false' hair, which remained wildly fashionable until *The Englishwoman's Domestic Magazine* sounded its death knell in 1876). Examine this blurry image more closely, though, and instinct will tell you that all is not as it seems. Something about her expression suggests that this young woman might not be entirely sensible of the world around her. Her eyelids are heavy and drooping. Her smile, stretched like a soft leather glove over bony knuckles, is more grimace than grin. The overall impression is of a woman – she was then 33 years old – who is acting a part. The part in question is excited bride-to-be, a leading role, and one that neither Harriet nor her mother, Mrs Butterfield, had expected ever to be in her power.

The novel you have just read, you see, is based entirely on truth. Harriet Staunton lived, and died, more or less as Elizabeth Jenkins describes. She was indeed – to use, as Jenkins does, the archaic, country word – 'a natural'. We can speculate that she was deprived of oxygen at birth, but whatever the cause of her disabilities, the real Harriet had what we would call learning difficulties. Careful tuition on the part of her mother – Mrs Ogilvy in the novel – meant that she was particular about her appearance. She was able to wash and dress herself, and was always – at least until her marriage – tidy and clean. But she found it hard to express herself in speech, and on the page. Sometimes, she would laugh loudly, for no apparent reason; sometimes, she would fly into rages. Her behaviour was, in the eyes of those who did not know and love her, distinctly odd.

Safe at home, though, her life was good. For Harriet had two great blessings. First, she had a mother who sincerely cared for her, for all that she was now married for the second time, with all the responsibilities this entailed (Harriet's father died when she was 12; her mother married the Reverend John Butterfield in 1858). Second, she had money: a legacy of some £5,000 (half a million pounds in today's money), under the will of her great-aunt, the Rt Hon Eleanor, Baroness Rivers. Her days were replete with shopping trips, and visits to relatives – and it was on one of these visits, in 1873, that she met Louis Staunton (Lewis in the novel). Thomas Hinksman, the son of Harriet's aunt, Mrs Ellis, had married a widow, Mrs Ann Rhodes, and thus had gained two step-daughters: Elizabeth, 23, and Alice, 15. Elizabeth had recently married an artist, Patrick Staunton, and his elder brother, to whom he was passionately devoted, was 23 year-old Louis.

Years later, Louis insisted that he would never have thought to play suitor to Harriet had it not been for the encouragement of one of her female relatives (presumably Mrs Ellis). But whoever put the idea in his head, he set about his wooing with alacrity and, after a brief courtship, he and Harriet were engaged. Mrs Butterfield was suspicious, but her opposition did no good. Harriet, enraged, left her parents' house to live with Mrs Ellis in Walworth. Mrs Butterfield, now seriously alarmed, attempted to place Harriet under the protection of the Court of Chancery as a lunatic. The application was refused, and Harriet and Louis duly made their marriage vows in Clapham, on 16 June 1875. Mrs Butterfield did not attend the wedding, but called on the couple three weeks later at the house they had taken in Brixton. This meeting was brief, but civil. Soon after, however, she received a letter from Harriet in which her daughter wrote that 'her husband objected to my calling upon her, and she thought I had better not come, to prevent any disturbance between them.' She also received a note from Louis: he would not, he said, have her in the house again. The next time Mrs Butterfield saw her daughter, in April 1877, she was in her coffin.

* * *

Elizabeth Jenkins, unlike some, seems to have believed entirely in the guilt of those who, in September of the same year, were found guilty at the Old Bailey of the murder by starvation of Harriet Staunton: her husband, Louis Staunton; his brother, Patrick Staunton; his sister-in-law, Elizabeth Staunton; and his lover, Elizabeth's sister, Alice Rhodes. Their crime involved, she wrote in her 2004 memoir, *The View From Downshire Hill*, 'almost unbelievable callousness and cruelty'. The Penge Mystery, as it was known, was an infamous case, one much written about, not only because the details were so horrible – the newspapers could not get enough of it, filling their pages with haunting illustrations of Harriet's final days – but also because the trial and resulting verdict hastened the establishment of a functioning Court of Appeal. Jenkins, though, only learned of its full horror – a horror that was to stay with her for many years – decades later, when her brother, David, a solicitor, lent her a copy of *The Trial of the Stauntons*, a volume in the highly popular *Notable British Trials Series*. The book had come from his office at Hawkins and Co, a firm established in the nineteenth century by a Mr Hawkins, whose son, Henry, went on to become a judge. Henry Hawkins' first case – 'the most sensational case I was called on to preside over' – was the trial of the Stauntons.

Jenkins, who had a lifelong interest in the criminal mind and was fascinated by trials, found herself completely absorbed – 'obsessed' – by the story of the Stauntons, which transmitted to her 'a powerful current of energy'. She decided to write a novel about it, a book that would turn out to be, as she later noted, 'one of the very earliest instances – if not the earliest – of a writer's recounting a story of real life, with the actual Christian names of the protagonists and all the available biographical details, but with the imaginative insight and heightened colour which the novelist exists to supply.' (In 1934, the same year that *Harriet* came out, F Tennyson Jesse, editor of several volumes of the *Notable British Trials Series*, published her novel, *A Pin to See the Peep Show*, based on the case of Edith Thompson and Frederick Bywaters, who were executed for the murder of Thompson's husband, Percy; however, she gave her characters fictional names.) Jenkins would call the story *Harriet*, after the victim.

The novel, her fourth, was not only her first commercial success; it also won the prestigious Prix Femina Vie-Heureuse (the runners-up were Evelyn Waugh's *A Handful of Dust*, and Antonia White's *Frost in May*). And no wonder. Though she later came to believe there was something 'blameworthy: a sort of flagrant breach of copyright' about keeping the names of people and place intact, *Harriet* is a remarkable and singular achievement: highly controlled, deeply revealing, quite brilliant. Read *The Trial of the Stauntons* and, though crammed with facts, it nevertheless confounds. Greed, a desire for financial gain, one can understand. But the locking away of a disabled woman in a bedroom of an isolated country house until she starves to death? This is a more difficult thing to hold in one's mind. While Harriet emitted her desperate animal cries, and scratched feverishly at her lice-infested skin, downstairs, the Stauntons carried on as normal, lazing by the fire, eating their veal chops and batter puddings. As crimes go, it is not only horrible. It is . . . *unfathomable*. Yet in Jenkins' hands, the quartet's unspoken complicity is deftly unpicked. She is a kind of psychological codebreaker, twisted logic a particular speciality.

She presents the Stauntons' crime not as a plan, but as a tacit agreement, one robustly underpinned by their peculiarly intense and protective relationships with one another: Patrick and Alice are in thrall to Lewis; Elizabeth is in thrall to Patrick, and anxious to protect Alice's reputation; Lewis wants – needs – to be adored by all three. Harriet's death is not so much an endgame as an inevitable staging point on a slippery slope – a moral gradient whose perilous trajectory is first marked, in the novel, when Alice considers how much more satisfaction she could get from a beautiful blue silk dress ('a deep jay's wing blue') than its owner, Harriet. (At this point, Harriet and Lewis are not even engaged.) Conscience is revealed as a shape-shifter: Elizabeth, for instance, finds that hers entirely approves of the lies she tells Harriet's mother. How else to protect dear Alice and Lewis? *Harriet* is a novel in which people turn away from the truth with the same ease that they might draw a curtain over a draughty window – as when Elizabeth sees Alice ironing pieces of the blue silk, now unpicked, and looks silently away. All four protagonists regard their own culpability (when they regard it at all) with polite distaste. Their lives remain quite delightful, unless they should happen to catch sight of their victim's shuffling, twitching form.

Jenkins' story grips because the horror takes place in familiar surroundings, and to a quotidian beat. Sometimes, in fact, everything is so very ordinary, it takes a moment for shock to register. The news that Harriet is going to have a child is dropped into the story casually, in conversation; so, too, is the fact that the child has been born. Only a sentence or three later does the reader, realisation dawning, consider what this means: that Lewis has slept with Harriet, a woman who knows nothing of sex, and whom he finds physically repulsive; that she must have found conceiving her child and giving birth utterly terrifying (Jenkins suggests later that Harriet hardly realises that her son 'was his as well as her own'). Jenkins resists the temptation to make what is happening to Harriet explicit right up until the moment when Alice notes that there is little point in asking a doctor to see her, for 'she will die anyway'. Instead, she slyly imbues everyday items with horror: the lurid and strongly perfumed sweets Lewis sends Harriet before they are married; the gloves Elizabeth pulls on Harriet's hands before they take her to Penge, the empty fingers dangling chillingly loose.

* * *

Elizabeth Jenkins was born in 1905, in Hitchin, Hertfordshire, where her father had founded the preparatory school, Caldicott. After school in Letchworth, in 1924 she went up to read English and history at Newnham College, Cambridge, where F R Leavis was then at the height of his influence. Elizabeth wrote an essay for him once (though he was not among her tutors, as has some-times been written), an experience she never forgot. Dr Leavis returned it a third shorter, 'showing me how what he had left expressed my view much more forcibly than what I had originally written.' In *The View From Downshire Hill*, she insists that she did not invariably act on this lesson thereafter. But examine any one of her books, and you will struggle to find a single sentence that could not be called beautifully concise.

Jenkins knew early that she wanted to be a writer – though her ambition was timid, and barely voiced – and, as she was leaving Newnham, its principle, Pernel Strachey (Lytton's sister), asked her if she would like to meet Virginia Woolf. Yes, she said. A note duly arrived at Jenkins' furnished bed-sitting room in Doughty Street inquiring if she were free to join the Woolfs at Tavistock Square one evening after dinner. Jenkins thought Woolf very beautiful, and was struck at once 'by her dignity and grace, and her complete lack of self-consciousness', but she was also some-what winded when, after some months of visiting the writer, she was unceremoniously dropped (during their last meeting, she records, Woolf's tone to her was 'contempt-uous and mocking'). Nevertheless, she pressed on, working hard to finish her first novel, *Virginia Water*, and it was finally published in 1929 by Victor Gollancz, part of a three book deal.

There followed, until her death in 2010, a long and vital writing career, one interrupted only by a brief stint as an English teacher and later, the war, during which she

****

worked at the Assistance Board, helping Jewish refugees and the victims of air raids (Jenkins never married). She wrote twelve novels – the best known is *The Tortoise and the Hare* (1954), which tells the story of the painful end of a marriage – and twelve non-fiction books, among them acclaimed biographies of Elizabeth I and Jane Austen. But her career was also, by today's standards, quiet, unshowy. Twenty-first century novelists are not allowed to be shy; they must be self-promoting, talky, able to address audiences on all manner of subjects. Jenkins, though, was diffident and self-critical. She knew her weaknesses, and accepted them. Many years after her last meeting with Woolf, she read the novelist's diaries, where she found *Virginia Water* noted as 'a sweet white grape of a book'. In one way, she was relieved about this; Woolf could be so scornful. But she knew, too, that she had put her finger on something: what Jenkins felt to be a lack of strength. 'This has always, I fear, come out in any novel I have written purely by imagination; a fictional version of a real story of real life, a transcript of experience or a straight-forward biography, has been needed to supply my deficiency.' My feeling is that, modesty aside, Jenkins was right about this – and this is why Harriet is so masterful. Forged from the unpromising prolixity of a Victorian courtroom, a powerful synthesis of truth and imagination renders it indelible. To call it the stuff of nightmares really is no exaggeration.

* * *

Some time after *Harriet*'s publication, Elizabeth Jenkins received a letter from an old lady, Mrs Atkins, who wrote: 'I think your story must be about the family that I was in service with when I was a young girl.' The two arranged to meet, whereupon Mrs Atkins told the author that, Patrick Staunton having died in prison, his widow had become, on completing her own sentence, the proprietor of a set of rooms called Llewellyn Chambers (perhaps named for the late Patrick Llewellyn Staunton) – an establishment used mostly by officers on leave from the Boer War. Elizabeth had married again, an older man, and it was Mrs Atkins' duty to take up a bowl of soup to his bedroom in the middle of the morning. One day, a little late, she arrived to hear him muttering from behind the screen at the foot of his bed: 'I shall get up. *I'm* not going to stay up here and be starved!' It was only on reading *Harriet*, or so she insisted, that Mrs Atkins realised the terrible import of these words. It was a story Jenkins clearly relished.

But did Elizabeth Staunton and the others deliberately starve Harriet to death? There have always been those who believe that they did not. They point to the evidence of Clara Brown, the Staunton's servant, who said nothing of her employers' abuse of Harriet at the initial inquest into her death, but then, at the Old Bailey, contradicted herself by giving a detailed account of their cruelty. And they question, too, Judge Hawkins' handling of the trial. He sent a jury out to reach a verdict late at night, when they were tired. In the case of Alice Rhodes, he pressed an insufficient case. Most crucially of all, he dismissed the

****

evidence of the doctors called by the defence – evidence which suggested that Harriet had died, not from starvation, but from cerebral disease, or tubercular meningitis. In this light, the Stauntons were guilty of criminal neglect, but not of murder.

The trial ended, with a guilty verdict and Judge Hawkins' passing of the death sentence, on 26 September 1877. Soon after, a campaign for the Stauntons' reprieve began. There were petitions and public meetings, and on 14 October, some 48 hours before the hangings were due to take place, the Stauntons' mother, Mary, travelled to Balmoral in the hope of asking Queen Victoria for a reprieve (no audience was granted, though the Queen noted her visit in her diary). However, it was a leading article in the *Lancet* on 6 October that changed everything. The piece reiterated the medical evidence, and called upon doctors to add their names to a 'memorial' to be submitted to the Home Secretary. Some 700 doctors went on to sign this petition, among them Sir William Jenner. The Home Secretary, R. Assheton Cross, could no longer withstand the pressure. On 14 October, the Stauntons' sentence was commuted to penal servitude for life. Alice Rhodes, meanwhile, was pardoned and released.

Patrick Staunton died of consumption in Knaphill Prison, Woking, in 1881, at the age of 28. Elizabeth Staunton was released from Fulham Reformatory by the order of the Home Secretary in November 1883, whereupon she set herself up, as Jenkins discovered, as an hotelier, and married an art dealer, Joseph Pool. She lived into her seventies. The son to whom she gave birth in prison in August 1877, named for his father Patrick, emigrated to Canada, and became a Christian brother (his twin sister survived only four days). Elizabeth maintained that Clara Brown was a liar, and that neither she nor the others, however indifferent to Harriet, had wanted her to die. Asked by the prison chaplain why she did not send for a doctor for her, she replied that they did not think her illness serious. They had also been unable to pay his previous bills. Alice Rhodes worked behind a bar in London after her release. The baby son to whom she gave birth in prison – Lewis was his father – died at the age of six months.

In Dartmoor Convict Prison, Louis Staunton was a model prisoner; every Sunday evening, he served the Mass in the Roman Catholic Chapel, and the priests who knew him apparently believed his penitence to be genuine. Shortly before his release early on the morning of 25 September 1897, Staunton spoke to the prison's deputy governor. He said that he believed he had been guilty of worse offences than murder – he had been a selfish young man, for sure – but he also repeated the claims he had made during the trial that Harriet was a drinker, and that it was this that caused her to refuse the food that was brought to her.

Louis Staunton left prison in a suit made to measure by his fellow convicts, and boarded a train to London. There, he met Alice, who had waited for him, and they were married. Alice died shortly before the outbreak of the First

World War, after which Louis married for the third time (in the end, he had thirteen children). He worked, with some success, as an auctioneer. He died, at the age of 83, in 1934, the same year that he achieved notoriety all over again, as the villain of a marvellous and terrifying novel called *Harriet*.

Rachel Cooke
London 2011